MEET JAKE TANNER

Born: 28.03.1985

Height: 6'1"

Weight: 190lbs / 86kg / 13.5 stone

Physical Description: Brown hair, close shaven beard, brown eyes, slim athletic build

Education: Upper Second Class Honours in Psychology from the University College London (UCL)

Interests: When Jake isn't protecting lives and finding those responsible for taking them, Jake enjoys motorsports — particularly F1

Family: Mother, older sister, younger brother. His father died in a car accident when Jake was fifteen

Relationship Status: Currently in a relationship with Elizabeth Tanner, and he doesn't see that changing, ever

By The Same Author

The CID Case Series

The Conspiracy

The Community

The Confession

The Cadre

The Company

The Cabal

The SO15 Files Series

The Wolf (coming 2021)

Dark Christmas (coming 2021)

The Eye (coming 2021)

St Paul's (coming 2021)

Power Station (coming soon)

School Attack (coming 2021)

Mile 17 (coming 2021)

The Wedding (coming 2021)

Arena (coming 2021)

The Terror Thriller Series

Standstill

Floor 68

The Jake Tanner Terror Thriller Series Boxset 1 (Contains Standstill & Floor 68)

THE CONSPIRACY

BY JACK **PROBYN**

ISBN: 978-1-912628-31-5

eBook ISBN: 978-1-912628-21-6

First Edition

Visit Jack Probyn's website at www.jackprobynbooks.com.

For Nana.

| PART 1 |

CHAPTER 1

THE CRIMSONS

They called themselves The Crimsons. And they'd been in the business of robbing banks for years. Nine, in fact. They had travelled the length of the country, raiding some of the largest banks and jewellers on the high street. And, in that time, they had become invisible – masters of deception and anonymity. Thanks, ultimately, to their excessive attention to detail. They left nothing uncovered – no escape unaccounted for. All bases of their heists were meticulously prepared. Not to mention that it helped to have certain friends in certain high places on the payroll.

But for their final heist, Danny – the eldest brother – wanted to go rogue. Off the books. Off the radar. And off the fucking chain. He had ingrained that modus operandi in them as soon as they began planning. He wanted to commit the worst robbery ever seen and be immortalised by the media coverage that had followed them throughout their nine-year career. And they were going to make it exceptional.

Danny was in the driving seat; Michael – the middle brother – riding shotgun. Michael was the strongest and biggest, declaring himself the brute force of the operation. Always the first one to enter the banks or jewellery stores, he could set the mood, the tempo, and scare the shit out of everyone in front of him. Anyone who tried to stand up to him rapidly wished they hadn't for fear of being picked up and thrown against the wall. Whereas Danny was the opposite. Slimmer. Shorter. And in his own words, more handsome. During their operations he had always seemed to be the most calm, the most relaxed, the most authoritative. He commanded control of the entire room with his voice.

Michael leant forward and switched the radio up full blast. 'Robbers' by The 1975 played.

Meanwhile, Luke – the youngest – was in the back, clinging to the shoulders of Michael and Danny's synthetic plastic seats. They neared a roundabout, and Danny showed no signs of slowing down. Instead, he pressed the accelerator and swerved the black Ford Transit round the bend, ignoring the horns and gesticulations from other drivers. The sudden force of the movement caused Luke to lose his grip on the seats and slam into the interior panels of the van, his head ricocheting off the metal.

'Fucking hell, Danny!' he shouted, leaning over to the dashboard and turning the radio off. 'Watch it!'

Danny snickered and looked in his side-view mirror.

'Sorry, mate. Didn't realise you were in the back there. You're so quiet.'

'Not that you'd be able to hear me.' Luke slapped Michael on the back of the head for nearly bursting his eardrums. 'Thought we weren't supposed to be drawing

4

attention to ourselves?'

'Can't you feel the adrenaline pumping?' Danny asked, glancing in the rear-view mirror. Luke glimpsed a fiery excitement behind his eldest brother's darkened eyes.

'This thing'll go off if you aren't careful.' Holding Danny's gaze, Luke pointed to the metal object covered in tarpaulin in the back of the van.

'The only reason it'll go off is if your fat arse sits on it,' Michael replied.

The two brothers in front chuckled as they continued on a straight stretch of road. On their left was a set of office blocks and the commercial entrance to the Friary Shopping Centre in the heart of Guildford.

A lorry pulled out in front of them. Danny swerved, narrowly avoiding the nose of the vehicle, and cursed beneath his breath. Luke recognised where they were – they had done a recce of the area a few days ago – and sat down, pressing his back against the metal frame his head had collided with moments ago. They were less than two minutes away, and a seed of emotion had crept into his mind. This time, however, he was sure it wasn't the excitement or adrenaline that usually accompanied him on their heists. It was different. Emotions that he'd never felt before. The adrenaline of a job usually ravaged his body, made him shake, made him smile, made him feel alive. But this time he was filled with worry, regret and a terrible premonition that something was going to go wrong.

And, right in front of him, was the thing that made him feel that way.

The device. It was diabolical. Evil. Vicious. Luke hadn't even been aware that sort of sinister equipment existed. But it did, thanks to Michael's research and Danny's handiwork.

Luke craned his neck over the seat and looked at the back

of Danny's head. 'You sure this is going to work, Dan?'

Danny veered the car to the left and then came to a stop. Luke knew from memory that they were at a set of traffic lights at the foot of the high street. The engine ticked over, coughing at them. 'Wouldn't be doing it if I wasn't, Lukey. Not flaking out on us now, are ya?'

'Nah.'

'Just think of how much pussy you're gonna get when this is all done, mate. There'll be seas of it.' Danny chuckled. 'Think how much pussy we're all gonna get.' He slapped Michael on the shoulder.

'You sure you ain't gonna miss Louise?' Michael asked Danny. 'Swear I saw you cry when you broke up with her.'

'Don't you worry about her, mate. She's long gone,' Danny answered. 'Just remember one thing though, boys.'

'What's that?'

'That, when this is all done and we're out of here, you guys remain loyal to me. You owe me one.'

'Where'd you get that idea from?'

'Louise. She told me to sack you lot off, but I said no. Nobody splitting me and my brothers up. So you better remember that, eh, Lukey!'

Before Luke was able to respond, the traffic lights changed, and Danny slipped into first gear and pulled up onto Guildford High Street. Luke's body tilted to the side as they climbed the steady incline, and as the van rolled over the cobbled pavements, his body began to shake violently. A deafening sound quickly filled the van, silencing all conversation. *Just as well*, Luke thought. He couldn't bear to listen to more episodes of Danny and Louise. *Even if they are broken up*.

A few seconds later, the vehicle slowed to a stop. Luke lifted himself up and glanced out of the windscreen. He checked the dash – 9:03 a.m. A few minutes behind schedule. By now, all the shops had opened, and the only people on the high street were either keen shoppers or employees running late for their shifts, hurrying down the hill. On their left, near the top of the road, was Bridgewater Jewellers. Their next hit. Independently owned. Hand-crafted jewellery. Made with emotion and love. All that crap.

'All right, lads,' Danny said, sliding the handbrake on, 'this is it. Get yourselves ready. Game time.'

Michael leant forward into the footwell, reached inside a gym bag by his feet and produced three masks. Their trademark. The masks were made from latex and depicted the face of the devil. Two large white horns protruded from the top corners of their heads and a black snake climbed between a set of fangs, exited the mouth and made its way up the cheek.

Michael passed them round, and they each took one. Danny placed his on his face and pulled his hood over his head, Michael tucked away what little of his fringe remained, and Luke pulled his full head of hair from his face, snapped the elastic band against the back of his skull and zipped his coat to his neck. They each wore crimson overalls, covering them from head to toe.

Simultaneously, Michael and Danny jumped out of the car and ran to the rear. A second later, the double doors opened, flooding light into the small space. Through the slits in the mask, Luke blinked away the brightness and restored his vision to normality. By his leg, lying on the floor, was a row of three Mini-Uzis, clamped down by cable ties to keep them in place. Beside them, a Stanley knife. Luke grabbed the knife, severed the ties, and handed them a weapon each. Danny had suggested using them as their weapon for the hit. They were small, compact, capable of rapid fire and easy to carry.

Luke loaded the magazine into his clip, aimed down the sights for good measure, then hopped out of the van. Shutting the doors behind him, he left the device in the back, ready and waiting to be used for the next part of their operation.

Bridgewater was open, as they'd expected. Danny strolled through, keeping his arm down by his side. Michael followed immediately after, then Luke. Neither of them protested that he'd disrupted the usual working order of things. This was Danny's heist – he was in charge – and if he was going to break their usual mould, then so be it.

The inside of the jeweller's was empty save for two cashiers behind their desks and another who sat in a half-opened booth in discussion with a client.

'Hands in the air!' Danny shouted, raising the gun. 'Now!'

'Move!' Luke screamed. 'Get down on the ground now!'

Danny made a beeline for the two workers standing behind the cash desk on the left-hand side of the room, while Luke rushed to the booth on the opposite side, pointing the gun at a brown-haired woman and a balding man. Luke's breathing raced and the sound of his heart pounded in his ears, drowning the screams and shouts surrounding him. All thought of fear and guilt had quickly dissipated, as though they had never been there in the first place, and were now replaced with pure, animalistic adrenaline.

'Don't even think about it,' Danny said.

Luke snapped his head towards Danny; one of the employees had her finger hovering over a panic button on the underside of the desk. If Danny's reactions had been a fraction slower, she would have pressed it and within seconds, their worst fears of being caught would have come true.

'Put your hands in the air now!' Danny screamed, his temper dwindling. 'Or I'll blow your fucking face off.'

The woman stared at him defiantly. She was blonde, portly and had a look on her face that Luke knew meant she had an attitude. Luke glanced at the badge on her left breast. Her name was Candice.

In the background, Michael was making his way around the shop, pilfering the contents from the cash register and window displays. Shards of glass splintered into a thousand pieces and rained down on the soft carpet, scattering across the floor. Michael lifted his gym bag beneath the cabinet, and with a sweeping motion, poured the jewels and diamonds into the bag, scattering some to the floor. Watches. Rings. Earrings. Diamonds. Necklaces. Charms. They had everything.

Luke's eyes danced between his hostages and Danny. Danny still held the gun inches from Candice's face, but his brother's arms were shaking. Something wasn't right. Something was happening that hadn't been part of the plan.

'Hey…' Luke said, snapping his head back to the woman and man in front of him. He switched the gun between them both, left and right like a tennis match.

'There's no need to panic, people,' Danny said, keeping his eyes maintained on Candice. 'This will only take a short while, and all you need to do is stand still and put your *fucking* hands in the air.'

Out the corner of his eye, Luke noticed Candice gradually raise her hands and breathed a sigh of relief. In all their years, in all their heists, they had never fired a shot on a single person. Though, for a brief moment, Luke thought that had all been about to change.

'There was nothing difficult about that, was there?'

Danny said through gritted teeth.

Candice spat at him, a globule of phlegm landing on his overalls and on the cheek of his mask.

Before anyone could react, Michael shouted, 'It's done. We've got everything, now let's go.'

Nobody said anything. Nobody moved.

Luke's heart pounded in his chest. By now, his attention was entirely focused on the dynamic between Candice and Danny. He lowered the gun without realising it and grabbed Danny by the shoulder. 'Come on! We've got everything. Let's get the fuck out of here!'

Danny remained still. The gun had stopped shaking in his grip. 'She's coming with us,' he said calmly.

'No! You can't!' came the cry of the staff member standing beside Candice. She lowered her hands and reached out for the gun, protecting Candice's face. 'Please, don't—'

Before she finished, Danny spun on the spot, pointed the gun at the employee's head and pulled the trigger. The deafening sound split Luke's ears in two. His body jolted and he blinked, stepping backward as the bullet tore through the woman's neck and buried itself in the wall at the back of the room. Blood sprayed against the shattered shards of glass and metal stands, sparkling in the fluorescent light overhead. Screams emanated from the booth in the corner of the room, and both the man and woman cowered underneath the table. But Candice did nothing. She remained perfectly still, her face freckled by flecks of the woman's blood.

Danny groaned, lowered the weapon, grabbed her arm and yanked her towards Luke and Michael. Michael hooked her other arm, and the four of them got out of there. Candice wriggled and writhed against their grip, but she was no match for them all, so she kicked and screamed, letting her body fall to the ground as if she were a deadweight. Michael stopped, handed Luke his weapon and shoved him away from her. Then he bent down, picked her up and hefted her over his shoulder in a fireman's carry.

Luke raced to the back of the van, his pulse racing, swung open the doors and held the nearest one open with Danny. Michael bounded over, ignoring the punches that Candice threw into his face as she struggled to break free. As he arrived, he bent his legs and launched her into the back of the van, throwing her into the chasm of uncertainty and despair.

As they were about to close the doors, in the street, to Danny's right, a middle-aged man with thinning brown hair advanced towards them.

'Hey! What are you doing!' he yelled, holding a phone to his ear. 'I'm calling the police!'

Everyone wants to be a fucking hero, Luke thought, and as the man approached them, Danny smacked him in the stomach with the butt of his gun. The man doubled over, dropped the phone and staggered forward; Danny grabbed him by the shirt and launched him into the back of the van to accompany Candice. In the background, a high-pitched scream pierced the air.

'Roger!' somebody called.

Panting, breathless, Danny threw the door shut.

Luke stared at him, his eyes wild behind the mask.

'What are you—?' Luke began.

'Shut up and get in!'

Luke did as instructed. He climbed into the back of the van with Candice and the Good Samaritan, and pressed his back against the van's doors, pointing his gun at them both. Less than two seconds later, Danny hopped into the front, started the engine and pulled away just as the sound of sirens filled the high street. The tyres screeched on the cobbles and the van shot off.

Luke's chest heaved. His heart raced.

They had just robbed hundreds of thousands of pounds' worth of jewels and diamonds.

They had just kidnapped the woman they needed for the next part of their job.

But there was a problem: they had another hostage with them.

And they were going to have to deal with him one way or another.

CHAPTER 2

EAGER BEAVER

Jake Tanner had never been to Guildford before. And, upon first impressions, it didn't seem like a place he'd want to spend much time in. At least, any more than was necessary. There wasn't much to see, nor was there a lot to do. Everything was surrounded by green and trees and fields and bushes; the closest he'd ever been to a jungle like that was when he'd been in a safari park as a teenager. He was a city boy through and through, and enormous expanses of space was unfamiliar to him.

The drive down from his home in Croydon had been long and monotonous, a far cry from the short and snappy distances he was accustomed to in the city of London. His Austin Mini Cooper had worsened the journey. It was more than double his age, and it showed. The suspension was non-existent, and it would cost him more than he paid for it to get it fixed. Still, it was his dream car, and he couldn't afford to replace it.

Jake pulled off Sandy Lane, leaving the row of overhanging trees behind, and entered the Surrey Police Headquarters car park. Mount Browne looked as though it had been a stately mansion in a former life, a host for aristocracy and the wealthy with its eaves, vaulted walls and several chimneys dotted on the roof. Now, however, it had been transformed into the hub of a vibrant and buzzing police force, the home of one of Surrey Police's satellite Major Crime Team divisions.

Jake climbed a small flight of steps, entered the foyer and wandered to the front desk. A pen chained to the surface dangled over the edge, and a few police leaflets were fanned across the surface.

'Morning,' he said to the unenthused member of staff on the other side of the desk.

'Name?'

'Temporary Detective Constable Jake Tanner,' he said. He knew it wasn't necessary to mention his rank, but he was proud of himself for achieving it and sought every opportunity to remind people of it. 'Here to meet with DCI Nicki Pemberton.'

Jake removed his warrant card from his pocket and flashed it in the man's face. The man dismissed it and, instead, reached for a clipboard and slid it across the desk's surface.

'Sign in.'

Jake did as he was told and scribbled his name, rank and sign-in time on the sheet. Passing it back to the reception officer, he asked, 'Is there a coffee machine anywhere?'

14

The man grunted and pointed to Jake's right. Then he leant over the arm of his chair, disappearing beneath the desk and returned a moment later with a polystyrene cup. 'Put it in the bin when you're finished with it. Nicki will be down in a few minutes. You can wait over by the cushioned seats.'

Jake acknowledged what the man had said, thanked him and moved over to the coffee machine. He prodded the button for a latte and waited. As the steaming water filled the cup, Jake read the literature on the corkboard in front of him. Dozens of leaflets dangled from the wall. '*An Introduction to Your Rights*'. '*So, You've Been Arrested*'. '*How to Report a Crime*'. '*How to Report a Police Officer*'. Jake had read them all. Back to back. Cover to cover. Police training 101.

Once the coffee machine finished, Jake found himself a seat on a small armchair so old and dirty that when he sat down, a plume of dust billowed in the air. Fighting to keep his cough down, he drank the coffee. It was bitter, too hot and made him gag. But it was enough to perk him up in the morning. For too long he had suffered restless nights and found himself becoming increasingly dependent on caffeine. Sure, having an eighteen-month old at home, and working a job that was unforgiving in his schedule and time, didn't help. But it was his life, his choice, and he was loving every minute of it.

Jake leant forward to place the cup on the table in front of him.

Someone called his name.

'DC Tanner.'

He flinched, almost knocking the cup to the floor, then composed himself before rising from the chair.

15

DCI Pemberton, a slim, experienced woman with a lob haircut, stood behind him, her hand extended. Jake, in a frantic rush as if he had just locked eyes with a celebrity, wiped his hand on his trousers and took hers. With his other hand, he brushed his black-and-grey-striped tie – the one that his wife had bought him the birthday before he joined The Met – centred it and pushed it deeper into his collar.

'Thank you for joining us,' Pemberton said. Her grip was powerful and firm, and she spoke with a certain authority he hadn't heard in a while. In a way, she reminded him of his mum, and at once he knew he wouldn't want to get on the wrong side of her.

'Thanks for having me. I hope I can be of some assistance.'

'So do I. I've heard some good things about you. You travelled far this morning?'

He shrugged. 'Only Croydon.'

'Enjoy the coffee?' Pemberton's left eyebrow rose.

Jake glanced over his shoulder at the bead of brown liquid running down the length of the cup. 'Yeah, it was nice, thanks.' He rubbed his cheek, massaging his fingers over the small scar that had prohibited any facial hair from growing around it.

Pemberton smirked, drawing Jake's eyes to her mouth. As he observed her, he noticed the residue of make-up on her collar. 'You're a superb liar,' she said. 'You should fit in fine here.'

Pemberton started off towards a set of double doors at the back of the lobby. Jake gave one last look at the cup of coffee, checked he hadn't left anything else behind and followed. Pemberton scanned her card, and they both waited until a green light flashed above the card reader and the doors opened.

She led Jake through a myriad of corridors and offices until they eventually stopped by a lift. Pemberton pressed the button, and, as they entered, chose the fourth floor of the building.

'This your first time working with us?' she asked as the doors closed.

'Yeah. First time I've ever been this far south of London.'

'First time for everything,' she said, smiling at him. 'You nervous?'

'The opposite. Hardly slept last night.'

'I think you'll find Surrey's a little more docile than London. Not a lot going on.'

'There's always something going on,' Jake replied exuberantly. He didn't care if he sounded like an excitable child. This was a big day for him. One that he'd been looking forward to for a long time. He was taking the next step in his career. And this was just the beginning.

The lift doors opened and revealed a vast expanse of office space. With a thin smile on his face, Jake crossed the threshold into the Major Crime Team, the beating heart of the building. The room stretched twenty feet wide and nearly eighty deep. Along the first half of the right-hand side was a series of offices. Closed-off. Private. Beyond that, in the far-right corner, was an even larger office space – almost the size of the entire floor. A long, wooden table sat in the centre of the room pressed against the nearest side of the wall. It was in the shape of a horseshoe. Inside, Jake noticed dozens of corkboards hanging from the wall, a television at the head of the room, and portable whiteboards on wheels in

17

the free space. The other side of the office housed the rest of the Major Crime Team. Jake counted another twenty bodies in the department, busy tapping their keyboards and mice behind their computer screens. He soaked in the atmosphere. There was a liveliness to it, a raw energy that enthused him. It signified to him that each day was new, and each day would bring about something exciting. In the time he'd been training as a detective constable, that was what he admired most about the job: the camaraderie, the friendships. Everyone within the team was a family. If one went down, they all went down.

'Welcome to Major Crime.' Pemberton nudged him on the shoulder then pointed to a desk in the far-left corner of the room, beside the office printer, which was larger than the desk itself. 'You're sat over there. Next to Danika.'

'She's here already?' Jake craned his neck in search of his colleague. 'I didn't see her name on the sign-in sheet downstairs.'

'She was here an hour before anyone in reception on the night shift had woken up. She's putting you to shame.'

Jake chuckled. 'I'm sure I can change that.'

Pemberton led Jake deeper into the room, past the other detectives who were busy working through their emails and filing paperwork. Some glanced up at him, curious, while some ignored him, as though he were just an intern that had no authority over anyone, or anything, in the building.

As they approached Jake's desk, Danika, Jake's colleague from Croydon Station, rose and waved. Her hair was pulled from her face by two kirby grips either side of her face.

Just as Jake was about to open his mouth, Pemberton said that she would leave the two of them to it, and that she

18

would return in a minute – there was something else she needed to sort out quickly.

'About time you got here, no?' Danika said, her Slovenian accent lacing her words. 'I was beginning to think that you might have got nervous.'

'Traffic was a nightmare,' he lied.

'You didn't fancy staying overnight, no?'

'I didn't want to leave Elizabeth alone with Maisie for too long. She's been throwing up all night, and ever since I left this morning.'

Danika sat, and Jake found his desk opposite her, their backs to one another. He pulled out the chair and reclined deep into the soft cushion.

'Is Elizabeth going to be all right without you?' Danika asked. She moved a few strands of hair behind her ear, revealing a studded earring and a mole on the helix of her ear.

Jake shrugged. 'She's got her mum to help. And mine's on standby as well if they need anything else. They only live a few miles down the road.'

'I'm sure she won't need that much help.'

'Well, you know what they say…'

'What's that?' Danika asked.

'That behind every good man is an even stronger woman – and a mum.' The sides of Jake's lips flickered skyward.

'And, equally so, behind every evil man is an even worse woman that is pulling all the strings.' Danika's eyes fell to the ground, and she swayed in her chair.

'Tony still threatening legal action?' Jake asked.

Before Danika could respond, Pemberton returned. 'You settled in yet?' she asked him.

Jake swivelled in his chair and glanced at the blank computer screen. 'I, er... I haven't had a chance to log in yet.'

'OK, never mind...' Pemberton turned as somebody in the distance entered the room. It was a tall, well-dressed man. He wore a suit, had a thin moustache and his Adam's apple was the size of a golf ball. Jake estimated he was in his mid- to late-thirties. And Jake had experienced enough men at that age around Scotland Yard to know what sort of person he was going to be: autocratic, arrogant and intent on setting the hierarchy in motion – especially because Jake and Danika were outsiders.

The man wandered over to them.

'Guys,' Pemberton began, 'this is DS Bridger... DS Bridger, this is DC Jake Tanner and DC Danika Oblak. Temporary DCs who have been seconded from the Met. From what I hear they've got plenty of experience with serious and organised crime so should be a lot of help to us.'

The man came to a stop beside Pemberton and wiped his top lip. He was flustered – his cheeks rouged – and he was out of breath. Light bounced off his shiny forehead.

'Still only temps and already you're moving up in the world?' Bridger asked. 'You must be good. Welcome to the best team in the country – and don't you let anyone tell you otherwise. Most people just call me Bridger.'

Jake shook Bridger's hand; it felt wet.

'Where have you been?' Pemberton asked, her voice neutral and plain, as if she were forcing herself to sound as though she cared.

'I just had to run a quick errand. Nothing major.' Bridger turned his attention to Danika, and he eyed her up and down. 'How long you two been training for, then?'

'Couple of years,' Jake said. 'Currently revising for the NIE – the National Investigators—'

Bridger held his hand up. 'Yeah, I know what it is, mate. I wouldn't be here if I hadn't taken it myself. You're leaving it late though, aren't you? Isn't the exam in a few days' time?'

Jake shook his head. 'Ours is September.'

'Eager beavers, eh? Revising for something three months away. I think I crammed in all my revision a couple of nights before.'

'And how did that turn out for you?' Danika asked, eyebrow raised. She carried about her the usual no-nonsense Eastern European attitude that Jake had grown to love and appreciate. The way she was able to shoot anyone down without even meaning to. The way she saw through any semblance of bullshit in the way people spoke. It was magical, and Jake wondered whether it had fully landed on Bridger, or whether there was still more to come.

Bridger smirked. 'I'm still here, aren't I?'

The conversation fell flat. Beside him, Danika excused herself. Jake watched her wander down the corridor over his left shoulder and turn into the toilets. As he spun his neck back to face Bridger, the telephones in the office started ringing. It was a deafening cacophony of sound, unlike anything he had heard at Croydon Station. Someone in the room's background answered the call while everyone else seemed to watch, waiting in high anticipation.

They waited. And waited.

Jake looked up at Bridger and opened his mouth in an attempt to engage his new colleague in more conversation. But it was useless; Bridger was too focused on the officer speaking into the handset.

21

The woman lowered the phone and rose. All eyes were on her.

'We've got ourselves armed robbery in progress on Guildford High Street. Bridgewater Jewellers. Reports of gunfire and a potential murder. First responders are already on the scene with paramedics. Scene of crime officers are pulling in as we speak.'

The atmosphere in the department instantly changed. Everyone stood and rushed to the other side of the room, concentrating their efforts on the Horseshoe. One of them grabbed a marker and began writing on the whiteboard. Jake looked around him and noticed Bridger had shot off; he hadn't even seen him go.

Jake rose out of his chair, trying to make sense of the flurry of activity that was taking place around him. At the head of the room, DCI Pemberton returned from behind a closed door and advanced towards the clutch of officers huddled together in the corner.

'All right, team. You know what to do. Set up the Incident Room. I want a key decisions log started and in my hands before I leave the building. DI Murphy – I want you as my deputy. I'm leaving you in charge of HOLMES and administering lines of enquiry while I attend the scene. Send in a couple more of the team once you've assigned their roles. DS Bridger – I want you to come with me. You're driving.' She stopped and searched the crowd. After her eyes fell on Jake, she said, 'And DC Tanner will be accompanying us. Grab your coat, Jake, it's time to go.'

CHAPTER 3

INTUITION

Jake stepped out of the car and closed the door behind him. They were halfway down Guildford High Street, and had been sat there for a few minutes, stuck in traffic, trying to turn onto the cobbled road just before the outer cordon that had been set up at the bottom of the road. Rows of shops and other businesses ran up the length of the street on either side. Overhead was a string of bunting advertising a farmers' market due to take place in a few days' time. And, just beneath it on the left-hand side, was the Guildford Clock, one of the few landmarks that Jake had researched after a quick online search in preparation for his visit.

Jake's eyes lowered. In front of him were four other police cars and two ambulances positioned awkwardly at different angles on the road. The entire street was cordoned off, and a uniformed officer stood on the other side of the white tape, his hands folded in front of him, his police cap pulled low over his eyes, his high-visibility jacket reflecting the early morning sun beating down on them from behind. It wasn't even 10 a.m. and Jake was already beginning to feel the sun's rays warming his back.

Jake, Pemberton and Bridger approached the uniformed officer. They flashed their warrant cards and signed in on the log he held in his hands. Everyone who attended the crime scene was instructed to register their time in and out, and the purpose of their visit. Jake nodded appreciatively to the officer as he ducked under the tape and moved over to the forensic tent that had been erected on the side of the street. Inside, Jake, Pemberton and Bridger grabbed a forensic scene suit – consisting of mask, hood, gloves and overshoes – and donned it. Jake hated wearing them – they always rubbed and chafed his hands and neck – but he also knew the importance of wearing them at the vital stages of an early investigation.

'Ready?' Pemberton asked, already on her way out of the tent, heading towards the crime scene. It was then that Jake noticed she'd left the incident log behind in the car.

Jake hurried after her. Outside the crime scene, a woman and a man were sitting on the edge of the van being checked over by a couple of paramedics. At the top end of the high street, a crowd had formed, and employees from other shops – replete in their multicoloured uniforms – along the street were still being funnelled out, moving to a safe distance. The sound of gossip and buzz and excitable conversation permeated the air like a dense fog.

As they arrived outside the jewellers, Pemberton turned to face them both, and said, 'SOCO have said it's OK for us to have a look. But we've got to be brief.'

They shuffled past the scene of crime officers at the front of the shop and entered. Pemberton first, followed by Bridger and then Jake. He was following the natural pecking order, and he didn't mind. He was there to learn. These people were his seniors, and he had to respect that. Though it didn't stop him feeling both nervous and excited about what lay ahead.

As they entered the store, treading lightly across the stepping plates that SOCO had placed on the ground, glass crunched underfoot and sent shivers up Jake's spine which branched out to the rest of his body like the splintered window displays. Three more crime scene investigators were huddled together in the centre of the shop, hovering over a body, snapping photographs of the gunshot wound to her neck. One of them moved closer to Jake and set an evidence marker down by the shell casing in front of him. Jake averted his gaze from the dead body and chose to observe his surroundings instead. The shop was no larger than his living room at home. On the left was a desk. Resting atop it was a computer, a cash register and a telephone. Behind that, a cabinet. And, on the right-hand side, a small booth with a desk in between the seats. Spread across the back wall was blood, dripping, forming streaks down the faces of the cabinets – it reminded Jake of a scene from *Carrie*. A few sparkling rings and bracelets and necklaces that had been dropped and abandoned on the floor, shimmered as Jake and the rest of his party distorted the ambient and artificial light above.

'Doesn't look like they were being too careful,' Bridger remarked, looking at the floor. 'It looks like they've thrown half of it about the place.'

'I think you should be more concerned with finding out who *"they"* are, Elliot,' Pemberton said, shooting him a disgusted and disapproving scowl.

'When are we going to find out who's in command, here?' Bridger asked.

A voice came from behind them. It startled Jake. He spun on the spot and searched for the owner of the voice. On the other side of the door, standing on the pavement, was a uniformed officer. The three of them exited the shop, shuffled past the investigators in the doorway and moved over to the officer.

'I'm in charge,' he said as they fanned themselves out before him.

'And you are?' Bridger asked.

'PS Byrd. Some of my team were the first responders.'

'Excellent,' Pemberton said, brushing past Jake to get closer to Byrd. She informed the officer that she was the SIO and that she was now in charge of the crime scene and investigation. 'What have you got for us, sergeant?'

'Armed robbery, ma'am. Witnesses report a group of armed robbers stormed the building just after nine, looted the contents and opened fire on one of the employees. The witnesses' clothes have been taken for further examination. Paramedics announced extinction of life as soon as they were on the scene. SOCO are securing the body and preserving as much evidence surrounding the body, as you can see. And the witnesses are currently being seen to by a paramedic. Reports are suggesting the robbers evacuated the scene in a black van and their exit route was at the top of the high street.'

'Very concise, sergeant.' Pemberton interrupted. 'Have you got scene logs for both of the cordons?'

Byrd nodded.

'House-to-house enquiries conducted and collated from the shops on the high street?'

Another nod.

'What about first accounts – have you obtained those yet?'

This time Byrd shook his head. He'd made it two for three, and from the discouraged look on his face, Jake assumed the officer had been hoping he'd be able to make it a full house by the time the SIO arrived.

'When can we speak with them?' Pemberton asked.

PS Byrd stepped to the side and gestured at the man and woman who Jake had spotted sitting on the back of the ambulance. Both were dressed in matching tracksuit bottoms and jumper a few feet from them. Their faces were ashen, their arms folded across their chest. The woman's body shuddered, and she rubbed her arms as if she were cold despite the warm sun.

'Thank you, officer. We will take it from here.'

Pemberton stepped in front of Jake. She held her warrant card in her hands. 'My name is DCI Pemberton and these are my colleagues. We are here to help you and make sure that you are OK and safe. I know this is a very stressful time for you both, but I'm going to need you to tell me what happened here?'

For a long while neither of them said anything.

'Anything you can remember now will be greatly appreciated.'

'It all happened so fast…' the woman replied, keeping

her head low, avoiding any of their gazes. 'We… We opened at nine. Just like every morning. This gentleman wanted to buy a ring, so I offered to help him. Just as we sat down, a black van pulled up outside. Three men jumped out with guns. They screamed at us. Told us to put our hands up. And that… if we didn't, then they would…' She paused a beat; there was a catch in her throat, and she coughed, clearing it. 'They shot Rachel. Then they took everything. All the money. All the watches, rings… everything. And then… And then…'

'What? Go on…' Pemberton urged gently.

'They took our manager. Candice Strachan. They drove off with her in the back of the van,' the employee replied. A tear formed in her eye, and she wiped her cheek with the back of her hand.

Jake froze. Until this moment, it had seemed like a normal armed robbery: guns, jewels, a getaway vehicle. But now there was another dynamic to it that Jake hadn't expected.

'Took her?' Pemberton repeated. 'What do you mean?'

'They kidnapped her. They abducted her and put her in the back of the van and then they drove off.'

Shit.

'Did you see which way they went?'

They both shook their head.

'How many of them were there?'

'Three,' the witnesses replied simultaneously.

'What were they wearing?'

'They were dressed in red. Lots of red.'

Double shit.

'Did you get a clear look at their faces?' Pemberton asked. 'Any defining features? Characteristics?'

'No,' Jake said before the witnesses had a chance to respond.

'Excuse me, Jake?' Pemberton snapped. Her inflection turned sour.

'They won't have seen their faces.' Jake faced the man and woman. 'Let me guess – they were wearing red devil masks as well, weren't they?'

They nodded. The only thing audible was the sound of Jake's heartbeat in his ears as the gravity of what their confirmation meant resonated around his head.

'How do *you* know?' Bridger asked. He seemed more annoyed at the fact Jake knew something he didn't than anything else. Until then, he had remained on the outskirts of the conversation.

'Is there something you need to tell us, Jake?' Pemberton asked.

'I've dealt with these robbers in the past,' Jake said. He hoped that would be all the detail he needed to offer, but it wasn't. Instead, they all gazed at him, silently pleading with him for more information. Sighing, he gave it to them. 'When I was twenty-one, I went to purchase my first car in Oxford. We were in the bank when a bunch of guys stormed in and robbed us. They took us all hostage and then got rid of us all...' Jake looked into each of their eyes before continuing. 'Except for me. Their leader – the others managed to escape – kept me with him, until eventually I convinced him to leave the bank with me, and then he got arrested. You've heard of them before. Everyone in the country probably has. They call themselves The Crimsons. I'm the reason their robbery in Oxford was a failure. I'm the reason their former leader, Freddy Miller, is in prison.

Nobody's seen them for years. And I think they've just claimed Guildford as their next victim.'

CHAPTER 4

THE DEVICE

Danny killed the engine.

'Nobody move,' he told them.

He slid himself out of the driver's seat, rounded the van and opened the back doors. The light poured in, forcing Candice and the Good Samaritan to shield their eyes with their arms. He leant in, reached for Candice, hooked his hand in the nook of her armpit and pulled her out of the van. As Danny hefted her to her feet, she stopped squirming, and he gazed out upon the mansion in front of them. They were outside Candice's house; for the next phase in their operation, they had forced her to give them directions. They had driven down winding, narrow country lanes, past large fields of green, and through a security gate to get there. The mansion before him was magnificent. Georgian. Elizabethan. Victorian. He didn't care. It was from one of those periods, and it was one of the most elegant properties he'd seen. Almost as large as the estate that he and his brothers had grown up on.

'Looks like we hit the jackpot here, lads,' Danny said, pulling Candice forward until she was in front of him, making them look as though they were new homeowners gazing out at their latest purchase.

Behind him, Luke shuffled out of the back of the van and grabbed the Good Samaritan by the collar. Luke groaned as he heaved the man out and up onto his feet.

'Please,' the man whimpered. 'Please, I… I don't want— You can't—'

Danny stopped and turned to face him, squinting behind the mask.

'What are we going to do about him?' Luke asked, pointing the gun at the babbling mess.

'I don't know,' Danny replied. 'Kill him.'

'No! Please! Please! No!' The man fell onto his knees and clasped his hands together, begging them.

'You were the one who wanted to be the hero, mate. You've done this to yourself.'

'I didn't mean to. I'm sorry. Please don't hurt me.'

Michael rounded the back of the van, sidestepped over the man and pulled out the device, wrapping it tightly in the tarpaulin. He clutched it in his arms and held it as though it were a cushion bearing wedding rings. Priceless. Delicate.

'Just carry on as planned, Dan. We'll leave him behind,' Michael added as he joined Luke's side.

'Names, you fucking idiot,' Danny snapped. 'What did I say about using names?'

Danny shut his mouth and exhaled deeply through his

nose, feeling the tension in his body release, but there was still a long way to go – especially if he wanted to continue with the next phase of his plan. Danny ignored his brothers and turned his attention to the house, bathing in its grandeur.

'How did someone like you afford a place like this?' he asked, only then realising that Candice was still locked in his grip.

'Husband,' she said. 'He was an art dealer. Somehow managed to sell art to Russians and other wealthy Eastern Europeans. Then he had a heart attack and left it all to me in the will.'

Danny led Candice to the house where she let them inside using a spare key hidden behind a brick in the wall.

The interior of the mansion was just as luxurious and opulent as the outside. Marble floors. Grand staircases. Glistening chandeliers dangling from thirty-foot ceilings. Mahogany cabinets housing glasses and plates and cutlery. The majority of the interior was old-school, old-fashioned, collectible. Something, Danny felt, that was out of the Middle Ages. Nothing too high-tech. No seventy-inch plasmas, million-pound fish tanks, self-flushing toilets, pool tables, indoor swimming pools, or Lamborghinis or Ferraris hidden in an underground garage. Nothing that would be worth stealing and selling on afterward.

'What the fuck is all this? Can't take anything in here,' Michael said, adjusting his grip on the device.

'Shut up,' Danny snapped. He stopped paying attention to the opulence of the house and the paintings that hung on the wall. There was a job to do, and time was running out. He didn't know how long they had left until the police

33

arrived. And he wasn't going to start pissing about to find out. He pointed to a spot in the middle of the foyer.

'Sit down,' he told Candice.

'Why?'

'Because I told you to.'

'You're not going to hurt me, are you?'

'Not directly.'

'What's that supposed to mean?'

Danny turned to Michael, then gesticulated with his finger to walk over to him. Michael removed the piece of plastic sheeting protecting the device.

At the sight of it, Candice's eyes widened, and her mouth fell open. The colour ran away from her cheeks, and she shuddered.

Perfect, Danny thought – it was the same reaction Luke and Michael had given when he'd introduced them to the idea it.

'What... What is it?' Candice asked, lowering herself to the floor; beside her, Luke pushed the man to the ground. He fell and landed hard on his shoulder; the momentum carried him, and he rolled onto his back. Danny paid him little heed; he had no need for the man, but he wasn't in the mood to kill him and give him any more attention than he deserved. The Good Samaritan could wait with Candice on the floor.

Returning his attention to Michael, Danny took the device from his brother and felt the immediate strain in his bicep.

'This... is a collar bomb.' He opened the mechanical lock and snapped it shut; it closed with a frightening *crack*.

'What does it do?'

'It fits round your neck. It should be a nice and snug fit.

34

There's a countdown inside. And four locks. Each lock requires a key. The keys are scattered around the place – if you can find them and remove the device *before* the countdown ticks down, you'll live, you get me? If not, the tiny charge inside this' – Danny knocked on the rectangular box of metal connected to the collar of the device – 'will spring six spikes into your neck and kill you instantly.'

Candice's body tightened. His invention was having its desired effect. This was going to be his final moment of evil. His final moment of heroism that everybody would remember The Crimsons for. This callous, destructive device that would impart doom on the bearer. It was genius.

He was a genius.

'Please,' Candice said, scrambling, her fingers clawing at the smooth surface of the marble flooring. 'No. There must be something else. Some other way. What do you want to come from this? Money? I have loads. Just take it. All of this stuff may look like a load of shit to you, but I promise you it holds its value. Take it now. Keep it. Sell it in a few years' time and you'll have hit the lottery. Please don't do this. I've got children. They depend on me.'

Danny smirked behind the mask.

'You don't get it, do you? It's too late. Soon, you'll be just as famous as us. You'll be the one people make documentaries about. Your face will be on the news. You'll be an icon – along with us. The final member of The Crimsons. Maybe they'll call you The Faceless Crimson because they won't even be able to identify you when that thing detonates. No one will know who we are, but they'll know you, and they'll know your name for all the wrong reasons.'

35

'B-But... do you not want them to know yours as well?'

'Did Jack the Ripper want people to know who he was? We want to be bigger than that. Bigger than him. We want to create a legacy. And you're going to play your part.'

Danny snapped his fingers, and Michael took the collar bomb from him and stuck the device around Candice's neck. She screamed and tried to wriggle away as Michael sealed the device shut, but her efforts were futile against the man who outweighed her two to one. Once the device was clamped around her neck, the corners of Danny's mouth rose.

'Don't panic. You'll have help soon – providing they can do their job properly and get here in time.'

Candice's chest heaved, raising the metal plate containing the small charge up and down against her breast.

'We'll make it easy for you,' Michael said, crouching down by her side. He reached inside his pocket, removed a piece of paper and handed it to Danny.

'The clue for the first key is written on here. The location for the others will be revealed as you discover the rest of them. Read the clues and decide for yourself whether it's worth the risk of going alone or waiting for the officers of the law to help you.'

Danny passed the letter to Candice, who inspected it for a beat. While she looked at the paper, Danny gave the signal to Luke, and at once his younger brother disappeared deeper into the mansion, climbing the steps behind Candice.

'How long?' Candice asked, raising her head.

'Till the boys in blue arrive?'

'No.'

'Until it detonates?'

Candice's expression remained impassive.

'You'll just have to wait and find out.'

Out the corner of his eye, Luke returned to the conversation. At the sight of him, Danny rose to his feet, picked up the tarpaulin from the floor and ordered his brothers to leave the house. They had done it. Now all they needed to do was to get out of there without being seen or arrested, and then head south where, in a matter of hours, they'd be free.

CHAPTER 5

LIKE OLD FRIENDS

As soon as the front door creaked shut, Candice dropped the paper to the floor and her body convulsed. Her breathing sped up, rapidly filling her brain with oxygen until the room began to spin, left and right, left and right, left and right, the sensation unrelenting.

The collar bomb drowned her. With each passing second – and each exasperated breath – the metal collar containing the spikes attached to her neck tightened, asphyxiating the oxygen in her brain. The box attached to the collar crushed her chest, paralysing the rest of her body. Her fingers clawed at the collar in a weakened attempt to alleviate the pain and pressure of it wrapped around her throat, but it was no use.

It was settled. She was going to die.

Then she closed her eyes and tried to control her breathing, tried to calm her nerves and staunch the overflowing emotions and thoughts bursting from her brain. But they wouldn't stop. And in no time at all the nausea returned with a vengeance. Her body reacted. Candice rotated to the side and projectile vomited on her mansion floor, the orange liquid spreading across the black-and-white stones. It dirtied the collar bomb and some of her clothes, though the latter was the least of her worries.

For a moment, she toyed with the idea of fainting, of passing out, of allowing the veil of unconsciousness to descend over her and drag her down so she wouldn't have to face her imminent death. But did she want that? No. Of course not. She had a family. She had a life. She had children. She didn't want to imagine how they'd react if they heard their mother died after being impaled by six spikes. Worse, she didn't want to imagine how they'd react after they found out that she'd done nothing about it; that she'd sat idle; that she'd died defenceless.

No. She wasn't going to let this thing defeat her.

Candice rolled onto her shoulder and lifted herself to her feet. But the stranger inside her house beat her to it. The man was already standing, his arms flailing as he clawed at the ground, trying to find a grip on the surface. As their eyes locked on one another, he stood and charged towards the front door.

'Hey!' Candice screamed after him. 'Where are you going? Help me!'

The man fumbled for the handle, stopped, babbled incoherently and, within a few seconds, opened the door and sprinted out of the house. As the door swung closed, it left a large-enough gap for Candice to watch the man reach the end of the gravelled driveway and disappear up the road.

Just like that, he was gone.

Stunned that she'd been left in this situation alone, left to die, Candice searched the floor for the note. She grabbed it, and, using her arms to balance herself, struggled to her feet. The blood rushed to her head, and she swayed from side to side, teetering on the edge of collapse.

A few seconds later, she regained steadiness and controlled her breathing once more. With the taste of acid burning her mouth and throat, she read the letter. It was folded in four, and had been handwritten, but the writing looked as though it had been stencilled over a printed version of the document. It was too neat and immaculate to be someone's own handwriting.

TIME TO PLAY A LITTLE GAME. YOU'VE BEEN CHOSEN AS THE STAR CONTESTANT. YOU HAVE NO OTHER CHOICE BUT TO COMPLY. FAILURE TO DO SO WILL RESULT IN DEATH. YOU HAVE A SPIKED COLLAR EXPLOSIVE STRAPPED AROUND YOUR NECK. INSIDE THE COLLAR IS SIX SPIKES THAT, WHEN DETONATED, WILL KILL YOU. TO UNLOCK THE DEVICE, YOU NEED TO FIND FOUR KEYS. YOU HAVE AN ALLOTTED TIME OF JUST OVER FOUR HOURS TO FIND THE KEYS AND SAVE WHAT'S LEFT OF YOUR LIFE. ONE HOUR FOR EACH KEY. IT SHOULD BE SIMPLE.

HERE ARE THE RULES, BEFORE WE BEGIN.

THE DEVICE IS BOOBY-TRAPPED. SO IF YOU TRY TO REMOVE IT BY ANY MEANS OF FORCE, IT WILL DETONATE AND KILL YOU INSTANTLY. OR IF YOU TRY TO CUT ONE OF THE WIRES INSIDE THE DEVICE, YOU

WILL MEET A SIMILAR FATE. DO NOT TAMPER WITH THE DEVICE. TO DISARM THE DEVICE, YOU MUST FIND THE KEYS.

THE KEYS MUST BE COLLECTED IN ORDER: 1, 2, 3, 4. THE FIRST KEY WILL LEAD YOU TO THE SECOND, THE SECOND WILL LEAD YOU TO THE THIRD, AND THE THIRD WILL LEAD YOU TO THE LAST ONE. YOU CANNOT SKIP ANY OF THE ABOVE STEPS. YOU MAY SEEK HELP, BUT WHOEVER AGREES TO HELP YOU IS ALSO BOUND BY THESE RULES. THERE IS NO NEED TO CALL THE POLICE, AS THEY WILL FIND YOU SOON ENOUGH. ALTHOUGH, IF YOU DECIDE TO GO ALONE, THEN THEY MAY NEVER FIND YOU. YOUR LIFE IS IN BOTH YOUR HANDS, AND THEIRS.

AND, SURREY'S FINEST, IF YOU'RE READING THIS NOW, GOOD LUCK. SHE'S GOING TO NEED IT.

I HOPE THESE INSTRUCTIONS HAVE BEEN CLEAR, AND I HOPE THAT YOU UNDERSTAND HOW SERIOUS WE ARE. IN LESS THAN FOUR HOURS' TIME, SHE IS GOING TO DIE.

THE GAME HAS BEGUN.

HERE'S YOUR FIRST CLUE.

THE FIRST KEY: WHERE CLOTHES ARE LEFT TO HANG AND DRY LIKE OLD FRIENDS.

Candice stopped reading. She had just over four hours to save herself. And in her current mental and physical state, she would never make it.

The thought made her nausea return. The world turned grey, and everything inside the house spun in a carousel of white and black. Her head felt light, and she vomited again, this time more violently, bringing up chunks of half-digested breakfast onto the floor.

As she wiped her mouth clean of stomach lining, a duvet of darkness descended over her, wrapping her gently around the body and pulling her into a void of sleep.

She was unconscious before her head hit the floor.

CHAPTER 6

PROMISES

'You're wrong,' Bridger said after a long pause. The atmosphere outside the jeweller's had been still after Jake finished explaining his encounter with The Crimsons. 'It can't be,' Bridger continued. 'Nobody's seen them for years.'

'Until now,' Jake replied. 'Maybe they've been in hiding.'

Pemberton cleared her throat. 'If that's the case, then what brings them back? Why have they chosen now – and here – to come back from whatever hole they climbed into?'

Jake took a moment to consider the options. 'Maybe they've run out of money,' he began. 'Or they're bored. Or they're using it as a distraction for something else – something bigger to come…'

'Easy, DC Tanner,' Pemberton said. 'We can deal with that in a minute. Right now, we need to find Candice Strachan and we need to find the people who have got her. We can only imagine the amount of danger she's in.'

Pemberton turned to the female employee. Two black snakes ran down her cheeks and red rivers warmed her eyes. Her countenance was withdrawn, and she chewed viciously on her thumb. Pemberton lowered her voice as she spoke. 'What else can you tell me about Candice? Anything you know about her. Any friends. Family. Someone who might know where they might have taken her.'

The woman nodded. 'We have employee files. She made us have one as part of our personal development. They're inside the office.'

At once, Pemberton called a SOCO over and instructed them to go inside the office and retrieve the folders. A few seconds later, the officer returned, lever-arch folder in hand.

'There's a lot of weird information in there. And a copy of her CV. She never really mentioned anything about any friends to us.'

'Family?' Pemberton asked.

'I think she had some. She didn't talk about them that much. She spent most of the time telling stories about her past, business strategies and that sort of stuff. I think she said she was writing a book on it.'

'Have you got an address?' Pemberton asked.

'Yes. Manor's Keep, Horses Way, Farnham. I pick her up on my way to work every morning.'

Jake pulled out his pocketbook and scribbled the address down. To his right, he sensed Bridger's gaze boring into him, judging him. He ignored it.

'Thanks,' Pemberton replied to the employee, reaching into her pocket. 'Listen,' she began. She produced a contact card which had her mobile number and email address on it.

'You've been incredibly helpful. Really, you have. These are my details. Please call me if you need anything. Or if you think of anything else. Soon I will be getting some members of my team to come and bring you into the station for a full witness statement. They're going to make sure you're well looked after. And you'll have your parents or other family members notified about what's happened. Does that sound OK?'

The woman and man nodded.

Pemberton smiled, ordered PS Byrd to send the evidence back to the station for evidence retrieval and then gestured for the three of them to head back towards the car. Jake hung back, waiting, trying not to step on Bridger's, or Pemberton's, toes. As he followed behind Bridger, the woman called after him.

'Detective…'

Jake stopped and spun on the spot.

'You'll find her, won't you?' Fresh tears filled her eyes, and another lump caught in her throat. The man beside her placed his arm round her shoulder, holding her, comforting her. Jake's gaze danced between them and his colleagues in the middle of the street. He didn't know what to say.

'Will you?' the woman repeated.

Jake swallowed before responding. 'Yes, we'll find her. We'll do everything we can.'

CHAPTER 7

PRINCIPLES

Jake hurried into the office behind Bridger and snuck away to his desk.

'How was it?' Danika asked, lifting her head from her screen as he arrived beside her. Jake perched himself on the corner of her desk.

'Jewellery store torn to bits,' Jake said, readjusting his tie clip, so it was perfectly horizontal. 'One fatality – shot in the neck. Blood everywhere. Glass all over the floor. And… they've taken a hostage.'

'Who's they?' Danika asked.

As Jake opened his mouth to respond, an officer brushed past him, rushed down the corridor and made a right turn into the kitchen. Returning his attention to Danika, he kept his voice low, and said, 'I think it might be The Crimsons. But—'

'Convenient,' Danika scoffed, rolling her eyes.

'Excuse me?'

'It is your first day here and look who chooses to rob a jewellery store at the same time.'

Jake stared at her in disbelief. He perched himself higher on her desk and leant closer, resting his left arm on top of her computer screen. As he neared her, he caught a vague whiff of her perfume. Jo Malone. It had been one of Elizabeth's favourites and, back when they had been students relying on their only source of income – student loans – he had bought her a bottle for her birthday. Since then, the realities of adult life and their ever-struggling finances had prohibited them from treating themselves to expensive luxuries. It was something he hoped to change in the near future.

'You think I don't realise how strange it is myself? The Crimsons strike on the same day I start here. I caught them once. I'll catch them again. But… if this is about being picked to go with DCS Pemberton and DS Bridger, then I'm sorry. I didn't have much say in it. I wanted you to come, but you were in the toilet. I couldn't have told them to wait for you, otherwise it would have looked weird.'

'Mmhmm,' Danika mumbled as she returned her attention to the computer screen.

Jake hadn't intended to upset her – and letting people down was one of the things he hated most. In fact, he'd wanted to give her as much opportunity as himself. They were both in the same situation, and they were both on the same career trajectory, so why did she think he would actively try and get ahead of her?

Jake placed his hand across the monitor, impeding her

47

view. 'Some witnesses are being brought in soon to give a statement. They were inside the shop – they saw it all. Put yourself forward to sit in on the interview with them,' he said, but there was no response. Danika continued to focus on her screen.

Sighing, he lowered his hand and cast his gaze across the room. The entire department was standing in the Incident Room. Pemberton moved into the centre of the Horseshoe and whistled, commanding the attention of the entire room – including Danika.

Jake and Danika slowly filtered in, standing in the doorway, out of the way and out of sight.

'Right, team,' she began, 'I trust you all know your positions and what your roles are throughout this investigation by now. And if you don't, then I want you to speak to DI Murphy – he's in charge when I'm not. We're now treating this as a Critical Incident and Category A+ murder investigation. Bridgewater Jewellers is the location of the incident. At 09:03 this morning it was raided by a group of armed robbers. They've shot and murdered a civilian, IC1, and have abducted another. Our second Nominal One, Candice Strachan.'

'Make that two abductions, ma'am,' someone from the other side of the Horseshoe called out, their hand raised. 'More reports are coming in that a middle-aged man was thrown into the back of the van with Candice Strachan.'

Pemberton nodded. 'Do we have a name for our second hostage?'

'Roger Heathcote.'

'Right… one confirmed fatality, two abductions. We can't let that number get any higher, guys. Whoever's the researcher in the team, I want you to create a victimology report on Candice Strachan in as much detail as you can. Why have they abducted her? Find out who she is, where she lives, what her skills are, education, qualifications, marital status, any relationships she might have, kids she doesn't know about, what she does for fun, whether she's ever had an STI in her life – I want to know everything about her.' Pemberton paused a beat to catch her breath. 'Then we're going to need ANPR on the registration for the vehicle they were abducted in, and any CCTV footage we can get our hands on. As soon as we get a hit, I'm coming with you all on the ground – I want to make sure Candice Strachan and Roger Heathcote are returned to their friends and families safely.'

A unanimous cheer came from the rest of the office, followed by a brief round of applause.

Before Pemberton continued, another officer raised her hand. She stood, juggling several documents. 'Ma'am,' she said, 'preliminary reports are coming in on Candice Strachan. That file she created is a gold mine. It's got her CV in it and everything.'

'I'm aware. What does it say?' Pemberton urged.

The officer cleared her throat and then continued, 'Years ago, she had a couple of stints as an actress. Performing in plays, and all that sort of stuff. Says here that her next of kin is her husband, an art dealer, but a quick check on his name shows that he died a couple of years ago from a heart attack and left everything to her in his will. He had some sort of investment in Bridgewater Jewellers, and eventually she bought the company out and now owns it.'

'Bet that was a comfortable inheritance fund,' someone

near Jake jibed. The man stood with his arms folded, and as he said it, he swivelled on the spot and glanced at Jake, a smile on his face. Jake didn't know why he'd looked over to him, but he didn't reciprocate the sentiment.

'All right, DI Murphy, that's enough,' Pemberton snapped, immediately stifling any disturbance that the comment was likely to provoke. She gazed around the Incident Room and waited until there was complete silence before continuing. 'While you're trying to find her, I want a small unit dedicated to focusing on her husband, too. He might have pissed someone off in the past and they're coming to collect an old debt. Also, it's worth checking out Candice Strachan's financial history. Whether she's run out of money in the past. Whether she's done anything corrupt or dodgy dealings.'

'What are you insinuating, ma'am?' DI Murphy asked. He was standing with his hands in his pockets.

'ABC principle. Insurance fraud. She might be overdue on payments, and with an elaborate robbery like this, she'll get an insurance payout that's second to none. That'll clear any debts she's got outstanding, and then some.'

Murphy shook his head. 'It's quite sophisticated—'

'But then the ones that always slip through the net are,' Pemberton interrupted.

He shrugged. 'I think it's unlikely.'

'But something we shouldn't rule out. Tangential thinking will help us solve this case, guys. And if DC Tanner is right, and we really do have The Crimsons committing another robbery – on *our* turf and for the first time in years – then we can't let them go. We must do everything in our power to capture them. I want another dedicated team to look into all of the previous Crimsons cases as a backup. Pull out eyewitness statements. Physical descriptions. Details. See if there are any links between this robbery and any of their previous ones. I want to be able to build a picture of these guys in my head so that, if I see them, we can bag 'em.'

'Sorry, guv,' Bridger said, his voice surprising other members of the team beside him. 'Hate to play devil's advocate and all that. But what if it's a copycat? You know, ABC, like you said.'

Pemberton stopped and cast her eye around the room. When her eyes fell on Jake, she called his name and waved for him to come over. Jake snapped his head left and right, making sure that she hadn't spoken to him by mistake. There was no accident. She wanted him, and what was worse, she wanted him to speak in front of everyone else. He suddenly felt as if he were back in school, preparing himself to be chided by the teacher for doing something wrong, and reading out what he'd written in his notebook was his punishment. Tentatively, he snaked his way through the small crowd of officers, taking care not to barge into anyone or trip over any dangling legs and the feet of those sitting on chairs.

'Sorry to have put you in this position, Jake, but you're the one closest to this. You know more about The Crimsons than the rest of us.'

Pemberton took a step back and pointed at a photograph of three individuals dressed in red coveralls, holding guns, on the corkboard behind her. Jake instantly recognised the picture. It was from the HSBC Bank in Oxford – the same one he'd been inside when The Crimsons last attempted a robbery. 'Can you please tell us what you know, and

51

whether we could be dealing with a copycat.'

As soon as Pemberton finished speaking, Jake seized up. He looked down at his feet and scratched the scar on his cheek before readjusting his tie, pulling it away from his neck and easing the tension it impacted against his throat. Everybody's attention was trained on him, and he sensed their judgemental thoughts crawling over his skin: that he was a nobody, a rookie, somebody who didn't even deserve to be in the building, yet somehow was the one in the limelight, at the forefront of the investigation.

'I… er…' He didn't know what to say. He wasn't feeling confident that the robbers were in fact The Crimsons; something wasn't right about Bridgewater Jewellers. In all of The Crimsons' previous heists they had never fired a bullet – there had never been a spent casing found at any of the crime scenes – and had never taken any hostages – except for him, of course, but that had been a different situation. But now they'd done both, and it filled Jake with dread at what might be next.

The ABC principle was simple. It meant that police officers should always assume nothing, believe no one and check everything. And Jake had fallen victim to the first one. He'd assumed it was The Crimsons from the outset, and he was backtracking. But he couldn't declare his reservations, could he? How would that make—

'Jake…' Pemberton insisted. 'Are we looking at a copycat, yes or no?'

Jake went with his gut. 'No, I still think it's The Crimsons, but they're going into uncharted territory, and I don't like it. They're doing things they've never done before, and I don't know where they're going to stop.'

Pemberton turned to Bridger and gave him a smug look before addressing the rest of the room.

'I still want you all to keep an open mind. At least until we get forensics reports and any other intelligence… Understood?'

Everyone in the room nodded. Jake was beginning to warm up to Pemberton. She was authoritative, commanding and intelligent. She knew what she was doing, and more importantly, she knew her team – she knew how they worked and what made them tick.

In the distance, the double doors to the MCT opened, and a few seconds later, a woman wearing a blazer appeared in the Investigation Room's doorframe. She looked flustered and her exasperated breath echoed over the silence that had befallen them. In her hand she held a piece of paper.

'Ma'am, had a ping on an ANPR camera go off. It matches the vehicle reg used in this morning's robbery. And we've had more eyewitnesses reporting seeing it on the road, driving erratically,' she said as she handed the sheet to Pemberton.

'Where?' Pemberton asked, still keeping her gaze fixed on the officer.

'Farnham.'

'Where's that in relation to?'

'Candice Strachan's house is just down the road from the ANPR ping, ma'am.'

CHAPTER 8

CELEBRATIONS

The never-ending, winding, bending country roads caused chaos in Luke's stomach and his knuckles whitened as he clung to the leather upholstery of Candice's Mercedes GLC. Before leaving, they had stolen the keys from her, changed the number plates using a set they'd already prepared in the back of their van, and hijacked the vehicle. For the next part of their operation, they needed to be in something more inconspicuous, something that wasn't wanted by the police, even though they all knew that, soon enough, with all the technology and knowledge that the police had, the GLC would become a very expensive beacon that would point towards them from every direction. But, for now, it would suffice until their next swap.

In all of their previous heists, The Crimsons would slip away from the crime scene unnoticed, swap cars several times until the trail was long enough for them to be confident that it wasn't being followed, and then they would trickle back into civilisation as serving members of the population. Now, however, things were different. There were three of them, following Danny's plan. And different didn't always mean good.

'Slow down,' Luke said, massaging his forehead to alleviate the nausea bouncing around his skull. 'I'm going to heave in a second.'

'Do it on the back seats – I don't care. This ain't my car, you get me?'

'But I—'

'Look at the cars in front of us or something. That usually helps. We've got a couple of hours to go. You're a big boy – I'm sure you can last that long,' Danny said, throwing his hands in the air. 'Or you can start putting the diamonds in the bags, if you want?'

'Do you want me to pass out? I'm no use to you if I'm unconscious, am I?' Luke replied, swallowing hard, fighting to allay the bile that rose in his throat.

Without warning, Danny slammed on the brakes, launching Luke forward in the seat. The seat belt holding him into position dug into his shoulder. Luke grimaced. 'If you don't slow down, we'll get pulled over. The cops'll be all over this car soon, remember?'

'Yes – thanks, Luke. I have done this before. I know what I'm doing; I don't need a kid like you telling me what to do,' Danny said. He gripped the wheel harder and rolled his knuckles back and forth.

Michael chimed in. 'A moment ago, you said he was a big boy, and now you're—'

Danny pointed his finger in Michael's face and then punched him in the arm. 'Don't start, Micky. Now's not the time.'

'Never seems to be a good time with you recently. You've been uptight the past few days. Why? You should be fucking buzzing!' Michael twisted in the seat and grabbed the open gym bag beside Luke in the back. 'We've just taken – how much do you reckon? Hundred grand? Two? Three?'

'Easy five,' Luke added.

'Exactly! You should be pumped. We don't want to miss out on a famous Danny Cipriano Celebration. Not on our last heist, eh, Luke?'

Just as Luke opened his mouth to respond, Danny beat him to it.

'As soon as we get on that boat,' he said, 'I'll be able to celebrate. Until then, we keep our heads cool and remain alert. Nothing's changed from the last four times – except that we're a man down, but that isn't going to have an effect on us, is it, Luke?'

CHAPTER 9

TICK TOCK

Candice awoke drearily. For a moment she wondered where she was, but then as her surroundings gradually came into view, she realised. She was lying on the floor, her legs and arms sprawled in every direction. Her face had frozen to the solid marble that her husband had insisted on purchasing, and she groaned as she peeled her skin away. Her body felt weak. Her breathing. Her muscles. Her bones.

Her arms shook in an attempt to support her weight. And then she remembered why.

The collar bomb.

It was heavy, weighing her down, slowly beginning to suffocate her.

As soon as she realised what it was, panic set in again. The envelope of unconsciousness hadn't afforded her an escape from reality. It hadn't been a dream; it was indeed very, very real. In her head she heard the invisible sound of the countdown ticking down.

Tick. Tock. Tick. Tock.

Bleep. Bleep. Bleep.

Seconds were passing her by rapidly, and she was doing nothing about it. She had no idea what time remained on the countdown. It could have been three hours. Two. One. Twenty minutes. Candice couldn't afford to wait around for someone to come and save her. If she was going to get out of this situation, then she was going to need to get herself out of it. She had never been defeated by anything else thrown at her before, so why should she start now?

Candice looked around her. Her eyes took in everything but focused on nothing. She stared at the spot where the man had been – the same one who had left her in the middle of her house. The same one who had left her to die. Before she could unleash a torrent of abuse directed at him for abandoning her, the white letter on the floor flashed in her eyes.

The instructions.

Her instructions.

Candice reached over, grabbed the paper and inspected it. She needed to read it again – the panic had stripped the details from her mind – but her hands shook violently, and she struggled to decipher the dancing letters on the page. The document felt thin in her hands, as though it had been ripped out of a notebook purchased at Poundland. That even the slightest abrupt movement would rip it in two and destroy any hope she held of finding the first key.

Eventually, she managed to hold it steady enough and read through what it said.

THE FIRST KEY: WHERE CLOTHES ARE LEFT TO
HANG AND DRY LIKE OLD FRIENDS.

That was good. Very good, in fact. It was closer than she thought. She was sure she had seen one of her attackers disappearing off upstairs somewhere. Feeling a new lease of energy and adrenaline, Candice started up the stairs as fast as her legs would carry her. She held on to the banister for support, lest her knees buckle under the weight of the device and send her cascading down the steps.

At the top of the stairs, Candice tore into the master bedroom – the place where she'd spent every evening for four months mourning the loss of her husband. It was the first place she thought to check, and every time she entered this room, it reminded her of him. The side of the bed that he used to sleep on. The family heirloom alarm clock that he'd owned for half a century and repaired more times than they'd had sex. The slippers that he placed on the floor that were ready for him every morning after he'd swung his legs out of bed. She hadn't had the heart, or the courage, to move any of it then, and she certainly wasn't going to start now. Since his passing, Candice had slept in the only room that faced the driveway, which was also much smaller. Perhaps it was because she felt safer there, as if the close proximity of the walls could protect her. Or perhaps it was because she was frightened that, every time she went to sleep, there would be someone trying to break in. Not that she would admit it.

A four-poster king-sized bed rested in the centre of the master bedroom, with bedside tables either side of it. To her left, on the other side of a beige door that matched the painted walls, was her walk-in wardrobe.

Candice approached it rife with apprehension. More than three quarters of the stuff inside was her husband's, but she banished thoughts and images and memories of him from her mind and began to tear at the clothes and shoes and jumpers and jackets and underwear inside the shelves and boxes and drawers. She overturned everything, searching each item of clothing first for the key before launching it to the ground. She poked her fingers into the nooks and crannies of the carpet and ran them over the skirting boards. After she'd overturned everything inside, she screamed. She'd found nothing.

Dejected, and becoming increasingly aware that time was running out on the invisible clock, she moved into the hallway to decide which room to inspect next. There were three more to choose from, including her own. In the end, she tried her room. It was the only logical location that had another wardrobe in use.

She stormed into the room, flung open the wardrobe doors and thoroughly searched inside. After decanting the contents onto the bed, she stopped. Panting. Her chest heaving. There was still no sign of the key.

'Where the fuck are you?' she yelled, gritting her teeth, small bits of spittle landing on the carpet. She sounded demonic, almost possessed. 'This is ridiculous!'

Her heart raced, and she became more irate and impatient with every passing second, and just as she was about to leave, the gravel in her driveway crunched. Candice clambered onto the dust-covered windowsill and stared ahead. In the distance, the gated entrance to the house had been left open. Four armed police officers, wearing Kevlar, helmets and carrying assault rifles stalked around the outskirts of the path that led to her house. They kept their bodies low, and their weapons fanned from left to right as they scanned the horizon, like flags gently swaying in the wind.

This was it! They were finally here! They had finally come to help her.

Candice charged downstairs, heedless of what effect it would have on the device; she was just glad to have someone there who could save her. She skipped down the steps and bounded to the door. Her foot caught on a small piece of vomit, and she bashed her shoulder into the door. It hurt – a lot – but now wasn't the time to acknowledge the pain. She needed to let them in. All of them.

Candice fumbled for the handle, found it and then yanked the door. She breached into the open and fell onto the front doorstep. The armed officers, at the sight of her, screamed, 'Armed police!' and ordered her to place her hands in the air.

Candice didn't hear a word of it. Her adrenaline drowned out the noise.

'Please!' she screamed. 'You have to help me! I'm going to die!'

| PART 2 |

CHAPTER 10

MOTHER OF GOD

'You have to help me! I'm going to die!' came an ear-piercing scream from across the driveway.

The firearms team was the first to arrive in front of Candice, keeping their distance to fifty feet. Their orders for her to remain still with her hands raised quickly filled the air. Jake watched on from Pemberton's car just outside the driveaway gates. He observed the armed officers saunter closer towards Candice's mansion and the blacked-out van that was used to kidnap her, with their weapons raised and eyes trained on her and the surrounding area. The sound of Jake's beating heart echoed around his head, and the sweat on his back multiplied.

The device strapped round Candice's neck filled him fear. What was it? He'd never seen anything like it before. It was some sort of collar. Metallic. Clunky. Thick.

Beside him was Pemberton, holding a radio in her hands. Static and distorted voices spoke to her over the frequency.

'The vehicle is clear. Approaching the property now, ma'am,' one of the voices said. Despite being a short distance from an unknown and potentially dangerous device, there was a high measure of calm in the firearms officer's voice.

'Understood. Approach with caution,' Pemberton replied, holding the radio against her lips.

In the distance, on either side of the road, a flurry of uniformed officers was setting up a cordon, cutting off street access. Directly next to them was the vehicle the firearms team had arrived in. Standing at the front of the vehicle was an officer holding a police dog on a lead.

Jake turned his attention back to the house. And then a few minutes later, they received the all clear from the armed officers.

'House is clear, ma'am. Safe to proceed.'

As soon as she received the order, Pemberton turned her attention to the officer holding the police dog. She wandered over to him and discussed something, just out of earshot. Moments after, she returned.

'We're sending in the dog,' Pemberton explained.

'What do you mean?' Jake asked.

'We don't know what that thing around her neck is. But we need to be able to communicate with her so we can help her and find out what it's for.'

Just as she finished speaking, the officer with the police dog arrived by her side. The dog was a German Shepherd. Jake's favourite. His family had owned one once, when he was a child, and it had been his best friend. But, due to the upkeep of the animal, Jake's parents were forced to get rid of it. They were gorgeous animals, loyal, trusting, and Jake owed his life to them for reasons not many people would understand. He longed to have another one ever since. *One day*, he told himself.

Attached to the dog's back was a small radio device that was frequently used in hostage negotiation. The dog's task was simple: give the radio to the hostage and come back. That way they could open up a two-way communication with the abductor and begin a negotiation. But this wasn't a negotiation in the traditional sense. There was no madman holding a gun to Candice's head making incredulous demands. Instead, there was an invisible enemy with no demands. Everything about the situation was unprecedented. And everyone was beginning to sense it.

Pemberton gave the order. The officer led the police dog through the gates, across the gravelled driveway and over to the perimeter that the armed officers had set for themselves. As they arrived at the firearms team, the officer bent down and let the dog off the leash. The animal bound towards Candice in a flash and stopped by her side. As soon as Candice picked up the radio and held it to her face, the dog hurried back.

'Candice,' Pemberton began just as relaxed as the firearms officer. 'This is DCI Nicki Pemberton from Surrey Police. We're going to need you to stay exactly where you are until we tell you otherwise. I need you to remain calm. We're here to help you.'

'Please!' came the hysterical response on the radio. 'They said it was like a b-bomb. They said it was going to k-kill me. But I don't know when it's going to g-go off.'

'We're here to help. Everything is going to be OK,' Pemberton said.

'No, it's not. I'm g-going to d-die if we don't st-stop it.'

A moment of silence fell on the vast driveway. Jake grabbed a pair of binoculars from Pemberton's car, tiptoed forward to the edge of the driveaway and squinted to inspect the device strangling Candice. A thick piece of circular metal was wrapped around her neck, like a giant handcuff. Attached on the bottom was a small metallic box, resting atop her collar bone. At the bottom of the metal box, on the underside, was what looked like a countdown timer and four holes.

'Mother of God, what is it?' he whispered to himself, afraid that he already knew the answer.

Candice replied, almost as though she'd heard him, 'It's a spike bomb. Th-th-they stuck it to my neck,' she stuttered. Her hands shook as she grabbed the bomb and attempted to yank it free.

'What does it do, Candice?' Pemberton asked as she joined Jake's side by the front gates.

'They said there's sp-spikes inside it. When it g-goes off, the sp-spikes are going to k-kill me.'

'Who put it there, Candice?'

'Th-They abducted me and sh-shoved me in the back of the van. And this other guy. They brought us into my house and… and… they stuck it round my n-neck. They said it would go off in a couple of hours. *Please*, you have to help me! I don't want to die.'

'Are you on your own here, Candice? Where's the other person who was abducted with you?' Pemberton asked, her voice clear, distinct.

'Gone. Ran away. As soon as they d-disappeared, he left me here to die.'

'OK, Candice, I'm going to need you to remain calm. Do you know who did this to you?'

'The Crimsons!'

At the mention of The Crimsons' name, Jake sensed a change in Bridger out the corner of his eye. The man took a slight step further away and reached into his pocket for his phone. A small wave of elation rolled over Jake – he had been right about his allegations – but it was soon dismissed as the severity of the situation slapped him back to reality. The Crimsons had upgraded their methods. Never in any of their previous heists had they abducted someone – let alone two people. And never had they used anything as devious and evil as a spike collar bomb.

'Are you sure it's them, Candice?' Pemberton asked.

'Yes. They told me it was. They said people were going to r-r-remember their name forever.'

'What else did they say?'

'They said it was booby-trapped. Consequences. Shouldn't be tampered with.'

Pemberton nodded and moved closer to Candice. She moved gracefully across the stones, looking as though she hovered above them a few inches. When she came to a stop halfway between the gates and the ring of armed officers, she continued.

'Did they say how to defuse it, Candice? Did they give you any instructions?'

Candice nodded, the whites of her eyes shimmering in the sun overhead. As she moved, the device bounced up and down on her chest.

'They left a note with some instructions on it. It's in the house. I can g-g-get it.'

Candice started to climb to her feet, but as soon as she moved, the armed officers raised their weapons.

'No!' Pemberton shouted. 'Stay where you are. Do not move. We're setting up a perimeter, and we need you to remain perfectly still. Just wait until I give you some instructions on what to do next.'

Pemberton twisted and spoke directly to Bridger. 'Get uniform to look for Roger Heathcote,' she called. 'He's got to be out there somewhere, and he might be able to help us track The Crimsons. Give them the witness report Mr Heathcote's wife gave us. And call in forensics and the bomb squad. I want them to confirm this thing around her neck is live and detachable.'

'Yes, ma'am.' Bridger nodded and walked to Pemberton's car, just out of earshot. He dialled a number and spoke into the phone rapidly.

Then Pemberton turned her focus to the nearest armed officer. 'I want you and your team to search the outskirts of the property. Make sure nobody's hiding in the bushes in the garden.'

At once, the armed officer adjusted his helmet, whistled to the other officers, waved his fingers in the air and headed down the right-hand side of the building into the garden. In the distance, Jake thought he saw the metal handrail of a swimming pool strutting out of the ground.

'You ever seen anything like this before, Jake?' Pemberton asked, distracting him.

Jake shook his head. 'Never. You?'

'That makes two of us. You still think it's your guys

behind this?'

'Honestly... I don't know what to think. They've never done anything this... merciless. But regardless of who it is, we need to find those instructions.'

'We can't enter the property until bomb squad have had a look at the device and confirmed it's safe,' Pemberton said.

'How long could that take?'

Pemberton twisted her neck backward and watched Bridger, who was pacing from side to side at the end of the driveway. He held his phone to his ear and appeared to bark orders into the handset. 'What's taking him so long?'

A few seconds later, Pemberton had her answer.

'Ma'am,' Bridger said, returning. 'Forensics are on their way. ETA fifteen minutes. Bomb squad are going to take even longer.'

'Why?'

'They're having to come from Reigate. And there's backed-up traffic on the M25. RTC involving a lorry and a busload of children.'

'My goodness. Is there no one closer?'

'Sorry, ma'am,' Bridger said, pursing his lips and shaking his head.

Pemberton sighed as she returned her focus to Candice. The woman was distressed, her eyes beading, and her hands still clung to the collar bomb. Jake had never seen one before, and he hoped he never would for the rest of his career. They were evil, malignant devices, dooming the person captive to certain death.

'What do we do now?' Jake asked.

Pemberton hesitated a beat before answering. 'Candice,' she said into the radio, 'a team of explosive experts are on their way down to help you.'

'You don't understand. There's a timer on it, and we still need to find the keys.'

'Keys?' Jake and Pemberton repeated simultaneously. 'What keys?'

'To unlock it. There are keys. F-Four of them.'

'Where?' Jake asked. He swallowed deeply.

'Everywhere. There's one in the house, but I... I can't find it... and then – then the rest are around Surrey. Please, we have to find the keys before this thing goes off.'

CHAPTER 11

PROVE YOURSELF

A wall of smoke lingered in front of Danika's face. The air was still, and the smell of chemicals and tar in the tobacco climbed her nostrils and plunged down her throat. She inhaled hard, her mouth tingling as she absorbed the toxins. She cherished the taste, the feeling, the relaxing sensation the cigarette incited every time she took a drag. It helped vacate her mind and offered a momentary release from the angst and stress of everyday life. She wanted more but knew she couldn't. Her husband would be able to smell it on her when she got home. No matter how much perfume she applied, the smell and taste lingered like burning rubber. And the less ammunition she gave him to use against her, the better.

The building's wooden double doors opened beside her, and another member of MCT appeared. He was handsome – his cheekbones prominent on his face and his jawline chiselled. He was dressed in a waistcoat with his tie tucked just beneath the buttons, and his navy shirt hugged the contours of his shoulders and arms. It was clear to see that he was in good physical shape. A man who took care of himself. A man who could protect any woman that he was with, given any situation. His only obvious flaw was the receding hairline that looked as if it were running away from his eyebrows.

The man reached into his pocket, produced a cigarette and placed it in his mouth. It dangled there as he frisked his chest and thigh pockets.

'Don't suppose I could borrow your lighter, do you?' he asked. 'Sorry. I left mine at my desk.'

Saying nothing, still reeling in the euphoria from her last hit, Danika reached into her pocket and pulled out a lighter. She ignited the flint and held the flame beneath the man's cigarette. He inhaled and an orange glow emanated from the end.

'Fourth one of the day, and it's not even noon,' he said, ejecting a cloud of smoke in the air. As he did so, the wind picked it up and wafted it into Danika's face. Two for the price of one. 'How many you on this morning?'

'Just the one.'

'Good. If Pemberton saw, she'd kill you. Hates fag breaks. But I'm a little more lenient. Can't blame her, really. Filthy habit. I've been meaning to quit. It's on my to-do list.'

'It is for everyone, no?'

'I like to think so.' He smiled at her and extended his hand. 'Mark Murphy. Detective Inspector.'

'Danika,' she replied, taking his hand. If there was ever any doubt about his manliness, the strength in his grip eradicated it. 'Temporary Detective Constable. I am in training.'

'That's right. I saw your name on the attendance list this morning. How did the witness statements go just now? Get some solid reports?'

'Good,' she replied. 'They did not tell us anything new though, which was a shame.'

'That's not always a bad thing. Means that the rest of us are doing our jobs properly.'

'Although, I'm almost certain that they were having an affair,' Danika said. 'The way they spoke about one another. Especially if all she was trying to do was to sell him a ring.'

'You can tell all of that by the way someone talks about another person?'

Danika shrugged. 'And the way they looked at one another in the corridor.' She flicked her eyes towards him.

'Be careful throwing allegations around the place. Some people don't take too kindly to them.'

'Forgive me. I am still learning.'

Mark chuckled, took another drag of the cigarette and said, 'I don't think I've ever seen anyone turn up to the office as early as you did.'

'What can I say? I am keen.'

'Suppose you've got to make a good first impression... but then there's *your* level of keen.'

'I was raised that way. My parents always told me that the best thing you can do every day is show up. No matter the occasion. No matter the circumstance.'

'Your parents did a good job.'

'It is easy to do if it is something you're passionate about.'

'And are you passionate?'

Danika retreated a little. In those four words he had been able to disarm her entirely. It was difficult to explain, but she felt very open, exposed, as if this man she'd only just met knew her deepest, darkest secrets.

'I'm a good judge of character,' Mark continued. 'And I've been watching you. Aside from speaking with the two witnesses, you've hardly spoken or interacted with anyone since you got here...'

Mark let his sentence hang in the air, and Danika hated him for it. He was right – she hadn't spoken directly to anyone in the office other than Jake and Pemberton, except for the monosyllabic responses she had given DC Johnson as they were sitting down in the interview room. The truth was, she didn't feel comfortable. She was nervous around people she didn't know. Especially at first. The awkward small talk. The sharing of life stories. How she would have to pretend that everything was OK. That her job – the one thing she loved second to her family – wasn't beginning to get in the way of what was in first position.

'I've been busy,' she lied.

'Well I've got plenty more things for you to be doing if you run out. If nothing else, this'll be perfect experience for you. How long have you been with the service?'

'Five years.' Danika took another drag of her cigarette, realised she'd finished it and lit another one. She hoped it would ease the pain of the obligatory small talk.

'I can tell it's going to be a busy day,' Mark said, nodding to the second stick she'd just sparked. 'What made you get into it?'

'My parents smoked.'

'No… I meant the police. How did you become an officer?'

'It's a long story.'

'Smoking can take a long time. And Pemberton's not here. She left me in charge of you, told me to make sure someone's looking out for you…'

Danika sighed before replying. She didn't want to tell this stranger anything personal about herself, but she also didn't want to come across as a rude and obnoxious bitch – she needed to make a good first impression. Besides, he was the only one in the squad who had acknowledged her existence – the rest of the team saw her as a burden, she was sure.

'My husband,' she began, 'he was a police officer. He joined when he left school. I met him a few years later. We worked together. Started a family together. A year after our kids were born, he was involved in an incident. Somebody threw him from the top of a building. Broke both his legs. He was forced to medically retire. He's been looking after the kids ever since.'

'That's heavy. I'm sorry.'

'You asked.'

A moment of silence washed over them. Danika enjoyed it. She relaxed in it. But Mark… well, it was clear to see he was hating every second. She sensed from his body language – his posture, his eyes, his mouth – that he had an arsenal of questions he wanted to fire at her.

He fired the first shot from the barrel.

'What about this Tanner guy? What's the low-down on him?'

'We came from the same borough.'

'You two close?'

'Pretty close, yeah. He tells me things. I tell him things.'

'How long's he been with us?'

'A couple of years, I think, no?' Danika shrugged and took another, longer, more satisfying drag of her cigarette. 'I forget exactly, but not many.'

'How does that work, then? Five years versus a few? You've been serving longer, and yet he's out there…'

She shrugged again. 'It is what it is.'

'Listen,' Mark began, turning to face her. She hadn't realised it, but he'd nearly finished his cigarette. 'I don't know what sort of stuff you've got going on at home. Maybe it's not my place to know. But you shouldn't let that – or what Tanner's doing out there on the road right now – stop you from excelling here, all right? You've got an opportunity to prove yourself. Learn all you can from it. The biggest criminals we've had in the country for a long, long time are on our doorstep. This is the most serious case I've ever worked on, and if you're considering taking the role further, there's no better time to prove yourself. And, hey, if you need someone to talk to up there, at least you've got a friendly face you can put a name to.'

Mark stubbed out the end of his cigarette on the metal ashtray screwed into the wall. 'It's something to think about. I'll see you up there.'

CHAPTER 12

CRICKET

'I'm sorry, Jake, but you're going to have to wait,' Pemberton told him. 'Nobody can do anything until the bomb squad arrive. I'm sorry, but this is a very delicate situation. I've never experienced anything like this in my career, and I need to come up with a strategy to work out how we're going to get her out her out of this device.' She paused a beat. 'I know you want to help her – and trust me, I do too – but we need to think about this calmly and logically. There's no guarantee that the device around her neck doesn't contain an explosive inside it that, when provoked, could kill all of us. It's too much of a risk.'

'OK,' he conceded, lowering his head. Perhaps he was going to learn more from her than he'd thought. On several occasions, at the beginning of his career as a bobby on the beat in the heart of London, he'd acted too rashly, too hastily, giving no second thought to his actions. In most cases, it had been to the detriment of the emergency call he was responding to. He'd been too excitable, too energetic. He wanted to help everyone and do everything he could to help them, even though he knew that wasn't always possible. He was the first to admit that it was one of his flaws as well as one of his immutable strengths.

After a few seconds of thought, he returned his gaze to Pemberton, and asked, 'So, what do you suggest?'

'I don't know. I need time.'

That's not a luxury we can afford, he thought, deciding to keep it in his head rather than voicing it aloud.

He shifted his weight from one foot to the other, then closed his eyes and suspended himself in a state of reflection. He considered – hard. About Candice, what she must be going through, standing there waiting, with the time bomb ticking down inches from her chest and neck. About how they needed to find the instruction sheet if they were going to stand any chance of saving her.

And then he had it, the seed of an idea.

Jake reached into his pocket and removed his phone.

'What are you doing?' Pemberton asked as he unlocked it and opened the camera.

'Candice can get it herself. She can use my camera to record the inside of the house. We'll see what we're dealing with and she'll be able to get the instructions.'

'I don't think that's going to—'

'Candice knows where the instructions are. And the property's been cleared by the firearms team. The more time we spend out here, the less time we have to find those keys and save her.'

Pemberton considered for a moment, sighed and then nodded in acknowledgement. 'How do you propose we deliver it to her?'

'I was good at cricket at school…'

'Has nobody got a chest cam?' Pemberton looked around her. The armed officers hadn't returned from securing the rest of the property, and the remaining emergency response units who had accompanied them to Candice's house were either setting up a perimeter further up the street or searching for the missing man who had been abducted. Jake didn't envy that job. He'd done it for long enough, and now it was time for a change in his career. This was it.

'I'm happy to sacrifice the phone,' Jake said.

'Someone *must* have a chest cam we can use around here instead?' Bridger repeated, surprising Jake. He'd been so quiet that Jake had forgotten he was still present.

'Like I said, I'm happy to sacrifice the phone. It serves the same purpose as the chest cam. This way we can monitor the inside of the property and her movements. She only needs to find the instructions, and then the rest of the work we can do ourselves.'

Bridger said nothing. His expression dropped and he scowled at Jake. It wasn't the first time that the senior officer had treated him with contempt, and Jake assumed it wouldn't be the last. He didn't care though. His main priority was Candice's safety and making sure she got out of there alive.

'Come on, stop talking about it and start doing it.'

Without warning, Pemberton snatched Jake's phone from him, called over the police dog, and strapped the phone to the animal's back. Just as she was about to finish, she remembered something. Then she removed the hairband from her wrist and wrapped it around the phone. As soon as the device was safely fastened in, the handler gave the order, and the dog hurried towards Candice. Using the radio, Pemberton explained to her what was going to happen next.

'Are you recording?' she asked.

'Yes,' Candice replied after having a check of the phone.

'And you know what to do?'

'Yes.'

'Repeat it back to me.'

'Find the instructions. Bring them back.'

'One more thing,' Pemberton said. 'Use the hairband to wrap the instructions around the phone.'

Pemberton finished and stepped backwards. Candice clutched the phone against her chest and disappeared into the mansion without saying anything. She ran off in such a way that, for a moment, Jake wondered if he would ever see the phone again.

CHAPTER 13

BARGAINS

Candice's pulse was pounding as she bounded up the stairs, clutching the phone against her stomach. It clanged against the collar bomb, sending a pang of fear up her body every time she heard it, but she carried on regardless.

She reached the top of the stairs and headed into the master bedroom, then paused.

The key.

For a split second she forgot what she was looking for and moved towards the wardrobe again, desperate to find one of the four items that would save her. She dropped the police officer's phone to the carpet by the foot of the bed. It bounced and landed just underneath a wooden dresser on the right-hand side of the room. She tore everything apart again, this time hoping the key would appear in a place she had seemingly overlooked. But there was still nothing. *You son of a bitch!* She threw a pair of shoes against the wall, narrowly avoiding a floor-to-ceiling mirror. *Where are you?*

Why couldn't she find it? It was supposed to be there. She was sure of it. They had told her so. They had told her it would be easy to find. Or was she just inept? No... they had hidden it too well. That was it. Unless they had lied to her and hadn't hidden it at all? Candice dismissed the thought immediately. It would do her no good to think such things.

A voice called her name from outside, telling her to hurry. She was running out of time, and the police were growing impatient – she didn't want to give them any reason to suspect her of anything. She wanted to be cooperative, to give them the help they needed to save her. And if she did anything to the detriment of that goal, then she would never be able to forgive herself. *Focus*, she told herself. She had a job to do. And so did they. They were going to find the keys for her – all of them. Of course they would.

Candice grabbed the note from where she'd dropped it earlier by the entrance to the walk-in wardrobe, picked up the officer's phone and exited the master bedroom, rushing along the landing and back down the stairs.

As she reached the bottom of the staircase, she wrapped the paper round the phone and tightened it with the hairband.

'I found it!' she said, elated. Her body tingled. Perhaps it was incipient hope, or perhaps it was adrenaline. She didn't know. But, either way, she didn't want it to be replaced with the sense of dread that she had grown accustomed to in the past ten minutes.

'Place the phone and the instructions on the dog's back, Candice. But remember to stay exactly where you are,' the female officer replied. She was the one in charge. Candice did as instructed.

She bent down by the panting dog's side, attached the mobile to the animal, and fought off the urge to stroke it. It was crazy how, despite the situation, there was something comforting about the dog that made her forget about what was happening to her. It put her at ease and made her feel calm. All she wanted to do was stroke its fur and play with it. But she knew that wouldn't be possible. *Soon*, she told herself. *Soon.* It was the little glimpse of hope she needed to help her get through it.

Bringing herself out of her trance, Candice gave the all clear, and the dog bounded towards the officers. She squirmed in celebration as the dog skidded to a halt on the gravel. Now she was one step closer to getting out of the collar bomb; she had kept her end of the bargain, now it was their turn.

All she could do was wait.

CHAPTER 14

BRIGHT IDEAS

Jake seized the note, photographed it and placed it in an evidence bag. As he stared at the image on his screen and read the note, the words filled him with fear. A sensation that made him want to run up to Candice and begin to saw the collar bomb free from her neck. A sensation that also made him want to run away and not have to deal with what lay before him at the same time. But he needed to remain cool and think logically – like Pemberton – if he was going to stand any chance of making today a success. He didn't want a dead person's blood on his hands after his first-ever case with Surrey Police. He was sure it wouldn't bode well for the rest of his career.

'Jesus Christ,' Jake said aloud without realising. He lowered his arm and handed the instructions to Pemberton, who continued reading. She was the type of reader who ran her finger along the line to help keep track of where she was on the page, and she was taking an age to finish.

'First things first,' she said eventually, 'find out where the hell forensics and bomb squad are.'

'Yes, ma'am,' Bridger said, stepping beside her. 'I'll give them a chase now.' He nodded at Pemberton before wandering off towards the black minivan. Jake observed Bridger peer inside the vehicle, pause and then step away and disappear to the other end of the driveway.

'Whoever's written this has got neat handwriting,' Pemberton remarked, holding the photograph aloft for a better view.

Jake followed her arm, his eyes half-closed. 'I think they've stencilled over a Word document or something. It looks almost immaculate. No one has handwriting that precise.'

'Send the original to the office. Tell them to get it investigated by the graphologist as soon as possible. Get them to cross-reference it with any documents and signatures in Bridgewater Jewellers... in particular those employees files they all seem to have.'

Jake nodded, hurried away and instructed a uniformed officer to deliver it back to the station. After the officer nodded, Jake raced back to Pemberton's side.

'This is insane.' Pemberton sighed and rubbed the bridge of her nose with her fingers. 'How are we going to get inside the property safely?'

Jake looked around him, taking in the minutiae of his surroundings. His head stopped as he glanced at the side of the mansion. 'The garden,' he said.

'Excuse me, Jake?'

'The garden. Move Candice into the garden where there's a lot of space – a *lot* more. That'll free bomb squad for when they get here, and it'll free forensics up to get inside the property without any issues.'

'You're full of bright ideas today, aren't you?' Pemberton said. She stepped from side to side on the balls of her feet as if she were waiting anxiously outside the school disco for the boy that she had a crush on to come and tell her that he loved her. Jake knew he was right; it was just about convincing her that he was right too.

Jake pointed at the instructions on the screen. 'This sheet changes everything. We've got just under four hours to find four keys.'

'Fine,' she said eventually. 'Add it to my log. We'll take Candice round to the back, while you and Bridger get yourselves suited up. Let's get you guys in there.'

CHAPTER 15

TOILET BREAK

As the three of them headed further south on the A287 through Beacon Hill, with the sunlight breaking through the arms and leaves of the trees hanging overhead, Luke constantly glanced behind him. His eyes searched for an entourage of blue flashing lights atop liveried police cars chasing after them, drawing closer with every passing second. But each time, he found none, except every now and then his mind played tricks on him. Cars miraculously changed colour and their roofs flashed incandescent blue and white. Even the sound of a horn from someone cutting someone else up turned into a police siren. It was relentless and it grated on his sanity.

'Pull the car over,' Luke said, clutching the back of Danny's seat.

Danny ignored him.

'Pull the car over,' he reiterated.

Silence.

'Dan – we've been in this car for too long. Way longer than we usually are. We need to pull over and switch. They'll have picked up the new plates by now. And I need a piss. Pull the car over.'

'We're not stopping,' Danny said, keeping his eyes trained on the road. 'Not until we get to Portsmouth.'

'I need a piss,' Luke said. He didn't care if he sounded like an insolent child. His guilt was getting the better of him. Images flashed intermittently in his mind's eye, vivid, visceral. Images of the dead woman Danny had shot in the neck. The lifeless eyes. The way her body slumped to the floor slowly. And then they moved to images of Candice, lying on the marble with the collar bomb attached to her neck. The screams. Shouts. Cries for help and mercy.

'Piss in a bottle or something,' Danny said, grunting loudly.

Luke scanned the back seats. 'There aren't any.'

'Piss on the seats then.'

'What? You can't be fucking serious,' Luke said. 'I thought you said no DNA? No trace? Just like every other time we've done this. Eh? So what makes this time different? Because it's Dan's Big Finale, Dan's Big Brilliant Idea, he thinks he can sacrifice those rules for everyone other than himself?'

Danny remained silent.

'Are we going to talk about the elephant in the room?' Michael said.

'What elephant?' Danny asked, his head snapping towards Michael.

'The fact that you fucking killed someone, Dan. Where did that come from? We never agreed to killing anyone. I don't care whether it was always Freddy's mantra not to fire a bullet. You could have at least warned us,' Michael explained. 'And what did she do to deserve it? She wasn't getting in the way of anyone. That's cold-blooded, Dan. I never expected to see that from you.'

'I did what I had to do.'

'I saw you pointing that gun at Candice as well... You almost shot her. We needed her – without her, this all goes to shit.'

A Ford Insignia pulled out from a rural road, cutting in front of them. Danny slammed on the brakes. Luke propelled forward into the back of Danny's seat, and as his brother gradually brought the car back up to normal speed, Luke locked himself into the seat with his seat belt. The engine roared beneath their feet. As they swerved in and out of the traffic, overtaking and undertaking at every opportunity, Luke glanced at the speedometer. It was cradled just above 80mph.

'There's only one lane of traffic,' he said, slapping Danny's headrest. 'Are you trying to kill us?'

'Don't tell me how to drive, Luke. You can't even pass your test.' Danny slammed on the brakes again. This time Luke saw it coming and tensed his legs while extending his hand into the back of Danny's seat to avoid any pain in his shoulder from the seat belt.

'Freddy said I was a decent driver,' Luke said, adjusting himself on his seat and gazing out of the window. It felt weird for him to mention their old friend's name. In fact, he had been more than a friend. A father. The dad they never had. It was as if Freddy had adopted them and led them onto the path they were currently headed down.

'Freddy ain't here now, is he? So you're going to listen to me instead.' Danny smacked his hand on the steering wheel. 'Christ – if only you both knew what Freddy was like. He's not the hero you think he is.'

'What's that supposed to mean?' Michael asked.

'He taught you everything you know. He taught *us* everything we know,' Luke added.

'And look where he ended up. Locked up for the next fifteen years. He ain't worth shit, you get me?'

'What did he do to you?' Michael leant forward and placed his hand on the dashboard, twisting to face Danny.

'Nothing.' Danny dismissed Michael with a wave of his hand. 'Leave it.'

They slowed as they approached a roundabout. To their right was a slip road that led onto the A3. Danny swerved the car around the bend, up the slip road and merged into the two lanes of traffic. The sound of the engine growling filled the still and silent interior. Luke continued to stare out of the window as he watched the world fly past in a mirage of green and grey, allowing his mind to wander momentarily.

For a long time, he had wanted out of his life as a career criminal. It was horrible – constantly turning your back on everyone you loved. Watching over your shoulder every step you took. It wasn't the life he had imagined he would have when he was growing up. He'd wanted to be an architect. An artist. A graphic designer. Someone who could draw. Someone who could make the world a better place with his art. But that had been a pipe dream. Something he

91

could never share with his brothers, especially not after they'd formed the group. How could he leave when they'd been so adamant about loyalty and trust and brotherhood? What sort of brother would he be if he turned his back on them? A terrible one, he knew. Neither of them would forgive him. But now there was a hope, a possibility. They were finally on their way out of the country – and out of this life forever. Now his passions had the chance to become a reality in the new lives they were going to make for themselves. Soon the three of them would be able to enjoy the rest of their time on earth doing what they loved, together. At least, that was what he told himself.

A road sign for a nearby service station flashed past less than a quarter mile away.

'Pull over here, Danny. I need a piss. *Still*,' Luke said.

Danny didn't respond; instead he expelled a puff of discontent from his nostrils.

'I think I saw one of those speed cameras flash a few miles back. This'll be a good place to ditch the car and get a new one.'

'OK, you can put those *skills* Freddy taught you to the test. Just don't fuck it up.' Danny's voice was replete with disdain, but Luke appreciated the poor attempt at trying to lighten the mood.

He eased into the comfort of the leather seat. His hand gravitated towards his crotch and applied pressure, relieving the burning sensation in his bladder. He shouldn't have downed that bottle of water before they left this morning. Danny moved the car across the two lanes of traffic, bringing the car down to a legal speed, and pulled off into a service station. He slid in to park behind an Audi A4 and yanked the handbrake on. The service station was surprisingly quiet, save for a few heavy goods vehicles that were parked up behind the building.

Luke placed his hand on the door handle.

'What are you doing?' Danny asked.

Luke glanced at the handle. 'I thought it was obvious?'

'Not dressed in your overalls, you're not.'

'Shit.'

'Get undressed. Mess your hair up. Put your hat on. Keep your head down. And try not to touch anything.'

In the back seat of Candice's GLC, Luke unzipped the front of his crimson overalls, slipped them off his body and shoved them to the side. He then reached inside the gym bag, sifted through the jewellery and found his beanie. Pulling it low on his head, he swept a few strands of hair out of his eyes and concealed the bag with his overalls before hopping out of the car.

Danny called back: 'You've got two minutes. Finish your piss and then come straight back.'

CHAPTER 16

MAKING THINGS WORSE

Michael watched Luke adjust his beanie and advance towards the Shell complex, hopping over the potholes in the ground.

The atmosphere inside the car was sour.

Michael waited until Luke entered the station before speaking. 'What was that all about?' he asked Danny, keeping his gaze focused on the building's revolving doors.

'What you talking about?'

'That Freddy bollocks you was spouting off to him. What aren't you telling us?'

Danny undid his seat belt buckle and folded his arms. 'Luke doesn't stop talking about that fucking prick. He worships him.'

'You know he thinks of him like a dad. I mean, can you blame him?'

'You seriously want to get into this again? The man who raised us was serving, defending our country. The man was a hero. Freddy was just a jumped-up little shit who was good at robbing places. Freddy's half the man Dad is.'

Michael sighed, grabbed the plastic handle on the door frame and said, 'You can't blame Luke for being born when he was. It's not his fault Dad missed him growing up. And it's not his fault Freddy was the only role model he had.'

'What about me?' There was pain in Danny's expression. As if the stresses and turmoil he'd been through his entire life were now showing up on his exterior. The lines in his forehead and sides of his eyes were beginning to grow, the bags beneath them darkening. 'What about me, Michael? *I* tried to be a good role model for that kid. You know I did. We're his blood. Freddy isn't. And I'll be fucked if he thinks Freddy is a better man than me. The bloke don't even know his own son.'

'I just hope you're not lying to him,' Michael said. 'Whatever you do. It'll only make things worse.'

Danny tutted, sighed and then shifted his attention to the cars pulling in and out of the petrol station. Michael knew his brother better than anyone, and he knew when Danny was hiding something from them. The only problem was working out what it was.

Out the corner of his eye, he watched Danny rub his forearm and squeeze the skin through his overalls. Danny didn't even realise he was doing it. But Michael knew what it meant. He'd seen the signs before.

'Oi,' he said, slapping Danny on the leg with the back of his hand. As Danny's gaze shot towards him, he pointed at his brother's arm. 'You all right?'

'Yeah.' Danny slid the sleeve further over his hand and placed his hands in his lap.

'Don't lie to me either, Dan.'

'It's nothing.'

'Did L—'

At that moment, the rear passenger door burst open and Luke fumbled in, a relieved smile beaming across his face.

CHAPTER 17

HIJACK

'What took you so long?' Danny jibed as Luke entered the car.

'I told you – I *really* needed that piss.' And he had. He had stood there for what felt like an eternity, waiting for his body to drain the urine in his system. But now that it was out of him, he felt as though he could run a mile.

'Come on. Get your gear back on,' Danny ordered. 'This Audi's been sat here for a while. Ain't seen anyone coming anywhere near it.'

Luke slipped back into his overalls, zipped the top up to his neck and pulled the hood over his head.

'Masks?' Michael asked from the front.

Luke reached across the seat and grabbed their red devil masks. They had become synonymous with The Crimsons, instilling fear in everyone who saw them. The masks were custom-made – a favour called in from one of Freddy Miller's contacts a few years ago – and Luke felt powerful every time he wore one. He could be anyone he wanted beneath it. He could don a new persona, a new way of life, a new outlook on everything. He could let the animal within him break free. And he revelled in the sight of watching their victims shit themselves as they stared down the business end of a barrel.

Luke pulled the strap tightly over the back of his head, tucked small tufts of hair in the sides of the mask and grabbed the gym bag next to him.

'Guns?' Luke asked, turning round to search the boot of the car.

'With me,' Michael said, before reaching into the footwell and producing Luke's Mini-Uzi.

Luke took it from his brother and bounced the weight of the weapon in his hands. It felt as light as a tennis ball, and as he tightened his grip around the handle, adrenaline surged through his body again. All notion of what had taken place in the past two hours flew out of his mind. They were too far gone now. It was time for a blank slate. As a result, his breathing quickened and he clenched his jaw, grinding his teeth together. It made him feel alive.

'Ready?' Danny asked. 'Is that everything? Luke – give Micky the bag. You're going to need your hands free if you're going to break into this car.'

'Does that mean I'm driving then?'

Danny hesitated for a moment. He looked at Michael, back to Luke, then Michael and back to Luke again. He shrugged. 'So long as you don't kill us.'

'Are you sure this is a good idea, Dan? It looks too open

to me,' Michael asked, placing a hand on Danny's back. 'Freddy always said to never—'

'Shut it. He's not here. The bigger the risks we take, the bigger the reward, trust me. Nobody's gonna know who we are. Now get on with it – somebody's coming.'

In the distance, a stocky man wearing a pink polo shirt, light blue Ralph Lauren jumper and brown boat shoes started towards them. Luke didn't know him, but he already thought the guy was a flash prick.

Wasting no time at all, Luke hopped out of the car, hurried to the driver's-side of the Audi and yanked the handle. Locked. Surprise. He reached inside his overalls and produced a long, thin piece of metal similar in shape and size to a ruler. As he slid the slim jim between the window and the door, Luke heard Danny and Micky hop out of the car and race towards the Audi's passenger doors.

'Fuck it!' Luke grabbed for his gun, gripped it in his hands and smashed the butt against the car window. The glass shattered and scattered inside the car and over Luke's overalls, but he didn't care. The adrenaline clouded his mind. He reached for the inside handle and swung the door open. Then he threw himself into the car and kicked open the plastic housing beneath the steering wheel.

Time was running out, and to make matters worse, the man in the ridiculous outfit shouted at them.

'What the fuck do you think you're doing?' he called.

Before Luke was able to react, erupting from behind the back of the car, was Danny, slowly approaching the man with his arm raised. At the sight of the weapon, screams and cries erupted from those who were standing beside cars in the middle of filling them with petrol, and tyres squealed as their owners floored it out of there.

'Give us the keys!' Danny screamed at the man.

There was no response.

'Give us the keys!'

Still nothing. The man froze with his arms in the air, paralysed by fear.

Realising they couldn't afford to waste any more time, Luke leapt out of the vehicle and over to the man. As he reached for the car owner's pockets, something inside the man changed. They tussled. But Luke reacted first. He was was determined to prove himself. He wasn't going to let this guy best him. And he wasn't about to have his reputation tarnished any more in Danny's mind than it already was.

Luke leant into the man, jabbed him in the stomach and caught a left hook with his fist. With one clean hit, the man fell to the ground. While he rolled on the floor, holding his face, groaning, moaning, screaming in pain, Luke fumbled for the keys inside his shorts' pockets. The man made a poor attempt at defending himself, but it was immediately stifled as soon as Luke flexed the Uzi. As he hurried back to the car, Luke barked at Michael to change the number plates of the Audi.

Luke dived into the vehicle and threw the keys in the ignition, slamming his foot down on the accelerator as it sprung to life. A few seconds later, Danny leapt in, and then Michael. The plates were changed. They were all together. And they in ready to go.

Cheers erupted and Luke slammed his hands on the wheel and dashboard as he merged back onto the A3.

'Fucking excellent, Lukey Boy!' Danny said, slapping him on the back.

'Job well done, son,' Michael echoed.

'For a moment then, I didn't think you'd pull it off,' Danny added. 'But you did good, kid. You did good.'

CHAPTER 18

FORTUNATE DISCOVERY

'That's it. Right there. Keep your arms high in the air for me, Candice. Don't move any further.' Pemberton gave the final order for Candice to stay exactly where she was in the centre of her acre-long garden. Fifty feet separated them from one another. 'My colleague, DC Tanner, is going to see if he can find the key for you. Is there anything you haven't told us that he might need to know before he goes in?'

Candice frantically shook her head.

'Jake,' Pemberton said to him, keeping her voice low, 'get inside there now. I'll stay here and send Bridger in when he gets back from whatever he seems to be doing.'

At that, as if on cue, Bridger returned, breathless and exasperated.

'Sorry, guv,' he began, his voice raspy. 'I couldn't find you.'

'It's not like we disappeared off to the Isle of Wight!' Pemberton snapped.

'Forensics are less than five minutes away. EOD ten.'

'You'd both better hurry then.'

'Why?' Bridger asked.

'The keys won't find themselves.'

Jake elected himself to go first and hurried to Pemberton's car at the end of the driveway. There, he dressed himself in his second full forensic suit of the day. The texture felt soft over his skin, but he knew that in a few minutes his hands would be slick with sweat. As he pulled the overshoes over his feet, Bridger arrived beside him.

'We should wear these as well,' Bridger said, holding a set of body cams in his hands.

Now we have a pair, Jake thought as he struggled to stop himself from rolling his eyes. He took one from his senior and strapped himself in. Once they were ready, they sauntered across the gravel carefully, paying close attention to the area where Candice had been stationed, and entered the through the front door. The splendour of the mansion took Jake by surprise and forced him to stop. He'd never set foot in a house as magnificent as this. Sure, he'd seen photos of them online – when he and Elizabeth played House Roulette, a fun game they'd created when they were bored one afternoon to see who could find the nicest house on Zoopla or Rightmove in their local area – but there was only so much that images could convey.

A glass chandelier dangled from the ceiling only inches from his head. To his left was a door that led into a living room; to his right, the dining room. Ahead lay the kitchen. The marble surface looked like something from a sci-fi film –

even with the pile of vomit splashed across it. Great wooden beams ran up the length of the walls, and the staircase to his left spiralled to the first floor.

Jake snapped himself back to the present. There was no time to stand and admire the property. He had a life to save.

'Come on,' he called, pointing at the stairs. 'This way!'

Jake leapt up them, two at a time, rapidly increasing the gap between him and Bridger so Jake was first to the top. A minor victory.

'Do you know what we're looking for?' Bridger asked.

'A key.'

'I know that. But what type of key?'

Jake shot him a derisive look. 'What type of key do you think? One that opens locks.'

'Shut up, Tanner. I meant is it a small one? Large? Long head? Short?'

Jake shrugged.

'Where is it?'

'If we knew that, we wouldn't be looking for it, would we?' Jake said, wishing he hadn't. It had been a Freudian slip, one that he regretted almost instantly. As he was getting older and more experienced in the police force, with the hierarchies and the internal structures within the teams he was working with, he realised he was more susceptible to small sarcastic comments accidentally slipping off his tongue.

As soon as Jake said it, Bridger grabbed him by the shoulder and pushed him back against the wooden banister. The wood creaked and bowed under his weight. Double his size and slightly taller, Bridger leant into him, pressing his body against Jake's and forcing him to arch his back over the edge. They were face to face, mere centimetres separating them. A concoction of smells assaulted Jake's senses: the lingering remains of aftershave, the stink of stale coffee on his breath and the faint chemical smell of bleach on Bridger's hands.

'Listen, mate. I don't know who you think you are, but you need to remember who you're in the company of. I'm your senior, so you can put your ego aside and stop your little power trip, all right? Just because you're getting excited like a little schoolgirl about your first-ever case with us doesn't make you the fucking Chief Constable, OK? Just because you've come from a strong operational background – or so they tell me – it doesn't mean you get to boss the orders around, all right?'

Pieces of spittle landed on Jake's mouth and cheek as Bridger shouted in his face. Jake didn't know what was worse: the fact that he'd just been verbally assaulted by a senior officer, or that he had let his mind speak for himself in the first place.

'I-I'm sorry,' Jake lied. 'I'm a naturally sarcastic person.'

That much was true, and it was one of the reasons that he managed to find himself in trouble more often than he'd like. But it was also true that he didn't like Bridger, and he didn't want to pretend he did. If the man was prepared to be unprofessional and inappropriate with his behaviour, then so be it. Jake was better than that. And now he had a point to prove.

Jake pointed to the master bedroom over Bridger's shoulder. 'If you wouldn't mind. We've still kind of got a job to do.'

The man's calloused hands tightened around Jake's

shoulders, forcing Jake to acknowledge what he'd just been told. In the end, Jake ceded and nodded.

Slowly, Bridger loosened his grip, shoving Jake into the banister one last time as he did so. He scowled at Jake for a moment longer before turning and heading into the master bedroom. Jake followed and stopped as he crossed the threshold. It was a mess; clothes, hangers, shoe boxes filled with old photographs and footwear littered the floor. If they'd had any chance of finding the key quickly, they were now greatly hindered.

'I'll take the bed, you take the wardrobe,' Jake said, stepping into the room. As soon as he was in, he blocked Bridger from his mind and paid little heed to what the detective sergeant was doing. The more he focused on the task at hand, the greater chance he had of finding the key.

Jake moved towards the bedside table, knelt beside it, yanked the door open and rummaged inside. There he found a small notebook, a Kindle, a jewellery box containing a watch and a cheque book. Disappointed not to find the key on the first attempt, Jake moved to the drawer beneath. Empty. He then moved to the other side of the bed, running his fingers underneath the mattress and duvet, feeling for anything hard and rigid against his skin. Meanwhile, in the corner of his eye, Jake glimpsed Bridger rummaging through the walk-in wardrobe, flinging clothes and shoes onto the carpet.

'Are you helping or just making more of a mess?' Jake asked, reaching his hand deep under the mattress.

'I'm doing my job.'

I'll believe it when I see it, Jake thought. He reached the other bedside table and sifted through the contents like a fox searching a rubbish bin. It was empty as well. He clenched his fist and scratched his cheek. What if the key wasn't in the bedroom at all? The note had said where clothes hang to *dry* after all, and the bedroom didn't quite fit that description. Then again, what if it was all a ruse? What if they had strapped the collar bomb to her neck knowing that she was doomed to die? What if there was no way they could save her, and they were wasting their time?

Jake dismissed the thought and occupied his mind with something else: the en suite, which was immediately to his right.

He wandered through. In front of him was the bathroom sink and above it was a mirror. The sight of his reflection caught him by surprise and made him jump. His body turned tense and his muscles tightened. He wasn't sure whether he let out a little gasp, but if so, he hoped that Bridger had been unable to hear it. To the right of the sink was the toilet, and beyond that was the shower. Everything sparkled and shone in the incandescent light overhead. The bathroom shower was pristine, as though it hadn't been used in years, and the toothbrush holder looked almost brand new. There was a small cabinet hanging on the wall beside a towel rack to the left of the sink, and the faint smell of cleaning chemicals lingered in the air. Everything was clean. Too clean. The rest of the bedroom's cleanliness didn't match the bathroom's. There was a disconnect, almost as if The Crimsons – or Candice – had cleaned the bathroom before leaving it.

Jake approached the cabinet on the wall and held his fingers underneath the handle. His breath steadied, and he inhaled through his nose and out through his mouth.

He pulled.

The cabinet was completely empty, save for two items resting on the middle shelf. A key. The size of his thumb, darkened and rusty. And, lying under it, a note.

Jake felt his entire body relax. He had found it. And he had done it without Bridger's help. Jake grabbed the key, along with the note, and read silently to himself before calling out to Bridger.

THERE ARE EIGHTEEN HOLES. EACH MORE CHALLENGING THAN THE LAST. ROLL THE DICE AND FIND WHICH ONE, OR THREE, WILL BE THE WINNER.

Jake read through the note a second time, assimilating the information, then paused, his attention gradually pulling away from the paper. Silence echoed around the house, and through the bathroom window, he heard Pemberton and Candice's distant chatter coming from the garden. Then he heard softened footsteps approaching him.

A second later, Bridger appeared at the door.

'What are you doing in—' At the sight of the key in Jake's hand, Bridger sauntered into the bathroom and took it from him. 'You found it. Well d— Why didn't you say anything?'

'I've only just found it.'

Bridger dismissed Jake with a wave of his hand and read the note.

'Any ideas?' Jake asked.

'Don't take a genius to work it out,' Bridger said, his Adam's apple convulsing as he swallowed deeply. 'You'll have to remember who we're dealing with, Tanner. These robbers aren't the brightest bunch.'

'Perhaps they're not worried about making you look intelligent as much as they are about escaping.' Jake smirked, but he suppressed it instantly at Bridger's burning gaze.

The senior officer spun on the spot and left the room with the key in his hand.

CHAPTER 19

TIMEPIECE

'Guv!' Bridger called, bounding over towards Pemberton. He skidded to a halt by her side and passed her the note.

'Oh my God! You found it!' Candice interrupted. At the sight of the key in Bridger's other hand, she rushed towards the three of them. Her breathing shook with excitement. 'You found it. You found it. You found the first key.'

Pemberton twisted and held her hands in the air. 'Get back, Candice. Keep your distance. It's for your own safety. I don't want to have to ask you again. We'll give you this key. But not until the bomb disposal team arrive.'

'No! You have to give it to me now! Please. We need to find the other ones.'

'And that's what we're going to do. You just have to be patient. We're not going to make any progress if you keep interrupting us every time we try to do something.

Understood?' Pemberton asked.

Candice said nothing and retreated a few paces.

Pemberton swivelled on the spot and faced Bridger. 'Get some extra uniform down here. We're going to need all the help we can get. Especially if she gets carried away with herself.'

'Yes, guv.' Bridger nodded and then left.

Pemberton returned her focus to Candice. 'Candice, I promise you, we *will* get these keys for you. But we don't know what condition your collar bomb is in. The instructions say it's trip-wired – for all we know, as soon as we fit the key inside, it may detonate.'

Candice let out a whimper. It was so visceral and raw it made the hairs on the back of Jake's neck stand on end. He hated this. What this woman was going through. The nightmare she was facing. And now Pemberton had just landed a truth bomb on her. And he sensed it wouldn't be the last.

'It's fine, Candice,' he added, hoping to ameliorate the situation somehow. 'That's what the explosive experts are for. They'll confirm there's nothing wrong with it, and that it's safe to use the keys.'

'Why aren't they here yet? We've been waiting ages!' Candice's make-up streamed down her face, and as she moved her head, Jake saw the redness on her cheeks and under her eyes from where she'd been rubbing the skin.

'They're coming. They'll be here any minute now,' Pemberton added, holding her hands in the air. But their attempt to allay Candice's fears was having little effect. Nothing would do that better than the bomb squad's arrival. Jake didn't believe they were nearby, and he was sure neither Candice nor Pemberton believed it either. But until the bomb squad arrived, Jake and Pemberton were going to have to do everything in their power to settle Candice's nerves.

'Do you know anything about golf?' Jake called to her.

Candice hesitated before responding. 'Only that there are eighteen holes in each game.'

'Then at least you and I are on the same page.'

'Is there a golf club nearby?' Pemberton asked.

Candice nodded and pointed in the opposite direction, towards the sun. 'That way. About five minutes away. Farnham Golf Club. You can't miss it. My husband knew the owner back in the day.'

'Thank you,' Jake said.

At that moment, Bridger returned, holding his phone in his hand. By now he had removed his latex gloves and had stripped down to his shirt and tie. Behind him was an entourage of scene of crime officers clad in white scrubs, their heads concealed by hoods and protective goggles. Jake didn't envy them wearing that in this heat. The sun was beating down on his back, warming his blazer and the top of his head.

'Finally!' Pemberton exclaimed, marching towards the SOCOs. She made it a few steps before turning and heading back to Jake. She stopped in front of him and placed a hand on his shoulder, then leant closer to his face and brought her voice down to a whisper. 'I need you to stay here with Candice. Make her feel more comfortable, at ease. Get her talking. But don't tell her anything she doesn't need to know. I'll be back in a minute.'

Before Jake was able to respond, she and Bridger had left

him alone with Candice, and he watched them disappear round the other side of the house with the CSIs. For a long moment, Jake just stood there, staring at the building, as though he were a dog pining after its owners, patiently waiting for them to return. He swallowed before adjusting his attention to the garden. The atmosphere was quiet, eerie – the sounds of the driveway muted as if they were coming from miles away – and all he could hear was the rustle of leaves in the soft breeze that flittered in and around him. Pivoting on the balls of his feet, he faced Candice, his gaze falling on her chest – for the first time, he didn't feel like a creep for doing it. Before him, a few metres away, was a potentially deadly bomb.

'How old are you?' Candice asked.

Her question took him by surprise.

He hesitated, stammered. 'Twenty-f-four. How old... how old do I look?'

'You're young. I didn't think they'd send someone your age into a job like this.'

'Sorry?' Jake lifted his right arm and scratched the side of his cheek.

As he did it, Candice's eyes widened. 'My son has that watch,' she said.

'Excuse me?' Jake hovered his arm in front of his face. On his wrist was the watch Elizabeth had bought him for his birthday last year. It had come at great expense given the little finances they had, and he'd begrudged her feeling the pressure to buy him something so nice for something that was over so soon, but he was appreciative nonetheless. It was a G-Shock GLX-5600-1JF. And it was one of his most prized possessions.

'Your watch. My son has that watch. You wear it on the same arm as him. The right. Few people do. Are you left-handed?'

Jake lowered his arm to his side slowly. The entire conversation confused him.

'I'm right-handed,' he corrected. 'I'm just awkward. I like to wear it on the right side. Always have done.'

'You look like him.'

Jake held his breath. 'Like who?'

'My son.'

'How old is he?'

'Similar age to you,' Candice said. 'He was taken from me when he was very young. Social services.'

Jake didn't know what to say. In the end, he settled on the only thing his instinct would allow. 'I'm sorry to hear that.'

'You're going to get me out of this, aren't you, detective?'

'I'm going to try.'

'You're different to them. To those other two. The ones you're with. *You* know what they're like, don't you? *The Crimsons*.' Candice said their name in a hush, as if saying it too loud would send a bolt of lightning from the sky to strike her. 'You know what you have to do, otherwise you know what will happen if you don't.' Her finger pointed at the collar bomb.

Jake took a step back.

'If you need help, you know who to go to, right?'

Jake said nothing.

'I heard on the news that there's one of them in jail, isn't there? One of The Crimsons. If you need help with what they're planning next, I'm sure... I'm sure he'll be able to help.'

'Freddy?' Jake whispered to himself, his attention moving away from the conversation.

Before he could say anything loud enough for her to hear, the sound of gravel moving underfoot distracted him. It was Pemberton. She came running back with Bridger beside her.

'SOCOs are in the building. Nobody else is allowed in or out until they've finished their investigations,' she said. 'Now, I want you both to go to the golf course. We've got to find this other key before EOD get here.'

'Yes, guv.'

Jake and Bridger sprinted over to Pemberton's car, Jake opting to hop in the passenger's side, allowing Bridger to drive.

'You're the directions boy,' Bridger said as he slipped the gearstick into reverse and pulled out of the driveway.

'Shouldn't be too hard considering it's only on the other side of this treeline.'

CHAPTER 20

DUSTING FOR PRINTS

The bedroom was a mess. That much was apparent to Charlotte Gibson, the first of the three SOCOs that had been positioned in the focal points of the mansion: the entrance, the bedroom and the black van stationed outside the house. Meanwhile, the rest of the team continued to set up their apparatus by the crime scene downstairs. Charlotte had been in the job for seven years, and never in her experience had she encountered a critical incident as jaw-dropping as this. The device wrapped around Candice's neck was unfathomable. But she had accepted the call to say that she would attend – it might have been the most diabolical case she'd worked on, but it was also the most interesting, the one that would put her name in infamy. This case – if she could prove herself during it – would skyrocket her career. Call it narcissism, call it vanity, call it whatever you want.

She didn't care. And if she helped solve it, then no one else would either.

Standing in the door frame of the master bedroom, she gazed about the vast expanse of space, lost for ideas of where to begin. There was too much choice, and the overflowing wardrobe to her left looked like the least appealing option. In her hand Charlotte held her camera and had her side bag full of everything she needed. Spare pair of gloves. Tweezers. Evidence bags. Brush. Powder. Pulling her hood over her hair, and lifting her mask over her mouth, she stepped into the room. When she stopped at the foot of the bed, she noticed the en suite to the right. Perfect. It was smaller and a much more manageable task than the rest of the room.

Upon entering, she surveyed the walls and furniture. It was clean. Too clean. As though it had been industrially cleaned only a few hours ago. Already her mind was beginning to imagine the last tenant, cleaning after themselves, moving about the bathroom, making sure nobody would find out what they'd touched and where exactly they'd touched it. Her old mentor had once told her that evidence was like a lover. Time and care had to be dedicated to it, and that it needed to be championed above everything else. But, more importantly, it needed to be respected.

Charlotte reached inside the bag on her hip, found her zephyr brush and flake powder, and set to work. First, she started with the sink, rubbing the fine animal hairs on the aluminium powder before transferring it onto the surface. A thin dust billowed into the air as it made contact with the porcelain, but she carried on regardless, methodically moving her way around the basin. Then she moved to the cabinet, wiping an extra load of powder on the bottom-left corner and on the shelves.

Within a few seconds, she had something. A thumbprint. Followed by another. And then another.

Charlotte leant closer and inspected the minutiae of the three prints. The bifurcation. The core. The delta. The pore. Smiling, she delicately set the brush aside on the bathroom sink, removed a piece of adhesive tape from her bag and set it on the first of the three prints. Then she peeled the tape free from the surface and smoothed it down onto a piece of Cobex – a thin plastic sheet. She scored the ends of the tape, signed and sealed the evidence in a plastic bag, and then repeated the process for the remaining two.

Within a few minutes, it was done. She pocketed her findings and headed downstairs. She was under strict instructions to notify the crime scene manager as soon as she'd found something of interest.

'Guv,' she said, holding the evidence bags in front of his face. His features were concealed behind the white mask. 'I found this. Fingerprints. From the en suite upstairs.'

'What's special about them?' he replied, deadpan.

'They're fresh from the cabinet. The en suite looks like it's recently been cleaned – especially in the last couple of hours.'

'Upload them to Ident1,' he ordered and turned his back on her.

As she started off, he pulled her back by the arm gently. 'Oh,' he began, 'erm... good... excellent work.'

Charlotte said nothing as she headed out of the house. The attempt at making her feel better was acknowledged but not accepted. It was just a shame she couldn't tell him what she really thought about him. If she could, she was sure she would have lost her job months ago, before everything else between them began.

CHAPTER 21

GOLF

Bridger skidded the car to a halt and switched off the engine, killing the sirens overhead. The noise, and their abrupt presence, alerted everyone in the vicinity of Farnham Golf Club's car park. Heads snapped towards them and some of the would-be golfers retreated a few steps; more to protect themselves from getting hit by the car and kicked-up gravel than anything else.

Jake jumped out, slammed the door behind him and jogged over to the golf club's entrance. Bridger followed, sliding into the building before the door closed. They were standing in the middle of what looked like an upmarket version of Sports Direct. Golf clubs dangled from the walls, trollies were placed neatly in a row beneath and there were racks of clothes, shirts, gloves and trousers in the centre of the space. At the other end of the building was a reception desk. A sign that said 'Restaurant This Way' hung above, pointing to another door in the far-left corner of the room.

'Can I help, officers?' a concerned voice came from behind the counter.

Just as Jake was about to open his mouth, Bridger slapped him on the shoulder with the back of his hand and shot him a look that said *I'll do the talking, all right*? before advancing forward.

'Are you the owner?' Bridger asked, reaching into his trouser pocket.

'Yes. James Atwood. This is my establishment. Is something wrong?'

Bridger flashed his warrant card. 'We're investigating a murder and a robbery in Guildford High Street. Have you seen – or has anyone handed in – a set of keys today? Or anything mysterious that may have been found on the course?'

'We've only been about open an hour. I doubt anyone's made it all the way round yet.'

'Is there... is there anybody who will know for certain?' Jake asked, trying not to sound too condescending.

James's face contorted.

'It's urgent,' Bridger said, feigning a sincere smile.

James arched his back away from them and twisted his head. 'Denise, love – has anyone handed in any keys?' he called down a small corridor to their right.

A second later, a distant voice cried back, 'Yeah. About half hour ago. Think I put them in the safe.'

James grunted and then ducked beneath the cash desk. The noise of a six-digit pin being entered into the safe sounded, and within a moment, Atwood reappeared.

'Is this it?' he asked. In his hand he held a small key, as brown and rusty as the one Jake had found in Candice's bathroom.

'Excellent. Yes. That's the one.' Bridger snatched it from Atwood.

'May we speak with Denise for a moment?' Jake asked before Bridger got too ahead of himself.

'I… I don't see why not.' James shrugged and called Denise again. A few seconds later, she arrived, drying a dinner plate with a tea towel.

'Would you be able to describe the person who gave you this key?' Jake asked.

'It was a woman. Young. Maybe in her mid-twenties. Said she found it in the car park.'

'Was she alone?'

Denise nodded.

'What did she look like? Do you have any CCTV footage?'

'Yeah.'

'Do you mind if we take a look?' Jake's eyes danced between James and Denise as he waited for an answer.

'Certainly. Please follow me.'

Denise started back down the corridor she'd just come from and Jake followed. She led him into a cramped office. In the centre was a computer monitor, showing the live feed from the CCTV cameras posted around the clubhouse and car park.

'Would you be able to go back to when the person entered the shop please?'

Denise did as instructed. As soon as she'd finished, she prodded the return key with an oversized finger and played the footage. Jake crouched so that the screen was at eye level and he rested his elbow on the desk, watching, waiting for the woman to enter.

And then she did.

Jake removed his pocketbook and made a note of the timestamp – 09:55:32. The woman entered the shop, sauntered up to the cash desk, handed over the key and then left, heading back to her car. Her face was hidden behind a baseball cap, and she wore a short skirt, a white shirt and held a gold club in her hand. At the back of her head, poking through the baseball cap, was a brunette ponytail.

Jake continued to watch the woman's movements. After she was finished with her car, she grabbed a trolley and wheeled it away, disappearing onto the golf green.

'Can you go back a few minutes please?' Jake asked.

Denise rewound the video, and Jake told her when to pause it. He leant closer, removed his phone and photographed the still, heavily pixelated image of the woman's face. He wasn't sure whether she was a suspect, or whether she was a Good Samaritan, but he was going to make sure he found out.

'Would you be able to zoom in on the car park?' Jake said as he adjusted his positioning to staunch the aching in his joints.

'I can try. The image isn't very good though.'

'I'm sure we can work with it.'

Once Denise had gone back to the image of the car park, Jake took another photo. This time of the number plate. He zoomed in on the photograph he'd taken. It was illegible.

'Do you mind if my colleagues seize this as evidence? I can get someone down here soon. We're working on a murder investigation.'

At the mention of those final two words, Denise's eyes bulged. Jake sensed that it was more out of curiosity and excitement than fear that a killer may have set foot on her golf course.

'Anything we can do to help,' she said, nodding excitably.

Jake thanked her, pocketed his phone and returned to the cash desk. As he returned to the cash desk, he caught Bridger and Atwood talking with one another. At the sight of Jake, Bridger thanked both James and Denise for their time, and then the two of them left. As they breached into sunlight, a wall of heat knocked him in the stomach, punching the air from his lungs. It was stifling.

Moving across the car park, Jake inspected the cars' number plates. From the footage, he'd been able to discern the make and model: he was looking for a silver Audi A3. And, in front of him right now, he was faced with a row of black Range Rovers and Volvos.

'She's gone,' Jake said, thinking aloud as Bridger unlocked Pemberton's car.

'You what?'

'The woman who returned the key. Her car's not here anymore.'

'Maybe she finished early. Maybe there was an emergency. We've got what we came for.'

'Hmm.' Jake was reticent. Something wasn't sitting right with him – something that was niggling at the back of his mind like the letter that was still on the table back home from HMRC telling him that he owed them a substantial amount of money that he didn't have. 'I think there are more keys out there.'

'What are you talking about?' Bridger slammed the door shut.

'The note. It said, "roll the dice and find out which one, or *three*, will be right".'

'You cannot be serious.'

'What if we go back to the house and realise we've got the wrong one – that it's one of the other ones we need?'

Bridger fell silent. His face turned red in frustration, and the sound of his increased breathing reached Jake. *Go on*, Jake thought, *say it – say you think I'm right.*

'OK. I think you're right, but we can't be here too long. We've got the other clues to find, too.'

'I haven't forgotten.'

Bridger was the first to move. He locked the car again, pocketed the keys and rounded the bonnet. 'I'll start at the first hole; you start at the last. Then we'll meet in the middle, yeah? Be quick.'

I don't need telling, Jake thought as he started off. He headed right, towards the eighteenth hole. The course was mapped out in a circle, and it didn't take long for Jake to lose sight of his belligerent partner. He sprinted to every course, checking inside the holes and the surrounding area by the flags. He found nothing in the first three. The course was surprisingly empty despite the weather, but for those he did interrupt, he apologised and then flashed his warrant card, silencing them before they could spout their obnoxious babble.

Jake jogged up and down the undulating surfaces, his legs quickly fatiguing as he covered the massive distances between each hole. Despair quickly sank in. He was on the fourteenth hole and he still hadn't found anything. But he was determined not to give up. Breathless, he slowed his pace to a jog that was more like a walk than a run.

On the fourteenth hole, Jake stopped by the course's sandbank. He scanned the surroundings, made sure he was alone and that there was no one else in the vicinity, then removed his phone.

'Danika?' he said, holding the device close to his ear as he ambled towards the next hole.

'Jake – are you all right?'

'I'm fine. What's going on your end?'

'It's busy. Non-stop. Loads of people have disappeared to the crime scene. I sat in the interview with the witnesses but I'm pulling some research together for the team now. Oh! And uniformed officers found Roger Heathcote in the middle of the road, collapsed.'

'Is he OK?'

'They found him passed out from exhaustion. He's been checked over at Royal Surrey Hospital already and they've just brought him. His wife has been informed.' Danika hesitated a beat. 'What's it like down where you are?'

'It's worse than we thought,' Jake replied. 'Much worse. We found Candice Strachan, but she's got a collar bomb strapped to her neck. The only way to disarm it is by finding four sets of keys. We're in the middle of sourcing them now.'

'*Jézus*.' Danika's voice was swamped with deep concern. 'What about The Crimsons? Where are they?'

'I was hoping you'd be able to tell me. Have there been any sightings of them?'

'Not that I've heard.'

'OK,' Jake said. He hesitated and looked around him one

last time, searching for anyone listening nearby, but he was alone. He swallowed before continuing and kept his voice low. 'Danika – I need to ask you for a couple of favours.'

'OK…'

'Firstly – Farnham Golf Club. We need this morning's complete CCTV footage. A civilian handed in one of the keys at 09:55. She's a potential lead in this investigation. Tell DI Murphy. He needs to get someone in the team to find her and question her on what she knows, if anything. I've taken a couple of photos as evidence – I'll send them to you now.'

'I will see what I can do.' There was a moment's pause. 'And what was the other thing?'

Jake scratched his cheek and started off again. 'Anything that comes into the office relating to The Crimsons, I'd like to know about it. I mean, we don't know for sure that it's them, or if it's another copycat group—'

'But I thought you said—'

'I know what I said. And I hope I'm right. But the way they've been behaving, the things they're doing… if it isn't them and I've convinced everyone it is, then it's going to be my arse – and reputation – on the line. It'll be over before it's even begun.'

On the phone, Jake heard someone in the office approaching Danika and stopping by her side. They asked Danika a question and she replied, quickly placating them and getting rid of them.

'Who was that?' Jake asked as he listened to the footsteps disappear in his ear.

'Just someone I spoke to earlier. It is nothing you need to worry about.'

'OK. Fine. There's one more thing.' Jake was expecting a

response from Danika, but when one didn't come, he continued, 'You're in charge of research, right? Good. I want you to find out *everything* you can about Candice Strachan.'

Jake reached the end of Hole 14 and entered Hole 13.

'What do you mean?'

'Something doesn't seem right. She started talking to me about my watch and the fact that I look like her son, and it just… it seemed odd. I just think it'll be worth investigating her, so we know she's kosher.'

'I'll do what I can.'

'Thank you. I have every faith you won't fuck it up.'

'You really are a prick sometimes, Jake Tanner,' Danika said and hung up. Jake felt a little lighter. Something about Candice had been niggling him at the back of his mind, and it felt good to tell someone about it. Especially someone he could trust.

Hole 13 was in sight. He jogged the remaining twenty feet and peered into the hole. An object glimmered in the sunlight. Jake reached inside and retrieved the key. It was almost identical to the one James Atwood had given them. The same size. The same colour. The same texture. And, beneath it, was another note.

Jake was too excited to read the note. He pocketed it, along with the key, and hurried round the rest of the course where he eventually met up with Bridger at the ninth hole.

'You got one as well?' Bridger asked, holding another key in his hands.

Jake smirked. 'Not just a pretty face, am I?'

'No one's ever said that. Except maybe your mum.'

'Hers is the only opinion that matters. Now, stop wasting time and let's get back to Pemberton.'

CHAPTER 22

TRIPWIRES AND TRIBULATIONS

Bridger eased the car onto Candice's driveway, leaving it in the same spot they'd picked it up from. By now, the forensic team had set up a perimeter around The Crimsons' van, cordoned off by tape, and small markers were dispersed around the vehicle, signalling points of evidence that were not to be touched. A group of three SOCOs clad in their white oversuits were inside the back of the vehicle. Flashes sparked from inside as they snapped photographs of new pieces of evidence.

Jake was the first out of the car and made his way to the garden. He came to a stop as soon as he realised it was no longer just Pemberton and Candice situated in the centre of the grass. In the time they'd been gone, four members of the bomb disposal unit had arrived and replaced the armed officers from before. The bomb squad were dressed in dark grey bomb suits – heavy-duty outfits designed to protect them from the threat of potential detonation – and helmets of the same colour.

'I'm glad to see you both,' Pemberton said as she approached them. It was clear to see she was no longer in control of the situation; that baton had been passed to the man currently standing inches away from Candice's chest, his hands fumbling around the device on her neck.

'What have we missed?' Jake asked.

'Right now, EOD are looking over the device to see whether we can remove it without blowing her face off.'

'And?'

'No luck yet. Did you find the key?'

Jake held his triumphantly in the air. Bridger did the same with the other two.

'Three of them?' Pemberton asked.

'That's what the riddle said. But only one of them works. Where's the one I found earlier?'

'It's with the guys over there. They're going to try it when they know more about the device,' Pemberton explained.

The three of them watched the bomb expert set a metal detector on the floor and remove a pair of wire cutters from his pocket.

Jake opened his mouth to speak but was too afraid to voice the question, too afraid to hear the answer he already knew.

'What happens if we can't use the keys?' Bridger asked with no such reluctance.

'With any luck we won't need them. But if they're useless, we'll just have to find another way to defuse it. Any word on The Crimsons' location?'

Both men shook their head. 'None yet, ma'am,' Bridger responded. 'HQ are running reports on Candice's stolen Mercedes. We're waiting on any ANPR and CCTV hits. But it's very possible they've changed plates, so it could be while until we find anything concrete.'

'Right. As soon as we hear something, I want you both to go after them.'

Jake's ears perked up. 'What about the keys?'

'You can leave that to us. There are enough uniforms here to go to the locations. But I want you both to follow and get after these guys. I've got a feeling we're not going to be out of this place for quite some time.'

Jake nodded. And then an idea popped into his head. 'Ma'am,' he said tentatively. 'Might I make a suggestion?'

'What?'

'Their old leader. Freddy. He's in Winchester Prison – it's just a few miles down the road. He might be able to tell us a thing or two. Do I have permission to speak with him?'

'What? No. I—'

'Ma'am, please. I've had dealings with Freddy in the past. I betrayed him – I'm the reason he's locked up. I don't think he'll want to speak to anyone except me. And I'm worried that this is all an elaborate plan for something else.'

'You think they're going to try and break Miller out of prison?'

Jake looked at her blankly. He shrugged.

Pemberton looked to the ground in a deep state of reflection.

'If you think you can muscle any information out of him, then yes. But I want a full update once you're done,'

Pemberton said. She stared deeply into his eyes. Her gaze filled him with a determination to succeed.

'You can't be serious,' Bridger added. 'You're going to let *him* speak with a former member of The Crimsons?'

'DC Tanner has a unique connection to this case, DS Bridger, so I have to manage these extenuating circumstances. It's my decision – I'm the SIO – and if you have a problem with my conduct, you know who you can take it up with. But how about you only do it *after* we're done here, eh?'

Bridger rolled his eyes. 'We don't even know for certain it is The Crimsons. Tanner admitted himself that they're acting strangely.'

'The same rules apply. We have to catch them, regardless of who they are and what colour outfits they like to wear.'

'They're more meticulous and methodical than any other robber I've ever come across,' Jake added.

'The pool of suspects is hardly big though, is it?' Bridger retorted, inching closer to Jake. 'You've only been doing this job for three hours.'

Just as Jake opened his mouth, Pemberton intervened. She stepped between them and ushered them away from one another.

'What is wrong with you two? Seriously. You're both acting like children. I've got two of my own to look after – I don't want to have to add you to the list as well. Don't make me regret my decision to involve you both.'

She turned to address Jake. 'I have news for you – they're not as meticulous as you give them credit for. A SOCO found fingerprint samples in the bathroom. They're being sent to HQ now. We won't know anything until the results come back. So you can both put your egos aside for now.'

Something moved in the corner of Jake's eye and distracted him. It was the explosives officer. He had stepped back from Candice's stiff, frozen body and started towards them.

'Ma'am,' he said as he neared, his voice barely audible through the thick helmet he wore. 'I've X-rayed the device. There's a small charge in there that's connected to the six spikes. When the charge goes off, it'll shoot the spikes into her neck. But other than that, there's no explosive.'

'What about the keys?' Pemberton asked.

'I think we're ready to try. From what I can tell,' the expert said. 'There's nothing to suggest the keys will initiate the device.'

'How certain are you?'

A pause. 'Seventy-five per cent.'

'We don't like those sorts of numbers, officer,' Pemberton replied. None of them did. They were far too low – far too low to be gambling with someone innocent's life.

'I'm afraid it's all I can give you at the moment, ma'am. If I had a little more time, I could be more confident.'

Pemberton glanced at her watch. Jake looked over her shoulder and saw it was 11:02.

'You have three extra minutes,' Pemberton said. 'Discover what you can, and then unlock it with the key.'

'The machinations in here are incredibly sophisticated. Whoever built it certainly knew what they were doing.'

'Yes, thank you for that,' Pemberton snapped. 'We just need to know how to stop it.'

The explosives expert fiddled with the device for the next couple of minutes before he took another step back and turned his focus to Pemberton, Jake and Bridger.

'It looks good to me,' he said.

'Is it safe?' Jake asked.

'As safe as a device of this malevolence can possibly be.'

'Use the first key.'

Paralysis gripped Jake as he watched the officer fumble for grip with his oversized flame-retardant glove. Eventually, he found purchase on the small key, steadied it against the lock and inserted it. Jake's palms dampened with sweat, the stress and paranoia finally beginning to take hold of his body.

The officer switched the lock. The sound was deafening, muting all other noise around them. And then everything seemed to stay still. Nobody moved. The breeze stopped. Jake's breathing stopped. Even the trees and small blades of grass stopped swaying. It felt like an eternity before someone said or did anything.

And then when nothing happened, they had their answer.

'It worked?' Jake asked hesitantly. He kept his voice low, lest he disturb the device and cause it to detonate.

'I think so,' the explosives officer said, taking a step closer to Candice.

As soon as he placed a hand on the device, everything changed.

An aggressive beeping sound emanated from the collar bomb, shouting at them, enraged.

Beep-beep-beep-beep-beep-beep-beep-beep.

'What's happening?' Candice asked, panicking. Her hands lashed at the top of the device and she strained her neck to peer over the top at the source of the noise.

Nobody responded.

Beep-beep-beep-beep-beep-beep-beep-beep.

'What's going on? Somebody tell me what's going on!' Candice's screech pierced Jake's eardrums. He felt useless. All he could do was stand there and watch.

'I don't know,' the officer said, struggling to keep the device still amidst Candice's thrashes and throes. 'Hold on! Stay still!'

Eventually, he steadied the machine and inspected it. 'The timer's gone down. It says we've got ten minutes left before detonation.'

Beep-beep-beep-beep-beep-beep-beep-beep.

'What?' Candice screamed.

'How can that be?' Pemberton whispered.

'Jesus Christ,' Bridger voiced aloud, throwing his hands into his hair.

Jake tried to say something, but the words fell over his teeth.

'Give me the keys,' the officer said. 'Let me try the other keys, for crying out loud! Hurry, before this thing goes off!'

Beep-beep-beep-beep-beep-beep-beep-beep.

Pemberton panicked. She mishandled the keys and dropped them to the ground. Cursing herself, she bent down. Jake knelt beside her and grabbed two by her left foot. He took the other one from her hand, hurried over to the expert and passed them to him, ignoring Pemberton's calls for him to retreat to a safe distance.

Jake watched the officer scramble for the lock and insert the keys one by one. By now, the sweat on his body had multiplied, and streams of salty liquid coated his skin.

The first attempt failed. As did the second. As Jake

watched the officer insert the final key – the one that he had found – he prayed, for the first time in a long time, that it would work. He didn't want to see Candice's head and brain and skull strewn all over the grass.

Beep-beep-beep-beep-beep-beep-beep-beep.

The officer inserted the key. Twisted. And then an eerie silence filled the air again.

Jake exhaled heavily. 'Did it work?'

'Yes,' the officer said hesitantly. 'It's gone back to the normal time.'

Candice let out a loud moan of relief, and then her legs buckled as she blacked out. The officer beside her caught her and eased her to the safety of the grass.

'Jesus,' Jake said. 'Is she going to be OK?'

'She'll come round soon enough,' the officer said.

'What happened just then?' Bridger asked.

'There must have been a setting in the countdown. As soon as we entered the first key, it required the second—'

'Which means we're going to need the third and fourth at the same time before we can do anything else…'

The officer nodded.

'Two down. Two to go,' Jake added.

Saying nothing, Pemberton turned and started towards the house. 'You two – with me.'

Jake and Bridger looked at one another before following behind her.

'What's the matter, guv?' Bridger asked.

Pemberton stopped abruptly and pointed at them. 'We need to move faster. Jake, get to Winchester. Speak with Freddy and see what he knows, if anything, about this robbery and kidnapping. Bridger, change of plan – I want you to look for the other keys. Forget what I said earlier. What happened just then has changed everything—'

Pemberton was cut off by her mobile ringing. She held a finger in the air to pause the conversation and answered the call. 'Yes… OK… Thank you… Understood… No. I'll be in touch if I need anything else… You've been a great help. Stand by for further instructions.'

She shut the phone off and turned to face Jake. 'Looks like you were right all along, DC Tanner. The fingerprint that forensics found in the bathroom came up with a direct match. A Mr Luke Cipriano.'

| PART 3 |

CHAPTER 23

OLD FRIEND

The cumbersome metal doors opened. On the other side was Freddy Miller, the former leader of The Crimsons. The man who'd held Jake hostage inside the HSBC branch in Oxford just over two years ago. The man who had been responsible for inspiring Jake to enter the police service. From that point onwards, Jake knew that he wanted to fight against evil, like he was some sort of modern-day superhero dressed in a suit and tie.

Freddy's face remained impassive as they locked eyes on one another. The bald man was ushered into the room by a prison officer and then allowed to walk the small distance to the desk in the middle where Jake was seated.

'I was wondering when you'd visit,' Freddy said, pulling the chair opposite from beneath the table. 'And in what capacity,' he added. 'I hear you bat for the other team now.'

Jake dipped his head slightly, glancing down at his suit. He straightened his tie and adjusted the metal clip. 'I've got a lot to thank you for.'

Freddy leant forward on the table, his face shining under the light. The man Jake had encountered during The Crimsons' last hit was completely different to the one in front of him now. There was no energy left in his face. No life. No vigour. The colour had gone from every aspect: his cheeks, his eyes, even his lips. His facial hair was messy and unkempt, and he looked as though he'd only just woken up. And he'd lost a lot of weight, too. So much so, in fact, that the prison-issue tracksuit drowned him, hanging from his shoulders and revealing half his chest hair. Jake reckoned he wouldn't have noticed Freddy if he'd passed him on the street.

'Have you really come all this way just to thank me. Or are you asking for help?' Freddy asked.

'Can it be both?' Jake said. He had never come face to face with a criminal in a situation like this. He couldn't believe he'd been allowed to speak with Freddy alone, but he had known it was the right thing to do. And, more importantly, so had Pemberton, which was all the authority he needed.

A smirk grew on Freddy's face. 'I know what this is about. They've done it again, and they've got you right where they want you, haven't they?'

'You've heard what's happened?' Jake asked. He had to be careful how to play it – give away too much and he would risk losing his hand to Freddy who, in fact, had Jake right where he wanted him: begging on his knees.

Freddy shrugged. 'I've heard things.'

'Where from?'

'The walls. You spend a lot of time in this place, they start talking to you. Begins to get quite scary after a while.'

'Perhaps you should see a doctor?'

'Shrinks aren't my friends.'

'I'm sure I could do an evaluation – I've got a degree in psychology.'

'You clever boy. I'm sure your parents were very proud.'

'My mum was.'

'And your dad?'

'Dead.'

Freddy leant back in the chair, folding his arms. He bounced on the plastic and placed his entire weight on it. He commanded Jake's attention in one move. 'How's that girlfriend of yours? What was her name?' Freddy touched his temples with his index and middle finger. 'Alice? Alicia? Eliza? Elizabeth! That's it. How's she doing? She still stuck around with a little shitbag like you?'

To Jake's surprise, he found himself chuckling at the remark. 'Yes. She's still with me, by some miracle. We've even got a beautiful little daughter together.'

Freddy clapped. 'You don't hang about, do you? Did you conceive her on the night we had our little foray? Testosterone levels running high. Ego through the roof. You really had a lot going for you that night, didn't you?'

'If only that were the case,' Jake said.

'Is the baby healthy?'

Jake nodded. 'Come down with something minor today, but Elizabeth's coping with it.'

'I'm pleased for you.'

Jake shifted the dynamic of the conversation away from

him to focus it more on Freddy. 'What about your little boy? Have you spoken to him?'

'Don't be fucking ridiculous. He's not allowed anywhere near here. I've written letter after letter, sent it to his mum's last known address, but have I heard anything? Fuck no.' Freddy made a *zero* gesture with his fingers. 'His mum wants nothing to do with me, so by default that means Sammy doesn't want anything to do with me either.'

Jake didn't know what to say. Now that he was a father, he could think of nothing worse than having Maisie ripped from him. Not seeing her every day, holding her, stroking her hair, kissing her goodnight at bedtime or when he got in late and she was already asleep. She was his everything – his entire world. And he would permit nothing to hurt her. Especially after he and Elizabeth had been told they wouldn't be able to become parents by a multitude of professionals in the first place.

'I'm sorry to hear that,' Jake said eventually, finding the courage to say the words. 'It must be horrible.'

'It is.' Freddy paused a beat. 'You know who I blame? *You*. You're the reason I'm in here. At least before I was able to watch my son grow up from the outskirts of his life. Now I have nothing, and no way of contacting him. He'll never know I existed, and there's fuck all I can do about it.'

There was an emotion in Freddy's voice that Jake hadn't heard before. When they'd first met, Freddy had told him about his son, but he hadn't expressed as much passion and adoration as he did just now. Jake was sure he saw the corners of the man's eyes glisten in the light.

'I don't know anything about what they've done,' Freddy said. 'This is all on them. *Their* heist. *Their* job.'

'I'm not here to ask you whether you know anything about this one.'

'What do you need from me then?' There was no expression on his face and no energy left in Freddy's tone, as if their previous topic of conversation had vacuumed it out of him.

'I need to know everything about the brothers. Their past. Their present. Their future. This job's different, Fred. This one's… more evil.'

Freddy stroked his stubble and smiled. It was clear who had all the power; Jake would have to change that.

'You don't ask for a lot, do you? And what do I get out of this little arrangement?'

Jake swallowed before replying. This was it. His ace card.

'I can get you to see your son. I can make that happen. I'll just need some time.'

CHAPTER 24

GOOD EGG

Dumf-dumf. Dumf-dumf. Dumf-dumf. Danika's beating heart thumped in her ears and drowned out the sounds of furious typing and chatter and laughter that surrounded her. The investigation was gearing up a notch. News and updates from Candice Strachan's mansion had begun to filter into the rest of the office; that the device connected to her neck was live and required a set of keys to defuse it; that DS Bridger and DC Tanner had already found two keys; that there were still a couple more, and that this was the most ingenious and difficult device for the explosives team to encounter.

But Danika already knew that. She had her informant telling her everything on the go. Jake. They had started the application for detective constable at the same time, and they had found themselves working in the same borough, developing their skills with one another, growing together.

But something about today had made her feel uncertain about him. Uneasy. And she couldn't explain what it was.

Perhaps it was jealousy. The fact that she was stuck inside the office, working behind the scenes, filing all the paperwork away while he was out on the front line, rolling with the Detective Sergeant and Chief Inspector. Not to mention that, for their first-ever case together, it was fortuitous that Jake had had direct experience with The Crimsons before. Of course, he'd given her that bullshit sob story of wanting her to be there with him when the original call came in earlier in the morning, and she had pretended to believe it. But she didn't. He knew what he was doing. Giving her tasks to throw her off the scent. But she wasn't doing it for Jake. No, she was doing it for the good of the investigation, the good of her standing within the team. She needed to stick out, draw attention to herself, make people aware that she existed.

It was time to look out for number one.

Danika propelled herself away from her desk, hurried to the printer and grabbed her documents. They were still warm. She paced across the room and stopped beside DI Murphy. Steam from his freshly brewed cup of tea floated in the air.

'Excuse me, Mark,' she said hesitantly. The smell of tobacco still lingered on his clothes.

He peered up at her. 'Ah, Oblak, what can I do you for?'

'I... I have the suspectology report on Luke Cipriano you asked for.' She handed him the pages she'd just printed out. Mark took them, and as he leafed his way through, Danika gave him the condensed version. 'His fingerprints appeared on Ident1 for several crimes when he was younger. He has

146

two brothers – Danny and Michael – and they were also arrested for anti-social behaviour when they were younger. They were abandoned as children and, from what I could see, they jumped from foster home to foster home.'

A smirk grew on Mark's face. 'Excellent. Stellar work, Danika,' he said.

His words filled her with pride. It wasn't often she was appreciated – either at home or in the job (policing was a thankless job at the best of times) – but whenever she was, she always stood there awkwardly, uncertain how to accept it.

In the end, she settled on, 'Thank you, sir.'

Mark turned his back on her momentarily, handed the documents to a female officer beside him and instructed her to write the information on whiteboards in the Horseshoe. Returning his attention to Danika, he said, 'I'm impressed. We'll make a good copper out of you yet. What else have you found?'

'Nothing at the moment, sir.' She hesitated, glancing back at her desk. 'DC Tanner asked whether someone in the team could investigate CCTV footage found at Farnham Golf Club? He believes a suspect may have handed in a key there.'

Mark's face illuminated. 'Yes... please... send the details to me... and I'll make sure somebody gets on it immediately.'

'Of course, sir. Is there anything else you need me to do?'

'No, that's everything for now.'

Danika nodded and thanked him once again. As she started away, Mark called her name and waved her back.

'Actually,' he began, keeping his voice low. 'There is

something. It's about Tanner... if he's not following the chain of command, I want to know about it. Information should be coming through either myself or DCI Pemberton. I want you to keep me up to date with everything he's telling you.'

'Of course, sir. No problem.'

There was a pause. Mark glanced down at her feet and then back into her eyes. 'Is he asking you to do anything else for him?'

Danika opened her mouth, but nothing came out. Her mind turned completely blank. Then she stuttered, 'He... yes... he wanted me to... to... Candice! He asked me to develop the victimology report on Candice.'

'What about her?' Mark asked, deadpan.

'He said that she was acting strangely – that there was something a bit off about her.'

Mark nodded approvingly. 'Right. Make that your next project. Anything you find, I want you to tell me about it, all right? I'll need to sign off on any information you choose to share. Can you do that for me?'

'Of course, sir.'

'Great. Thanks, Danika. You're a good egg.'

CHAPTER 25

BIRTHPLACE

MONASTERY, O MONASTERY, WHERE FOR ART THOU, O MONASTERY? HIDING IN THE THREE PILLARS OF YOUR MIND.

Bridger lowered his hand and gazed at the police constable Pemberton had assigned to accompany him. It was a bullshit decision he didn't agree with. He didn't need someone to babysit him. He was an experienced detective. If anything, it was Bridger who was doing the babysitting. The officer's name was Smithers. He was young, fresh out of school, with a youthful set of legs and keen eyes. He was full of life and excitement. Eager. Like Bridger had once been before the stresses and inane politics of the job had withered him down to nothing but the miserable bastard he was.

They were at Waverley Abbey, a few miles south of

Candice Strachan's mansion. After reading the clue, Bridger had deduced that it was the destination for the third key.

'What do you reckon?' he asked Smithers. 'We in the right place?'

Smithers shrugged. 'I don't know.'

Of course you don't.

He reread the instruction, confirming in his own mind that he was right. It wasn't the most eloquent thing he had ever read, or the most accurate, but it had been fairly obvious. It wasn't as though there were a plethora of monasteries to choose from in Surrey. And if there was one thing he had learnt from the previous two clues, they weren't designed to be impossible.

They reached the end of the slight incline leading to the abbey. Before them, three hundred feet in the distance, was the remains of the abbey. Knots of tourists and families ambled the grounds, marvelling at the magnificence of the site, shielding themselves from the sun by using umbrellas to cast shadows over their heads and backpacks. For a moment, Bridger contemplated evacuating the site entirely, but decided against it; it was unlikely that anyone would have found the key and taken it for themselves. It wasn't in the nature of the type of people who visited these sorts of sites; he always found they were more a "look but don't touch" type of community.

Bridger started off towards the structure directly ahead. It was a small building, constructed from stone, with a roof that cleared his head by a few inches. Arches split the building in two, and holes in the shape of windows interspersed the length of the structure. To the left of the building was another, with a tree beside it.

'I want you to watch here, OK?' Bridger said, holding his hand up to Smithers. 'Make sure nobody disrupts us. I'm not expecting it to be heaving with people in the next thirty seconds, but if anyone gives you any lip, get them out of here. They start launching verbal assaults on you, come and let me know. I'll take care of it.'

'Of course, sir,' the officer said. He sounded almost robotic, and Bridger remembered the early days when he used to sound like that himself. Subordinate. Inferior. And now look at him. He was the one barking the orders.

Bridger left the young man alone and headed towards the other historic remains. As he entered, he slowed to a halt and absorbed the surrounding atmosphere. It seemed as if the ghosts of everyone who had ever set foot in there were alongside him now, gazing at the wall with three window holes running down it in front of him. He carefully edged forward, looking down at the ground beneath his feet. The rocks and grass squashed under his weight. He wanted to savour every moment, but then he remembered what he was there to do. The key. The note. Candice.

He removed the instructions from his pocket and reread the final line.

Hiding in three pillars.

'Gotcha!' he whispered triumphantly to himself.

Bridger approached the wall and pulled on a new pair of latex gloves. He studied it for a moment. Observing. Uncovering the secrets before peeling back the layers. And then he moved a piece of rock he'd noticed nestled at the bottom of the window frame. He placed it delicately on the ground and returned his attention to the window. Hidden beneath the rock was the key, wrapped tightly in another strip of paper. Bridger let out a small celebratory fist pump.

Now all he needed to do was keep it safe.

Bridger pocketed the small piece of metal against his breast and unravelled the fourth note.

RUNAWAY, RUNWAY, RUNAWAY – YOU ARE NOT WANTED HERE. SEVENTEEN MILES OF TARMAC FROM TAKE-OFF SEPARATES YOU FROM TOUCHING DOWN SAFELY BACK ON EARTH.

CHAPTER 26

CHANGE OF PLANS

'I thought you were looking after the kids tonight?' Pemberton snarled into the phone. She kept her voice low and shifted from one foot to another, struggling to find a comfortable standing position.

'I know,' her husband replied. 'But something's come up with work. They need me to come in.'

'Can't it wait?' She nestled the phone in the crook of her neck and rolled back her sleeve to check the time. She had only been on the phone for a minute, but it was already beginning to feel like ten.

'Leakages tend not to wait, love,' he said, his voice deadpan. 'Especially if they're your biggest client.'

'And no one else is available to do it?'

'No. I've tried.'

Pemberton sighed in despair and ambled away from the

crime scene to the conservatory at the end of the garden, lest she draw any unwanted attention to herself.

'When will you be gone?' she asked.

'Soon. I'll need to come back to pick up the boys from school, but then they'll need someone to look after them afterwards.'

'Well, I'm sure as anything not going to be able to leave on time. Nowhere near it. I could be here all day.'

'So, you've already had to cancel with the girls anyway, no?'

'I'm definitely going to need a drink after the day I'm having,' she said, folding her free arm across her chest and planting her hand under her armpit, 'regardless of what time it is. They'll wait for me. Even if I only get to see them for five minutes.'

'Then what do you suggest we do?'

'You need me to tell you?'

'I—'

'Book a sitter.'

'No.'

'Come on. Someone we trust.'

'No.'

'William – stop being ridiculous. How many times do I have to say it? Not everyone we hire to look after our kids is going to turn out to be a predator. That was one time—'

'Which was your fault. You convinced me to let him into our home.'

'We were desperate. I'm not getting into this with you again – I haven't got time right now. I'm stressed to the max, and the last thing I need is to get into an argument with you over something so trivial and something we've both discussed a thousand times already.'

Pemberton paused. There was silence in her ear, save for the sound of her husband's wheezy breathing. She had won... at long last. But it was bittersweet.

'Like I've told you before, if anything happens to our children under the watchful eye of a babysitter, I will not stop until I find them and hurt them. Just like last time. Surely there's someone we know who we can ask?'

'I'll find out,' he said and hung up on her.

Before the call disconnected, she was already scrolling through her address book, searching for another number to call. This was a call she wasn't looking forward to. She was going to have to cancel the plans she'd been looking forward to for weeks; it was a nightmare trying to organise anything anyway, let alone an evening for them both to be together without the risk of children and husbands interrupting.

Pemberton found the mobile number in her address book and dialled. The phone rang and rang. Rang and rang. Until it clicked through to voicemail. She sighed and tried again. This time, the person on the other line answered within the first ring.

'Ma'am?' he said tentatively, as if he were uncertain it was her on the other end.

'Mark – where are those files I requested? It's been a couple of hours now,' she said, cupping the microphone on the device with her hand.

There was a brief pause as DI Murphy registered what she'd said. 'Sorry, ma'am,' he replied. 'I've been swamped. I'll have them over to you by the end of play today.'

Pemberton sidled further away from Candice and the explosives officer and moved towards the patio doors of the conservatory. She peered in, trying to focus on the inside of the building and not the reflection of the garden behind her. From what she could see, there were four chairs positioned around the edge of the structure, facing the centre. In the middle was a small fireplace, with its chimney protruding from the top of the conservatory.

'Ma'am?' Mark insisted. 'I said I've been swamped. I'll have them back to you as soon as.'

Pemberton snapped to reality. She shook her head and focused. 'Something's come up.'

'What?'

'I have to cancel tonight. William's been called into work and I might have to look after the kids.'

'You're shitting me?'

'I wish I was. I tried to argue against it, but he doesn't want to consider getting a babysitter.'

'Idiot. The guy's a tool. You need to break it off with him.'

'It's not that easy. You know I'm trying. Slowly.'

'He's such a flannel.'

Pemberton shuffled her feet from side to side. She hated letting Mark down like this. It had happened on too many occasions, and she was beginning to think that she might have to fake her death to even get a chance to speak with him in a non-professional capacity. They had even tried romancing their time together at work after hours, but even that had been interrupted by late-night staff and the cleaning crew. And there were only so many training weekends she could fabricate as an excuse to get away from her husband and kids.

'What have I said before, Mark?' she continued. 'William's a good guy. And I have my reasons for doing what I'm doing, but you don't need to make sarcastic comments like that, OK?'

'Sorry, Nic. I was just really looking forward to seeing you.'

'And so was I. I know we've had tonight organised for weeks.'

'It is what it is,' Mark said, his voice rigid.

'Don't be like that,' Pemberton replied, casting a glance over her shoulder. 'It's going to be tough, but I'll make it worth your while when I do eventually get to see you. Maybe we'll just have to find a nice quiet place in the toilets tomorrow night after work – after everyone's gone home. Not the most luxurious place. And we'll have to make sure we don't have a repeat of last time.'

'Depends on whether your arsehole husband decides to throw a fit again.'

'It'll be all we can afford to risk at the moment. Listen – I'll speak to him tonight whenever he gets back from work, and we'll reorganise something soon, OK?'

'I won't hold my breath.'

Pemberton sighed and pinched the bridge of her nose with her fingers. 'Don't be like this – please. I do want to see you. I really do.'

'You sure? Because so far, it doesn't seem that way to me. I'm always second best.'

'I have a family – a husband and kids to think about.'

'A husband you no longer care for and kids you hardly see? Yeah,' Mark said. 'That's what I thought. Sounds like a real happy family to me.'

He rang off, leaving Nicki to stand there blankly, staring into her reflection in the window. She closed her eyes, swallowed and exhaled.

She had hoped he wouldn't say that. She loved her family – her husband, Damian, Jules – but things hadn't been the same for a long time, especially with William. The arguments. The late nights. The black hole that her libido had fallen into. The revulsion she felt every time he tried to touch her. But there had been a light at the end of it. Mark. He made her feel things she'd forgotten existed. Made her feel things she wanted to feel every day. Her marriage had stagnated, and the only thing keeping her from being with Mark was the crippling guilt she felt every time she was with him. The situation itself was a minefield: she was his senior, and if word spread, she could lose her job, and everything she'd ever cared for.

A voice behind distracted her.

'Ma'am.' It was the explosives expert, carrying his helmet under his arm. His short black hair was damp, and thin beads of sweat bubbled on the pores of his nose.

'Yes?' she said, forcing the debilitating thoughts and images of the future from her mind. She needed to be present at the crime scene; she needed to save Candice Strachan. 'What's the latest?'

'I need to have a word. I don't think she's going to make it.'

CHAPTER 27

TIME FOR A CALL

One thought occupied Danny's mind as he stared out of the window. The woman who was waiting for him at the port in – he checked his watch – two hours' time. She had agreed to travel abroad with him, to another country with him, to another way of life with him. She was happy to do all that with him, and he couldn't wait. They had been dreaming of this day for months, ever since they'd first met. *Louise.* Even the thought of her name sent shivers running up and down his spine. He was besotted with her, and she had a hold over him like no other woman had been able to maintain. He counted down the minutes until he would be with her.

In the front of the stolen Audi, Luke blasted the radio. He drummed along to the beat of the song, tapping his fingers on the steering wheel. Luke was driving conservatively. Perhaps a little too conservatively for Danny's liking, but his brother was in control, and he was doing a good job of it, so he wasn't going to interfere. There was still a long way to go.

'You feeling all right, Lukey?' Danny asked. He placed his palm on the back of Luke's headrest.

'I got this.'

'That's not what I asked,' Danny said.

'Have we crashed yet?'

'Don't tempt fate, mate.' Danny returned his attention to the outside word – outside the confines of these four walls of glass – and considered his future life. 'Any news on the boat?'

'Last I checked it was fine. Still scheduled to leave on time,' Michael said, unlocking his brand-new iPhone.

'Assuming the police aren't waiting for us down there.' Luke glanced at Danny in the rear-view mirror.

'Why you always got to put a downer on everything?' Danny said. 'They won't. Trust me. Nobody saw our faces. Nobody left any DNA. Nobody knows who we are. Who said we needed Freddy, anyway?'

'You fucking shot someone, Dan. There'll be gunshot residue all over that place.'

'I thought I told you boys there's nothing to worry about. I'm in charge. Besides, if you're really that worried about it, we've got our help, remember?'

'Yeah. And you know how successful the last little piggy was,' Michael said, tutting.

'That was an anomaly. That fucking prick Tanner got in the way last time. It won't be happening again.'

'And what about the rest of the stuff?' Michael asked, rotating in his seat and peering back at Danny. 'Has that all been picked up?'

'Yes, Micky. It's all under control.' Danny checked his watch again. 'My contact should be picking it up right about now, in fact. Relax.'

Nobody said anything for a while, and the sound of tarmac passing beneath them filled the car. In the driver's seat, Luke shuffled. His eyes flicked repeatedly to Danny in the rear-view mirror.

Eventually, Luke cleared his throat. 'You sure this is going to work, Dan?' It was evident to see he was sceptical. In fact, it was clear he'd been sceptical since the beginning, and it was Danny's job to change that.

'When have I ever let you down before?'

'You really want him to answer that?' Michael glanced back at Danny, facing him but not looking directly at him.

Danny hesitated a moment before continuing. He swirled his phone in his fingers like a toy and then dangled it between the two front seats so they could see it.

'I think it's time to give them a call,' he said.

'Who?' Luke asked.

'Luke Skywalker and the Rebellion... who fucking else, dickhead?'

The A3 widened into four lanes as it gradually turned into a motorway. They were just on the outskirts of Portsmouth, and Danny estimated they had less than twenty minutes until they arrived at their next destination.

'I don't approve of this,' Luke said.

'I don't know why you think this is a good idea,' Michael added. 'You're just shooting us in the foot.'

I don't care, he thought. This was his job. He was in charge. This was going to be his biggest achievement yet. One that everyone would remember him for. They – his inferiors, those who had doubted him, and those chasing after him – would think about him every waking moment of their day. He would haunt them. The one that got away with one of the UK's largest heists.

And now it was his time to speak with them directly.

He unlocked the phone and dialled 999.

'Nine-nine-nine, what's your emergency?' came the operator's voice moments later.

'Yes. This is The Crimsons.'

CHAPTER 28

BETTER NEWS

Pemberton's heart caught in her mouth, and for a moment, she wasn't sure whether she'd vomited or not. She swallowed it down, and then, for a long while, stared blankly into the officer's face.

'What's your name?' she asked.

'Armitage, ma'am.'

'And you're sure? There's nothing we can do to save her?'

Armitage glanced behind his shoulder before turning his attention back to Pemberton. 'The device is intricately manufactured. The locks are all connected to different wires. When we used the first two keys, it severed the cables. I followed where they led to… nowhere. We just cut open two pieces of copper wrapped in plastic. That was it. There also seems to be a tripwire on the edges of the device, so that if we try to open the seal, whatever's inside will detonate for sure. But I also found something else…'

'What?' Pemberton asked, her mouth dry.

'A phone.'

'A phone?' Pemberton asked.

'A phone.' Armitage nodded as he said it.

Pemberton's skin went cold. 'Why wasn't this picked up when you inspected the device?'

'It was hidden, ma'am, behind a solid piece of metal. I just thought it was a part of the design. But since we introduced the keys to the device, it opened – almost as if it were some sort of treasure that we unlocked.'

'What does it mean for the device?' Pemberton asked, even though she already knew the answer. 'That it can be remotely detonated?'

'It looks that way, ma'am.'

'What are the keys for then? Why go to all that trouble if they're going to remotely detonate it anyway?'

'I don't know. Maybe they're a decoy. Something to keep us occupied. But I wish I had better news for you.'

'No,' Pemberton said, stunned. She found herself struggling for the words that would have usually come so easy to her. 'You're doing a fantastic job. Keep up the good work.'

CHAPTER 29

INCOMING

The telephones in the office bleated. Each device played together in a symphony of noise across the room. Danika lunged forward and grabbed the phone. It was an instinctive reaction, one that had been ingrained in her from her time as a receptionist back in Slovenia. But as she held the phone in her hands, she regretted the decision to pick it up. She was new, untrained and knew nothing about any of the goings on in Surrey Police.

'DC Oblak,' she said carefully, making sure not to pronounce her name wrong.

'Is this Surrey MCT? Have I come through to the right department?'

'Yes. Who's calling, please?'

'Forgive me, I'm calling from Surrey control. We've just received a suspicious call from someone claiming to be a member of the organised crime group called The Crimsons… I understand you're dealing with the robbery in Guildford?'

Danika's attention narrowed in on the microphone in her ear; she drowned out all the ambient noise and listened intently to the woman's voice. This was her chance.

'Our officers are dealing with the case right now.'

'They said they needed to speak with the SIO. They said someone's going to die if they don't speak with them.'

Sránje. Sránje sránje sránje. Her heart beat fast and her mind fogged. She was panicking again. That was going to have to stop if she was going to progress any further in her career. She couldn't afford to be fazed by the earliest signs of trouble. *Miren. Inhalirati. Odviti. Calm. Breathe. Relax.* She inhaled and exhaled slowly through her nose and mouth.

'Thank you for letting us know,' she said. 'I'll find the right person for you to speak with. One moment please.'

Danika looked at the phone console. Her eyes searched for the mute button and eventually found it a second later. Holding the phone in her hand still, she leapt up and scanned the office for someone to help. Those nearest to her were either on the phone already or walking away from her.

She looked for Mark. He was the Deputy SIO, he would help.

As soon as she spun around, he appeared.

'You look frightened,' he said, bearing a big grin. 'What's up?'

Danika explained.

'You're joking?' he asked, his brow creased.

Danika shook her head.

'I'll call Pemberton.' He dialled her number and held it to

166

his ears. Within seconds she answered.

'Boss? Hello? It's me. We've got an issue. One of The Cipriano brothers has just called 999 and is asking to speak with you directly... Yes?... I don't know. You're right. OK.... That'll take a moment to set up, but we can do it.'

Mark hung up and disappeared towards the other end of the room. She watched him bark orders to other members of the team, and a clutch of them came rushing over to her desk.

'What are you doing?' she asked.

'Tracing the number. If we can get that, we trace the call and find them.' He gestured for him to use the phone in Danika's hand. Reluctantly, she ceded control.

'This is DI Murphy, acting SIO,' he said into the receiver once the wiretap was set up. 'What's the mobile number and the IMEI that the civilian is calling from?' He made a note of the number and flagged it to everyone else around them. 'Please hold a moment while I put you through to the right person.'

CHAPTER 30

AN EYE FOR AN EYE

'This is DCI Pemberton.'

The words sounded like a song in Danny's ear. After just under five minutes of waiting, he had finally managed to get through to the person in charge.

'Good afternoon, DCI Pemberton,' he said, keeping his voice monotonous and deep.

'Who am I speaking with?'

'Names aren't important.'

'I've given you mine.'

'Quid pro quo? Is that how you want to play it? Like Hannibal Lector and Clarice Starling?' There was no response. 'Do you need me to silence the lambs, DCI Pemberton?'

Still no response.

Danny was testing how far he could take Pemberton's

temperament. Dipping his toe in the waters of sarcasm and belligerence. And he was revelling in the excitement of it.

'You still there, officer?'

'I don't think the line's very good. You must be in a bad signal area?'

'Nope. Don't think so.'

'Where are you?'

'Somewhere we won't be for too long.'

'You still haven't told me your name. If we're going to give a tit for tat, I need to know you're fully on board.'

'Danny.'

'And what do you want, Danny?'

Danny smirked. 'What do you think of the collar bomb? Spectacular, isn't it?'

'Depravity is what it is.'

'I'm disappointed you don't appreciate it. A lot of time and effort went into making that. Aren't you lot supposed to take an objective look at things?'

The car slowed to a gradual halt and the number of vehicles either side of them increased. Danny leant into the centre of the car and peered through the windscreen. Traffic stretched in front of him for as far as he could see, and more cars were beginning to pile up behind them as well.

A car horn sounded beside them.

'What's that noise?' Pemberton asked. 'Are you in a spot of traffic. Let's hope we don't catch up with you.'

'You won't.'

'You sure of that?'

'You like wasting questions, don't you? Would you have wasted them if I'd told you that you only had three to begin with?'

'What are you—'

'Are you sure you want to use that as your final one, detective?'

There was a long pause. Danny waited, but he soon became bored.

'How far behind us are you? With the keys, I mean. Find any?'

'We've only found the one.'

Danny pulled the phone away from his ear, placed DCI Pemberton on loudspeaker and opened his text messages. He opened the first chat at the top and scrolled through the latest texts.

'Danny? You still with me?'

Danny snapped to. 'You say you've found one key?'

'Yes,' she replied.

Liar. Evidence suggests otherwise, love.

'Which one did you find? The one inside the house?' Before Pemberton had a chance to respond, he continued. 'We wanted to make it nice and easy for you.'

'We've got a lot to thank you for.'

'You sound unappreciative.'

'That's a habit of mine. My husband tells me it's something I need to work on.'

'You been together long?' Danny probed.

'I'll tell you that when you answer my question: what's going to happen to Candice? We know about the mobile… the remote detonation.'

Well, shit. Danny hadn't expected them to discover the mobile so soon. He had tried his hardest to bury it deep within the complex inner workings of the bomb.

His hand moved to his overall pocket. Inside was a small

key. It was metallic and cold to the touch. His thoughts turned to Candice, crying on the floor, squirming, begging for her life in front of Michael and Luke and the Good Samaritan. He squeezed the key in his hand until it dug into his skin.

Danny exhaled deeply. The traffic hadn't moved while they'd been talking, and the idle sound of the engine purring underneath reminded him they were still a long way away.

'If you didn't appreciate the collar at first, then hopefully by the end of it all you will,' he said softly.

'What do you mean?'

'There are three layers to it. The keys. The timer. The phone. If you get all the keys, you disarm the charge. If you do it before the deadline, you disarm the charge. And if you find the phone that detonates it remotely, you'll disarm the charge.'

'How do we find the phone?'

'I have it. I'm calling you now on it. The only way you'll get that is by arresting me.'

'Nothing would give me greater satisfaction right now,' Pemberton said. 'But how do I know you won't just detonate it now?'

'I like to play fairly. I'll give you some time. My recommendation would be to find the keys instead. You've got three more to go and not long left on the countdown.' He rubbed the key in his hand. 'Although, I have a sneaky suspicion you'll struggle with the final one. I made it extra difficult to find.' He whispered so that his voice was inaudible to Luke and Michael over the sound of the radio. 'Especially if I've got it in my pocket,' he said. Returning his voice back to normal, he continued, 'If you're not quick

171

enough, detective, Candice is going to die today. Soon she'll be nothing more than a lifeless body without a head. And her blood will be on your hands. Goodbye.'

Danny hung up the phone, removed the SIM and snapped it in half. He rolled down the window and threw it onto the motorway. There was no way the police would be able to track them now.

CHAPTER 31

MAIDEN

'Luke, Danny and Michael Cipriano. That's who you're looking for,' Freddy said, with a cup of water in his hands. 'But not in that order. Danny's the eldest, Luke the youngest. Five years separates them. And there's not a hint of Italian in any of them, other than their surname and strong family bond.'

'What about their parents?' Jake asked. He sat with his elbows resting against the edge of the table and his hands knitted together. He had a pen and paper in front of him, but he made little use of it. The most important information would be stored in his brain.

'Both English.'

'That's not what I meant… what did they do?'

Freddy eased deeper into his chair and rolled his left sleeve back, revealing a wrist so skinny Jake saw the tendons and river of veins disappearing into the material. 'The dad was in the military. And the mum did a runner on them when they were really young; she ran off with some other fella. He had money and, I can only assume, a smaller cock. It had to compensate for something, I guess.'

'What happened when the dad was in the military?'

'He gave them up to a foster home. He couldn't afford to look after them *and* serve his country. It would appear he favoured the Queen and all her horses more than he did his own flesh and blood.'

'Where did he serve in the army?'

'Afghanistan. I don't know which regiment exactly, but I know he dealt with explosives of some description.'

Jake nodded. 'That explains where the spiked collar bomb came from.'

'That thing that Danny created is a technically difficult device to conceive of, let alone make. I'm surprised he managed it.'

'You and I have got very different philosophies on praising people. How do you know it was him that made it?'

Freddy rolled his eyes. 'He never shut the fuck up about it when we were working together. All the time. How he wanted to build something – *do* something – that would make him one of the most notorious armed robbers in existence.'

'He must have had help from somewhere?'

'Not that I know of. And not me, if that's what you're insinuating. I wanted nothing to do with it. Besides, I haven't seen them boys in years. Not even a letter or anything.'

'I'm sure they've got their reasons. Least of all trying to

lay low. As soon as they come to visit you, the first thing someone's going to do is arrest them.'

'But not even a letter?' Freddy rolled his right sleeve higher up his wrist. 'They could have done that anonymously. I kept them safe while I've been in here. Protected then. When I was interrogated, they offered me a leaner sentence in exchange for information on them. But I didn't give it to them. I gave my life for those kids. I kept quiet. And now look at the thanks I get.'

'Don't worry,' Jake said. 'We'll catch them.'

'I'm not worried about you catching them. I'm more worried about them doing something stupid. They've not followed the usual pattern. Before, we liked to keep things simple. Rush in, scare the shit out of people with the guns, and then get back out again. But this time's different. This is the first time Danny's been in charge of a raid, and it follows none of the patterns from our previous ones. He's gone rogue. I mean, they've fired shots. They've spent cases, something we never did when I was in charge – you can vouch for that.'

Jake nodded.

'Danny's gone more sadistic. And I doubt they're following the protocol for after the heist, either.'

'What was the protocol?' Jake asked.

Freddy leant forward in his chair. Two feet separated them now. Face to face.

'Have you got a map?' he asked.

Jake looked at him perplexed. When he arrived at the prison, he'd handed in all his possessions – including his phone and wallet. 'I don't have my AA map with me unfortunately.'

'Well, you're going to need one,' Freddy said.

Exhaling deeply, Jake lifted himself out of his chair, hurried over to the door and spoke with the officers standing guard outside. He ordered them to bring him a map, and within seconds, they returned. As Jake scurried back to the desk, he was already unraveling the pages.

He set the map of England down on the table and placed his hands on the corners to stop it from folding itself over.

'Our first hit was here.' Freddy pointed to Newcastle. 'And then we moved down to Leeds, Leicester, Oxford and now Guildford.' Freddy pointed to each corresponding location as he went through the list. 'For each hit, we had a designated extraction point – somewhere we'd go and hide the fuck away from everything. Once it had all died down, we'd just slip out of the city and stay somewhere else. That's how we got away with it. Nobody knew who they were looking for. And we always had extra help.'

Jake's ears perked up. 'Extra help?'

Freddy slid the map back to Jake and made a pig noise. The sound reverberated around the walls.

Jake said nothing; his face fell flat, bemused.

'Come on, Jake,' Freddy began, 'you didn't seriously think we could do it all on our own? All those years. Never a single arrest.'

'I...'

'We had help from the inside every single time. But you were the anomaly we weren't counting on. There was a cockup with our contact. He got delayed and then you decided to be a hero and got in the way.'

'What about now? Have they got someone helping them?'

A smile grew on Freddy's face.

'You see, now this is the part where you need to make good on your guarantee that I'll be able to meet Sammy while I'm in here.'

Jake bit his lip. 'You know I can't force them to do anything.'

'You'd better find a way.'

'I will. I'll speak with her in person.'

Freddy paused a beat. He raised his eyebrows, winked and said, 'Make sure you tell her I'm helping you out. Make me seem like a good guy for once. That I want to atone for my mistakes. Some bullshit like that.'

'I think you're well past that point, Freddy.'

Freddy snorted and wiped his nose with the back of his hand. 'Anyway, in answer to your question: I don't know. This hit was organised *after* I got sent down. I wish I could tell you more.'

Jake lowered his gaze to the table, looked at the map and ran his finger down the country. As his finger fell over Oxford, an idea popped into his head. He glanced up at Freddy.

'All of your heists… each one got further and further south?' he said.

'Exactly. Why do you think that is?'

Jake shrugged. 'Because there's more money down here?'

Freddy brandished his middle finger and aimed it at Jake. 'Think bigger. Think differently. You're an intelligent guy – I'm sure you can work it out.'

Jake looked at the map again. His eyes ran along the south coast of England from right to left. Brighton. Portsmouth. Southampton. Bournemouth. His eyes went back to Portsmouth. Dozens of thin blue lines ejected from the city in a spider's web.

'Port,' Jake said slowly. 'Portsmouth Harbour?'

Freddy nodded. 'Distinction. Top of the class. Well done. When we started, we made a pact. We decided that we would head down the country, taking more and more money with us, taking bigger and bigger risks, and then we'd get the fuck out of here like a whore in the night. Your boys, if there's nothing else they've made good on, won't be staying still. They'll be on the move. They'll be heading towards a ferry that'll ship them out of the country. And then you'll never see them again. How much did they take in Guildford?'

'I don't know. Couple hundred thousand? Half a mil? Maybe more. It was a jewellery store.'

Nodding, Freddy said, 'Add that to what we took in our previous hits and they're going to be smuggling over two million out of the country. Easy.'

'How? How are they going to smuggle that much?'

Freddy smirked. 'You're so naïve, Jake. You've got a lot to learn. I can tell the past couple of years have taught you nothing.'

'Just tell me how, Freddy.'

'A few ways: the friends in high places, the friends in low places and the friends in middle places. They'll have contacts who can facilitate the expatriation of all that money. They'll be looking to export a lot of bags out of this country.'

'Where are they going?' Jake asked.

'I don't know.'

'Bullshit.'

'It's true.'

'Come on, Freddy. You expect me to believe that you never discussed where you would end up after this was all done?'

Freddy held a hand in the air. 'We discussed it, yes. But we never settled on anything – or anywhere – concrete. They could be going to Australia for all I know.'

'Would they have booked the tickets under their own name?'

Freddy shook his head. 'Unlikely. We all had fake passports – purchased them from a guy called Mick "The Mandate" – just in case you guys did manage to identify us.'

'What were your aliases?'

'They've changed by now. You've got to give them some credit. We had a rule that, if one of us was caught or anything happened to us, we would change everything like that, in an instant, just in case someone grassed to the police.'

Jake hung his head low.

'I know it's not the breakthrough you were looking for, but it's all I can give you.' Freddy twisted his neck left and right, clicking the joints. 'But there is one silver lining…'

Freddy let the comment hang in the air.

'Go on…'

Freddy cleared his throat before continuing. 'If there is one name they would have changed it to – at least one of the brothers – it would be their mother's maiden name.'

'Which is…?'

'Harrington.'

CHAPTER 32

MUG

The engine revved beneath Bridger's feet. The muscles in his body clenched – especially his hands wrapped around the steering wheel – as he tore through the seventeen miles of tarmac that separated them from their next destination: Dunsfold Aerodrome.

It had taken him some time to work out the fourth clue, but with a little help from the Internet and Smithers, he'd got it.

As they pulled into the airspace, Bridger was taken aback. He leant forward and gawped at the enormous hangar in front of him.

'This place is huge,' he said, switching off the engine.

Dunsfold was not on par with Heathrow or Gatwick certainly. But if their search was for a key the size of a thumbnail, they would be there for hours – if not days. The runway was in the shape of a triangle, and a series of air hangers ran along the west side of the track. On the opposite side, decommissioned aeroplanes were left to rot and rust, weeds and patches of grass sprouting from the ground offering a welcome change in colour to the monotonous grey that surrounded them.

'Any ideas where it could be?' Smithers asked him.

'Let me see the note again,' Bridger said, holding his hand out.

Smithers removed the note from his pocket and passed it to Bridger; the sergeant reread it.

'No clue. And there's no one around to help us.'

'Maybe we could—'

Bridger cut the man off with a wave of his hand. He had an idea. He pulled his phone from his back pocket and dialled Pemberton's number. It went straight through to voicemail.

'Maybe we could ask to check the CCTV? One of the brothers would have had to enter this place to leave the key here. They must have been picked up on something...' the officer continued.

'Assuming they have CCTV.' Bridger dismissed the man's idea. What was it with junior officers making suggestions? This constable was the second to try it today, and it was beginning to seriously grate on him. He was the one who had put in the years of hard work and dedication to get to where he was now. He was the one who had licked as much arse as he could to get to the point where he could make important decisions. He didn't need some red-nosed, baby-faced arsehole telling him how to do his job.

He tried Pemberton again. This time she answered.

'What is it now?' she snapped.

'Boss, I—'

'What do you want, Elliot? We've just had direct contact from The Crimsons.'

'Oh shit.'

'Oh shit, indeed. Now, what do you want?'

'What did they say?' Bridger asked. He sensed the urgency and dread in her voice.

'Where are you?'

Bridger looked around him and admired the brilliant feats of machinery in the background of the airfield. 'Dunsfold,' he said. 'This place is too big for us to find anything in time.'

'You won't find anything,' Pemberton added. Her voice went hoarse as she said it. 'I have reason to believe the final key isn't where the instructions say they are. I believe Danny Cipriano has it.'

'What makes you believe that?' Bridger asked, stepping away from Smithers so that any residual noise of their conversation was out of earshot.

'The fact that he told me over the phone... I think he wants Candice Strachan to die. Bomb squad found a phone inside the collar device which means it can be detonated remotely. Danny has both the phone and the key. The Crimsons never intended for us to save her.'

'It was all a distraction?'

'Yes.' Pemberton's voice sounded weak.

'Where are they? Did they tell you where they're headed?'

'We set up a trace on the call, but we lost it as soon as the call ended. The number disappeared – he must have switched the phone off. I'm told the last ping from the cell tower was somewhere near Portsmouth.'

'Portsmouth? Why?'

'Maybe they're trying to smuggle themselves out of the country.'

Bridger hesitated before responding. 'Have you heard from Tanner?'

'No. Not since he went to Winchester,' Pemberton finally replied.

Bridger took a step away from Smithers and lowered his voice. 'Do you think we need to be careful around him?'

'What do you mean?' It was clear to him that she wasn't in the mood to defend or fight anymore.

'How do we know he's not in with them?' Bridger began. 'I mean, think about it. The first time he comes across them is on their last robbery in Oxford, and he sets one of them up to take the fall. I read the paperwork on the case after it happened, and he never explained what really happened inside that bank. How do we know they didn't plan something? Freddy took the rap so Jake could get out free and become the new leader of the gang. It worked out perfectly. Now Tanner's getting cosy with the police, while working on the side with The Crimsons for today's hit.'

'You have an overactive imagination, Elliot.'

Bridger paused a beat to catch his breath. 'Think about it, Nic – he rocks up today on his first day with us. And, on the same day, The Crimsons strike. Seems like too much of a coincidence to me. And Danika as well – both of them, here together. I'm certain she's got something to do with it too – feeding him information that comes into the office. And why do you think he wanted to speak with Freddy alone? They're working together, and they've taken us both for mugs.'

A long silence followed. Bridger didn't know whether he'd lost signal, or whether Pemberton was in a deep state of reflection. Eventually, a light groan told him it was the latter.

'What do we do?' she asked.

'I say we need to keep an eye on him. Keep him close. He knows something he's not telling us.'

'I... I just can't see it happening.'

'It's the people you least expect to hurt us that do.'

'And if you're wrong?' she asked.

Bridger shifted the phone from one ear to the other and scratched the side of his head where the phone had just been. He glanced up at Smithers.

'We'd better hope I am.'

CHAPTER 33

HARRINGTON

Danika had been sitting at her desk for hours and her lower back was beginning to flare up. It was an annoying sensation, deeply rooted in her spine – as if someone was constantly prodding and poking it – and no matter what angle she positioned herself in, the tiniest movement set it off and sent a shockwave of agony up and down her body. She winced, clenched her fist and allowed her palm to absorb the brunt of the pain. On a few occasions, she had drawn blood, but it was nothing a quick wipe on her trouser leg wouldn't sort out.

Less than ten minutes had passed since the surprise call from one of The Crimson brothers. Since then, the office had been sent into a hive of activity. A trace had been placed on the number and emergency responders were being sent to the location rapidly from the local Hampshire police force.

Information was being dug out on Danny's, Michael's and Luke's lives. But Danika had paid little attention to the goings-on in the office. She had doubled down on her own investigation, focusing her efforts on the life and times of Candice Strachan.

As she reached across the desk for a highlighter, an email popped into her inbox. It was one of the information requests she'd submitted. She opened the email and read through the report, her eyes widening as her mind absorbed the text.

She had something! Finally. Something of use to the investigation. But where was Mark? She craned her head over the desk, searching for him, but he was nowhere to be seen. In fact, she hadn't seen him since the phone call had ended.

Before she could do anything, her phone vibrated. She answered it without checking the caller ID.

'Can you talk?' the voice asked. It was Jake. His voice sounded hoarse and dry, as if he'd been talking for hours without a break.

'This is a bad—'

'The Crimsons are heading south,' he interrupted. 'I've just got out of a discussion with Freddy Miller, and he confirmed they were trying to get out of the country.

'We've just had a call from one of the brothers. Danny—'

'Cipriano,' Jake said, finishing her sentence for her. 'What did he want? What did he say?'

'He spoke with DCI Pemberton. He told her that there are several ways to detonate the collar, and that he's got the final key. After the call we traced the number to the outskirts of Portsmouth. But that's not everything,' Danika said. She was getting excited now. All thought of Mark had flown out of her mind. She was getting a kick out of sharing her findings – her ego needed massaging just as much as anyone's. 'I've got some of the information you requested on Candice Strachan. Turns out her recent movements have been incredibly suspicious. In fact, everything about her has...'

'I'm listening,' Jake said in her ear.

'SOCO found a tonne of bank statements and financial records of hers in her house – both personal and business. According to them, she loved shopping. A lot. But I'm not just talking about any old shopping sprees, I'm talking thousands of pounds' worth of transactions, luscious trips abroad, expensive restaurants—'

'None of this sounds incredibly surprising, Danika.'

'Wait. Let me get to the point and stop interrupting. All of that *normal* behaviour was used to mask something else.' She ran her finger down the page. 'On the twentieth and twenty-fifth of last month, she made a trip to the local bank and B&Q store.'

'Right?'

'This woman has never been to a B&Q in her life as far back as her bank records go. And, to make it worse, her debit card registered the payments in Oxford.'

'Do you know what she purchased?'

'I've spoken with the company, and they confirmed that, in accordance with their records, she purchased a set of four separate locks.'

'You're shitting me.'

'I wish I was. But that's not everything.'

'What?'

'I've looked into her records a little further, and I've

noticed that, in the past year, Candice has been renting a storage unit in Southampton. It's all in her name.'

There was a long pause.

'Oh my God. Freddy Miller just told me that the brothers are going to be smuggling their money out of the country. They're using Candice's storage units to do it,' Jake said.

'You're not suggesting what I think you're suggesting, are you?'

'Did you ever follow up with that CCTV request from the golf club?'

The change in conversation stunted her. 'Yes... I, er, I passed it to DI Murphy. He told me to run everything by him.'

'And you've not heard anything back?'

'No. I...'

'Danika,' Jake began, 'who else knows about the storage units?'

At that moment, her thoughts turned to Mark, and then she remembered that he'd instructed her to run all information by him first before sharing it with Jake.

'You're the only one who knows about this.'

'Keep it that way. When I spoke with Freddy, he told me that they always used to have inside help. I think you need to be very careful about who you can trust.'

Danika lowered herself into her seat, wincing as the bolts of pain shot across her lower back. She surveyed the room, observing those around her, scrutinising their every move.

Jake sighed and then the sound of a car engine sounded in her ear.

'I need you to find something else out for me, too,' he said. 'I need to know Candice Strachan's maiden name.'

Danika leafed frantically through her notes. She knew she'd scribbled it down somewhere – it was just a case of finding it. Even though he didn't say anything to her, she sensed his patience dwindling.

'Yes!' she screamed, brandishing the small Post-It note she'd scribbled on. 'I found it earlier.'

'What is it?'

'Harrington.'

CHAPTER 34

HARD SHOULDER TO CRY ON

Danny fidgeted in his seat and scratched the back of his neck. The traffic hadn't moved since he'd hung up the phone with the woman named Pemberton and every fibre in his being was on high alert. What if the police had blocked off the A3 and were charging towards them now? What if those helicopters he heard in the distance were looking for them? It would have been his fault. Every part of their plan so far had been meticulous. They had left no trace, and they had left nothing behind that would lead the police to Portsmouth. So what was taking so fucking long?

Danny slapped the back of Luke's chair in anger.

'We better not miss this boat,' he said.

'What time's it leave?' Luke asked.

'Two p.m.,' Michael answered. He spun a zippo lighter between his fingers. Danny sensed his brother was dying for a smoke. In fact, they all were. But none of them had any with them.

'We're going to have to move. Otherwise we'll be late. Luke – pull out and go into the hard shoulder.'

Luke, taking his orders as he should, rotated the steering wheel and started turning the car to the left. He was quickly stopped by Micky's hand on the wheel.

'As soon as you do that, the traffic will start moving. It's sod's law.'

'I don't give a shit,' Danny said, throwing his hands in the air. 'Sod sod's law. None of this traffic is moving anyway. If we go into the hard shoulder, we'll be the only ones actually doing something.'

Michael shook his head. 'I think it's the wrong decision – it's not that much further to Portsmouth. There's still time.'

Leaning forward in his seat, ignoring the biting seat belt in his shoulder, Danny said, 'Well, why don't we ask Luke – after all, you're a grown man now, Luke. You've proved that much today. You get to make the choice on your own.'

Luke licked his lips as he contemplated for a moment. His answer was obvious: he slipped the car into first and swerved through a thin gap between the car beside them and the hard shoulder. They bumped into the car as they manoeuvred their way through. A cacophony of horns travelled up and down the traffic. The three brothers cheered as they drove past everyone who had been forced to sit there. Danny contemplated sticking his middle finger out at the rest of the world but decided against it. The world of technology was growing at an alarming rate, and the last thing he wanted was his face to appear on social media because some little shit with a smartphone had decided to snap him.

Their excitement, however, lasted a matter of seconds.

Luke was the first to notice the flashing lights of the police vehicle behind them. Then Danny, and then Michael.

'It's fine. Just play it cool. Is this the first police car we've seen?' Danny's pulse raised as he spun in the seat, peering out the back window.

'I think so.'

Luke continued to drive for another hundred yards.

'Pull over, mate,' Danny said. 'See if they go past.'

Danny grabbed for the gun on the other seat and placed it on his lap. He glared out of the rear window. The saloon was right behind them, giving them no space to breathe.

Slowly, Luke eased the car from the tarmac onto the stretch of grass that climbed up a steep bank. He slipped the handbrake on and, under Danny's instructions, kept the car in first gear. There, the three of them waited, but when the police car didn't drive past them, Danny's throat drowned with fear. Through the window, Danny saw the police officer exit the vehicle and saunter towards them.

'Fuck, fuck, fuck,' Danny said, spinning round in the seat. His chest heaved and he closed his eyes, forcing himself to relax. 'Micky – you sure you put those plates on properly?'

'Course I did!' Michael snapped.

Danny composed his breathing through long, rhythmic sighs. 'Luke,' he began again, 'keep calm. Do as I say, OK? Don't do anything stupid. I'll handle this. Just roll down the window and remain calm.'

Luke rolled down the window.

'Good afternoon, sir,' the officer began, stepping into view. The officer instantly froze as soon as he saw Luke,

Danny and Michael in their crimson overalls. 'May I see some identification please?'

'What seems to be the issue?' Danny asked, leaning forward, concealing the gun in his arms.

'You can't drive along the hard shoulder. You know that, right?'

'I do now.'

'Show me your identification.'

Luke unzipped his overalls and reached inside for his wallet; Danny and Michael shared a quick glance. They both knew that, if neither of them did anything, they were fucked. Not only had they stolen the vehicle, but they'd also forced Luke – the learner driver – to take the wheel. And then, to make matters worse, they'd driven along the hard shoulder. It was a catalogue of errors, and Danny needed to be the one to get them out of it.

Luke handed the man his forged learner's licence through the window.

'You're not supposed to be driving this vehicle, Mr Harrington,' the officer said.

'We're teaching him. We're practising. We're his brothers,' Michael said, leaning across the dashboard.

'Without any learner plates?'

'We had them on,' Danny said. 'They must have fallen off.'

'Even so. You're still driving unlawfully...' As the officer inspected Luke's license, his radio bleated.

'*All units be cautious of three IC1 males wearing blood-red overalls in the Portsmouth region. Wanted in connection with armed robbery and murder in the Guildford area. Be aware they are armed and dangerous. Last reports claiming they were driving*

along the A3 in a stolen Audi A5. Confirmed reports of their
names are Danny, Michael and Luke—'

Danny reacted quickly. He moved his arms, raised the gun and aimed it in the man's face. The officer's reactions were lightning quick, and he swerved just as Danny pulled the trigger, so only one of the bullets propelled from the gun caught him. A spurt of blood sprayed from his neck like something from a Quentin Tarantino movie and he fell to the ground clutching his throat, landing with a dull thud.

Danny wasted no time in screaming at Luke to floor it. 'Get us out of here! Go! Go! Go!'

Luke lifted the clutch and stamped on the accelerator. The small Audi tore off, leaving the officer on the ground behind them.

Danny turned back to see the devastation he'd caused. Strangers were jumping out of their cars, tending to the officer. The last thing Danny saw, before they drove out of sight, was the officer alive and breathing, reaching for the radio strapped to his shoulder.

CHAPTER 35

CONFRONTATION

'I don't believe you,' Pemberton said to Jake on the phone, throwing her hand to her mouth. She didn't want to believe it. Couldn't. Like the time her sister-in-law had been diagnosed with Parkinson's disease. It wasn't fair, and neither was this.

Candice Strachan had been taking them for fools. Lying to them. Manipulating them. All of them. Especially her.

'I wish it wasn't true, ma'am,' Jake said loudly in her ear. He was inside his car, awaiting further instruction.

'I need hard facts though, Jake. I can't just go in there and accuse her of being involved with all of this.'

'I've asked Danika to check them over multiple times,' Jake said. 'They're solid.'

Pemberton was standing on the driveway, outside the front door of Candice's mansion. She'd left Candice alone with Armitage and the rest of the explosives experts. She needed breathing space. Meanwhile, the SOCOs continued to remove dozens of bags of evidence they'd found in the house and surrounding area to be sent back to the station.

'This is not the sort of situation I want to be in, Jake.'

'Is there a way we could get her to confess?'

'What are you talking about?'

'If she's in on this, then she'll know the spikes in a collar is a fake. She'll know the charge inside it won't be live. The whole point of chaining that thing to her neck has been to distract us this whole time. All you need to do is try and take it off. Gauge her reaction. Tell her that we can't find the final key. Tell her that Danny called and told us that we'll never be able to find it, so we're going to try it that way. And if, for even a second, she believes that it's true, then she'll panic. She'll know that she's been betrayed.'

Pemberton nodded as she listened to Jake. She shuffled her feet in the gravel and watched her foot disappear underneath the stones. 'How did you know about the call from Danny?'

There was a moment's hesitation. 'Danika just told me. Why?'

She ignored the question. 'Leave it up to me. I'll deal with it my own way.'

'Wh-What do you want me to do now?'

'I don't know, Jake. Speak to Bridger. Help him find the key – if by some miracle it does decide to show up, I want you both together.'

'Where is he?' Jake asked tentatively. The vigour in his voice had gone.

'Dunsfold Aerodrome.'

'And how long until the timer runs out?'

'Just do it,' she snapped. 'Just meet with Bridger and he'll instruct you there.'

Pemberton hung up before Jake had a chance to respond.

CHAPTER 36

REVELATION

Pemberton strode round the side of the house and over to Candice Strachan. The helpless woman now sat on a garden chair that one of the explosives officers had brought across for her. She had her arms folded on her lap, and her expression remained still. Nothing had changed in the few minutes Pemberton had been gone.

'Is everything OK, detective?' Candice asked.

Pemberton paused a beat before responding. How much did she want to let on? Should she trust Jake and follow his suggestions? Or should she deal with it her own way? She had too many voices inside her head clouding her judgement.

'No, Candice,' she said eventually. 'You and I both know it's not OK.'

'What's that supposed to mean, detective?' Candice's

head frantically darted between Pemberton and both the explosives officers beside her. 'You're scaring me. What's happening?'

'Tell me about your acting career, Candice,' Pemberton said plainly.

Candice's eyes widened in horror. 'What— I… er… what do you mean?'

'You know, your acting career. The one you had when you left school. The one when you were in your twenties.'

'I… It didn't last long.' Candice swallowed, and her throat convulsed. 'I had a couple of auditions for plays. Had a few minor parts, nothing major. I had to leave the industry.'

'Why?' Pemberton asked without giving Candice an instant to carry on.

'Because…' Candice swallowed again, this time lowering her head into the metal plate of the collar bomb. She sniffed hard and her chest started to heave. 'Because the director… I was starring in this Hollywood production. It was a small thing. Nothing… nothing major. Nothing like on the big screen. But it was *my* big break. And then… then the director called me to his dressing room one time after we'd just finished shooting for the day. He said I'd done really well. Said I was a real talent. Had a real career in acting ahead of me.'

'Bet that was nice to hear.'

Candice glanced up at Pemberton and scowled.

'It was. But he took it one step too far. He raped me.'

'And what did your husband have to say about it?'

Now the tears came. Candice sobbed, cried, sniffled and when Pemberton gave her no sympathy, she stopped. 'I

199

never told him.'

'Must have been quite a burden.'

Pemberton thought for a second. How Mark Murphy had told her on the phone that all three brothers were genetically linked. How their dad had been a soldier in the army. How Candice had just lied to her face.

Pemberton bent down on her knees, taking care not to split her trousers in two. She placed a finger on the grass for extra balance.

'You know what they say about actors, don't you? They make very good liars. After all, that's what you're doing, isn't it? Lying? Pretending to be someone you're not. And getting paid to do it as well. I think the director was right, you are a good one, and you probably did have a great career in front of you.'

Pemberton let the statement hang in the air in front of Candice's face.

'Please,' Candice implored. She reached out and clawed at Pemberton, who threw the woman's arms away. 'You have to get this thing off me. You have to find the key. You have to save me.'

'There is no key, Candice. We know what's going on.'

The whites of Candice's eyes brightened, and her pupils darkened and dilated.

'Wh-Wha-What do you mean there's no key?'

'Your eldest son, Danny – he told us as much.'

At the mention of Danny's name, Candice's face dropped. It was a picture: the colour that rushed from her cheeks, the muscles in her face that contorted into a frown, and her bottom lip that quivered. Never before had Pemberton seen fear strike someone so coldly; she just wished she had a camera with her so she could relive the moment again and again. She took a mental image instead.

Candice shook her head frantically. 'No. No. No, no, no, no. I don't understand. *You* don't understand.'

'You can stop the act now,' Pemberton said, standing. 'The play's over.'

'No – you don't understand.' Candice scratched her scalp with her fingers and rubbed her eyes with the other. 'You *need* to find the keys. Please.'

'I told you, there are no keys.'

'Find the fucking keys, you bitch!' Candice's voice carried across to the other end of the garden. 'Can't you realise I'm going to die if you don't get this thing off me.'

'What are you talking about?' Pemberton asked. 'There are no spikes in there. There is no charge inside. You know it.'

'There is. There are. For Christ's sake there are. There's really an explosive in there!'

Pemberton retreated slightly, holding her hand out, as if it would defend herself against the force of an explosion.

'Explain yourself,' she said.

'I lied. The-They're my sons. All of them. The Crimsons. Danny. Micky. Lukey. I gave birth to them at a bad time in my life and I hadn't seen them for years. But after my husband died, they made contact, and I was ready to accept them for what they were. And then we staged today. But I had no idea that Danny was going to shoot Rachel. I had no idea. Each of them were all in charge of doing the keys. Luke did the first one, but he hid it in a different place in the house – it wasn't where we'd agreed. Micky was responsible for the golf course and Waverley Abbey ones. Danny should have left his key on one of the runways. He promised he'd leave it in plain sight,' Candice said. Something caught in her throat and tears began to well in her eyes.

'But he hasn't, has he?' Pemberton asked. 'What's he done with it?'

'He's kept it. Or put it somewhere else.'

Candice choked. Her chest heaved rapidly. She grabbed the collar and began to shake the device free from her neck, alerting the explosives officers. They rushed to her side and pinned her arms behind her back.

'What happens now, Candice? Stop resisting!' Pemberton whistled two nearby police constables to rush by their side. They straddled her legs and placed handcuffs around her wrists behind her back. 'What happens now, Candice? We're trying to help you.'

'Get this thing off me!'

'Tell me about the device. What will it do?'

Panting heavily, Candice said, 'I don't know. Danny built it. He told me the keys would defuse it.'

'But how do you know there's a charge in there? Why would he build it to be live? Why would he want it to detonate?'

'I-I-I don't know. We agreed that the keys would disarm it, but when I heard you talking on the phone about remote detonation, that was when I knew that he wanted to kill me. I should have seen it coming when we were in the jewellery store. He held that gun in my face for too long. He had the opportunity to shoot me dead there and then, but he didn't take it.'

'Why would he want to kill you, Candice? Why would he do such a thing?'

'For the years he's been alone. For the years they've all been alone. I thought this was a way for me to rebuild their trust. A way for me to come back into their lives. After my husband died, I had nothing, no one. But when they made contact with me, I thought we were going to be a family again. We were all going to leave the country and never look back.'

'Leave the country?' Pemberton repeated, her voice turning shrill.

'That's what we agreed. To get on a boat out of here.'

I don't believe it. 'Where?'

Candice shook her head. 'Please. You have to get this thing off me. I'll help you find them. I promise I will. Whatever it takes. I don't want to die. I'll help you – but I need you to promise me something first.'

'What?' Pemberton asked. Her mind wasn't with it. She was in disbelief. Jake Tanner had been right about everything.

'I want you to promise that nothing will happen to them if they're caught. I'll take the rap for everything. It was all my fault.'

'And if we refuse that?'

'Then you won't find them.'

'And you won't be alive to see their trial.'

| PART 4 |

CHAPTER 37

INERTIA

'Drive! Drive! Drive!'

Danny slammed his fist on the back of Luke's chair, but it made little difference. Traffic enveloped the three of them. In the time since he'd shot the police officer a few hundred yards back, those stuck in the traffic jam had pulled into the hard shoulder in front of them, blocking their exit. Now they were trapped, and there was nowhere else for them to go.

'Fucking drive!' Danny screamed, small bits of spittle and phlegm expelling from his mouth and landing on his arm.

'What do you think I'm doing?' Luke hissed back.

'Ram into them if you have to.' Danny turned to his middle brother. 'Micky – how many bullets you got left?'

Michael glanced back at him, fear filling his eyes. 'Why? What are you going to do with them?'

'Just tell me how many bullets you've got left. We don't

have time for this.'

Michael inched further away from Danny. 'I've not used any. You're the only one who's used them.'

Danny extended his hand. 'Give it to me.' He spoke as calmly as he could, but his brother's hesitation made him want to scream and beat him into submission.

'Micky,' he began, 'don't make this any more difficult than it already is. Just give me the gun,' he enunciated, hoping that his composure would appease Michael. But when his brother didn't move, Danny screamed, 'Give me the fucking gun!'

'There are kids in these cars, Dan. Don't shoot—'

Danny lunged across the seat, slapped Micky on the back of the head and snatched the Mini-Uzi from him. He gripped the light machine in his hand, unwound the window and hung out of it. Donning the mask, he swung the weapon around in a wide circle. Petrified faces stared back at him, and those hidden behind the confines of their cars tucked beneath their windows. Danny knew their efforts were futile; the bullets would undoubtedly penetrate the glass and side of the doors. There was nothing that could save them.

He steadied the gun and depressed the trigger. Bullet fire rained down on the already battered and beaten 4x4 family van whose driver had decided foolishly to be a hero by pulling out in front of them. The small lumps of lead ripped into the boot, tearing the number plate in two, and smashing the rear window; sprinkles of glass descended to the floor. One of the bullets tore into the right rear tyre and sunk the car. Danny screamed in euphoria as he felt the weapon bounce mini shockwaves up and down his arm. The sound of his voice and his rapid heartbeat drowned out the ringing in his ears.

'Ram into them,' Danny ordered, leaning back into the car.

Luke did as he was told and slammed the Audi into the back of the family van. The brothers lunged forward with the collision, while the engine beneath screamed and the tyres squealed. A few seconds of inertia passed, until eventually the torque from the Audi was strong enough to nudge the 4x4 along. Luke lowered his foot to the floor and Danny watched the rev counter climb into the red.

The Audi started to move faster now. Danny reached forward, grabbed hold of the steering wheel and swerved the car to the left, banking onto a small incline. There was a gap, large enough for them to fit through, and he wanted to take the opportunity. It was now or never.

Luke clipped the wing mirror as he sped past the 4x4. Danny chanced a look inside the vehicle. The family were cowered over the chairs – the parents leaning across the seats to protect their children. It was pathetic really. That they thought you could get in the way of The Crimsons. Why did people think it was OK to interfere?

Danny couldn't comprehend their need to be heroes.

'Well done, Luke,' he said, congratulating his brother with a pat on the back as the 4x4 became a small dot in the rear window. 'Now get us the fuck out of here and down to the port.'

CHAPTER 38

AHEAD OF TIME

'Where are you?' Jake asked into the phone.

'Dunsfold,' Bridger replied. He was abrupt and dismissive.

'Have you received any update on The Crimsons' location? Pemberton said something about them heading down to Portsmouth,' Jake said eagerly. He was feeling a resurgence of passion and desire to catch The Crimson brothers before the end of the day surge through his body. He just hoped he'd get the outcome he wanted.

'Why don't you ask your little friend?' Bridger asked. He said it with so much malevolence and anger that Jake felt as though Bridger was sitting beside him.

'Excuse me?'

'Ask your buddy – Freddy. Or do you like to call him Fred?'

'You're being childish.'

'I bet he told you all sorts of things, didn't he? I know what you two are up to.'

Jake rolled his eyes. *Don't rise to it*, he told himself. *Don't rise to it.* But it wasn't that simple. Bridger had been pushing him and pushing him and pushing him closer to the edge all day, until eventually, at some point, he was going to... snap. He was going to have to stand up for himself. And Jake was more than happy to deal with the consequences afterwards if it meant he could save his integrity now.

'A woman is going to die if we don't do anything to save her,' he began. 'And three of the country's most notorious criminals are going to escape if you don't stop this behaviour. It's completely unprofessional. I've every right to make a complaint to the Professional Standards after all of this is done. And I'm not even going to entertain your insinuation that I'm somehow working with Freddy and The Crimsons. It's completely unjustified.'

Jake breathed heavily. He'd stopped caring. Bridger's opinion of him mattered none; there were more important people to impress.

'All right, all right. Calm down, princess. Can't you take a little bit of banter?'

'There's a difference between banter and bullying, sarge.'

'Well, if you give me a reason to trust you then I will. But until I see it, I'm keeping a close eye on you.'

'Do whatever you have to do,' Jake snapped.

He clenched the mobile in his hand with anger. He was close to snapping the device in half. Instead, he hung up the phone in anger. He slammed his palm on the steering wheel and threw the phone into the seat beside him; it ricocheted and bounced off the door frame and landed in the passenger-side footwell. He swore aloud and reached over to inspect its damage.

'Bitch!'

A thick crack splintered from the top right of the screen to the middle. His most expensive possession – by a long margin – was destroyed, and it was his fault. It was then that Jake felt a panic attack strike him. It was a dizzying sensation he hadn't felt for some time, born from a horrifying avalanche Jake found himself in when he was twenty, on a snowboarding trip that had been organised by his university. The wall of white had encompassed and suffocated him then, and it was beginning to encompass and suffocate him now. His body tensed, a thin layer of sweat formed on his skin and he became incredibly hot. His vision turned to white and his head felt light. He closed his eyes and pressed his palms into his eyeballs, attempting to calm the rising pain in his head.

His phone vibrated in his hand, immediately clearing the white veil and bringing him back to reality.

Dazed, he answered without checking the caller ID.

'Hello?' he asked.

'It's Bridger. We—'

Jake groaned as the headache fluctuated and bounced around his skull.

'You OK?' Bridger asked.

Jake blinked away the pain, but it was useless. It only resided as far as the back of his brain – just out of reach, like the memory of a long-forgotten friend.

'I'm fine. What do you want?'

'We've got a location. We've just had reports come in that

211

they opened fire on uniform on the A3, and then they turned the fire on the rest of the traffic.'

Jake remembered what Freddy had told him; that this was unchartered territory for The Crimsons. That they had never done anything like this. Which meant they were dangerous and even more volatile than Jake originally thought.

'Any other casualties?' he asked, starting the engine.

'None. *Yet*. The uniform was shot in the neck. I don't know if he's going to make it. He's on the way to hospital now. But there haven't been any confirmed civilian casualties. The ambulance service is already on the scene.'

'Where were they spotted?'

'Outside Portsmouth.'

It's really happening.

'What does that mean for the motorway?' Jake asked.

'It's fucked, in a word. It's backed up about ten miles apparently, and it's going to be stuck there even longer. Nobody's going anywhere. Head towards Portsmouth, but you're going to have to try the back roads or the long way round. It's under Hampshire Police's command now, so we have to follow their rules and procedures. They've got helicopters in the air hunting them down – apparently, they stole a vehicle from a petrol garage along the A3. They've got them on CCTV and the number plate running through ANPR.'

'What's your ETA?' Jake asked, entering the address into his onboard Tom-Tom.

A pause.

'Thirty-five minutes. Yours?'

Jake waited as the satnav calculated the results. The

screen informed him it would take forty minutes for him to travel via the motorway to Portsmouth.

'I can be there in twenty.'

CHAPTER 39

DIFFICULT DECISIONS

Never before in her illustrious career had DCI Pemberton been forced to make as tough a decision as the one in front of her now. Candice Strachan had just confessed to being a member of The Crimsons, to having a role in their robbery and kidnapping, to helping them smuggle themselves out of the country, to aiding and abetting their crimes. And Pemberton hated her for it, for lying to her and the rest of the police for so long. But now Candice *was* the victim. She *was* going to die. The collar would detonate if the final key wasn't found. There wasn't enough time on the countdown for Jake or Bridger to retrieve the key from Danny and return to Farnham. There wasn't enough time to find Danny and the rest of his brothers, arrest them and then bring them back to the collar bomb. Whichever way she looked at it, it wasn't possible. And then what would happen? Candice's blood would be on her hands. It would be her decision to leave her stranded there in Surrey.

'PC Mooney,' she called to one of the uniformed officers who'd been standing on the outskirts of the garden; he came rushing over.

'Yes, ma'am.' His face beamed and his cheeks shimmered with a thin layer of sweat.

'I need a vehicle. A police escort vehicle. Something big. Something that's going to be able to transport Ms Strachan over there.' Pemberton nodded in Candice's direction.

'Are... are you sure, ma'am? Would we not be able to use the OED's van?'

Pemberton shook her head. 'It's not the right kind of vehicle. That's just a Transit. We need something that we can isolate Candice in. The same thing we use to transfer criminals from prison to prison. You know what I mean?'

Words weren't making sense to her. It was like the events of the past few hours had destroyed the synapses in her brain that controlled all thought processes and communication. All her training and police jargon had flown out of her head.

'I think so...' PC Mooney said, nodding, uncertain of himself. 'Leave it with me. I'll sort it out. When do you need it?'

'Ten minutes ago.'

PC Mooney started off, speaking into the radio pack on his shoulder. He was authoritative and calm and, to Pemberton's surprise, able to concisely tell the person on the other end what they needed. A prison transport vehicle. *Of course it was, idiot.*

Pemberton wandered back to Candice, who was still

215

sobbing and pleading on her knees.

'Pl-Ple—' she began but was cut off by Pemberton's hand.

'Stop. Just stop. We're doing everything we can for you. God knows you don't deserve it,' Pemberton added. She had lost all prudence in her voice; it was now filled with disdain. She no longer cared for the spite and malign in her words. 'I've had an idea that's going to get you out of that thing.'

Candice looked up at her; her eyes were beady and bloodshot. 'What is it?'

'We've received reports that your sons have stolen a vehicle, shot a police officer, opened fire on a family and—'

'Oh my God,' Candice whispered, her voice trembling as it turned into a whimper. She tried to move her hands, but they were still wrapped behind her back.

'We figured,' Pemberton continued, 'that because you're a part of this, you know where they're going. You know what their next moves are.'

Candice shook her head frantically. 'No. Honestly, I don't. You think they were going to tell me anything after they've done this to me? I was never going to get on that ferry with —' Candice's face bulged.

Pemberton smiled. She made no mistake in showcasing her smugness.

'Which ferry are they getting on, Candice?'

Candice muttered the word 'shit' under her breath, then shook her head.

'I can't remember.'

Liar.

'Do you remember when I told you that I had an idea?'

Candice nodded.

'Your survival hinges on your next choice. Do you

216

understand?'

Candice nodded again, but this time she pulled her gaze away from Pemberton.

'We have a special vehicle we can transport you in. Now, we would usually move you to the station, but these are extenuating circumstances. And I'm the person in charge of making the decisions for said extenuating circumstances. How lucky you are.' Pemberton was enjoying this; she felt like she was getting payback on the woman who had betrayed her. 'This vehicle… it's safe, robust and will keep you isolated. It's got a lot of petrol inside it, and it's fast. Do you know what that means, Candice?'

Candice didn't reply. Pemberton eyed her for a moment before continuing. A part of her wanted to leave Candice there, stranded, helpless. To use it as a form of punishment. It was what she deserved. It was her own fault for becoming an accomplice in such a heinous crime in the first place, regardless of her motives.

'It means that we can transport you to wherever your sons are. You might want to protect them but remember who put you in this situation. They did. So it's in your best interest to tell us where they might be, because if we can find them, we can find the key, and if we can find the key, we can get you out of this – and then you'll be able to live longer than the countdown timer indicates. How does that sound?'

Candice opened her mouth and voiced something, but it was weak, inaudible.

'Excuse me?'

'Yes.'

'Yes what?'

'Do it!' Candice screamed, thrashing her body left and

217

right. 'They were talking about boarding a ferry in Portsmouth sometime in the afternoon. They needed to give themselves time to get there.'

'And were you supposed to be joining them?' Pemberton toyed between placing her hands on her hips or folding her arms. In the end, she went with the former.

'Yes. I'm s-s… I'm sorry.'

'It's a little late for that now.'

PC Mooney arrived behind her.

'Ma'am,' he said, hovering a few feet away. 'I've just spoken to HQ. The vehicle you requested is on its way. ETA five minutes.'

CHAPTER 40

ONCE AND FOR ALL

Jake's experience driving at high speeds was limited; he had only been in the force two years and had seldom encountered such driving circumstances in the middle of gridlocked London. But, according to his satnav, he was fifteen miles away. He was on the M27 heading south towards Southampton with mile upon mile of open road. He blitzed the first twenty miles in just over ten minutes, only having to brake heavily on a couple of occasions, chiding the cars that decided to pull out in front of him. Their driving was irresponsible and reckless.

As Jake passed over the River Hamble, his mobile rang. He answered on the handsfree.

'This is DC Tanner,' he said, peering into his wing mirror, glancing to see if there were any cars behind him.

'Jake?' It was Elizabeth.

'Liz? What's wrong? Is everything OK?' At once his paranoia erupted; they had a rule whereby she would only call him during a shift if it was an emergency.

'Can you talk?' she asked slowly. He sensed, from the reticence in her voice, that she was hiding something.

'Of course I can. I'm driving, just in case the signal drops out. What's happened?'

'It's Maisie. She's still throwing up. She's got worse.'

'OK…' Jake said, concentrating equally on the road as much as the conversation with his wife. He didn't want to have to choose a priority. 'Have you spoken to your mum? What's she said?'

'She… She's not here. She couldn't come. She had something with work,' Elizabeth explained.

'I thought she was on leave. What did she need to do?'

'I don't know, all right? I didn't want to ask too many questions.'

Jake paused a beat and sighed. 'Probably still dealing with the Detson Tower fire backlash.'

'Leave it, Jake. Our daughter is more important than your issues with my mum,' Elizabeth said as Jake slowed behind the car in front of him. He sounded the sirens and immediately the car veered across the lane.

'What other symptoms has she got?' Jake asked, returning to his previous speed.

'Fever. She's gone a bit pale. And she's been vomiting.'

'Any diarrhoea?'

'Lots.'

'What has she had for food?'

'We just had some baby food a couple of hours ago.'

Jake's mind raced. He tried to recall everything he'd

220

learned at the antenatal meetings about childbirth and having a first child and what to expect. He tried to remember everything he'd learned from the books on becoming a father for the first time. He drew blanks on both. Their baby was precious. She was their Little Miracle, as they liked to call her, and he didn't want anything to ever happen to her.

'Can you come home?' Elizabeth asked. Now the fear in her voice came flooding out in droves.

Jake hesitated before responding. 'I can't, Nelly. I'm sorry. Something big's come up.'

Nelly was his nickname for Elizabeth. After she'd told him that her favourite animal was the narwhal, it was the first thing that came to mind. Nelly the Narwhal.

'Where are you?' Elizabeth asked.

'Portsmouth.'

'Are you driving alone?'

'Yes.'

'God. Please be careful, Jake. I don't want something to happen to both of you. Not in the same day.'

'Everything's going to be fine. Keep calm – we don't know anything is seriously wrong with Mais. Have you called my mum?'

There was a pause on the other end that told Jake all he needed to know.

'Give her a ring. She's only ten minutes away. Five if the roads are quiet. She'll be the first to help – and, more importantly, she'll be the first to know what's wrong with her; she raised three kids. Just don't tell her I called her an expert.'

'But I feel bad—'

'Listen,' Jake said as the car topped 85mph, 'before Maisie was born, I told her we're going to need all the help we can get. She's going to be on call 24/7 and she's fine with that. That's what mums are for. Shame the same can't be said about yours.'

'Jake!'

'Sorry, Liz. I'd love to come back and help – it's killing me that I can't. But there are things I've got to take control of first. It's my first day and I'm dealing with some old friends.'

'Old friends?'

Jake paused a moment before continuing. He checked both his mirrors and tightened his grip on the steering wheel. 'The Crimsons. They're back. And this time they've killed someone and taken a hostage.'

'Please be careful... don't put yourself in any unnecessary danger. I want you home in one piece.'

'I'll be safe, I promise. I'm going to end this once and for all.'

CHAPTER 41

ON THE OTHER SIDE

Within minutes, they'd reached the end of the A3 and were on Queen Street, right in the epicentre of Portsmouth. The streets bustled with life – students, families, groups of teenagers, boys, girls, men, women, children, all enjoying the sun and summer temperatures in their t-shirts and shorts and skirts. Directly ahead of them was a tower block that jutted out of the flat skyline like a pimple on a teenager's face. To their right, was HMS *Nelson*, Portsmouth's home to the Royal Navy. Danny glanced out of the window and glimpsed a short view of the base's gate. A sense of elation washed over him. The finishing line was in sight. Everything that had happened up to this point was paying off. Everything that they had done had led them to this moment. It had all been necessary, even if nobody else believed it.

As they sped down the road, nearing the end of Queen

Street and the block of flats that towered against the skyline, Danny pointed to a junction a few hundred yards away. 'Swing a left up here.'

'I thought we needed to go straight,' Luke began.

Before he knew it, they were at the junction, and Luke showed no sign of following his instruction. Danny lunged forward between the seats and yanked on the steering wheel. The car swerved to the left, and the two brothers fought over control.

'I said turn left,' Danny hissed. 'There's been a change of plan.

'What do you mean, change of plan?' asked Michael, twisting in the seat. 'Since when?'

Danny ignored his brother and pointed to another sign ahead, hidden behind a tree. 'There's a car park up there. Follow the signs for it.'

'Danny – what is going on? Where are you taking us?' Michael repeated.

'Shut up and wait,' Danny snapped.

A few seconds later, Luke pulled into the car park. It was old, disused and riddled with potholes. At the back of the car park was the rear fascia of a car wash. Luke found a free space in the centre of the park and slowed the car to a halt. He cut off the engine and waited. The air around them fell silent, save for the pounding pulse in Danny's neck which drowned out the sound of sirens and helicopter blades in the distance.

'You've got some explaining to do,' Michael remarked.

'We're not getting the ferry here,' Danny said plainly.

Both brothers looked back at him, eyes wide. Michael opened his mouth, ready to unleash an expletive, but Danny allayed him with a wave of the hand.

'Let me explain, before you start kicking off. The police aren't thick – they'll have worked out where we're going by now, you get me? Even with our help from the inside. It's not long until this place will be on complete lockdown – they're already above us. So, we needed another way out of the country. And I took the liberty of booking another set of tickets for us.'

'Where?'

'Southampton.'

'*Southampton*?' both brothers repeated.

'All we need to do is get out of this shit heap, change our clothes, hop on a bus and get on the boat. Perfect escape. The police will find this thing, immediately search it and the rest of Portsmouth Harbour for us, and then look on the ferry. By the time they've done all that, we'll be long gone,' Danny explained. He felt the smile on his face growing larger. But he was the only one smiling.

'You lied to us, Dan. When were you going to tell us?' Michael said.

'I just did?'

'Yeah, right at the last fucking minute. What else aren't you telling us?'

Danny's fingers ran over the key in his pocket.

'What about Mum?' Luke asked, his voice weak, almost childlike.

Danny clipped him round the back of the head with his free hand. 'Don't call her that. That woman has never been a mum to us. Just because she turned up now and helped us with this, doesn't mean she gets that privilege.'

Michael twisted in the seat and glared at Danny, his

nostrils flaring. 'Answer the question, Danny. What about Candice?'

Danny broke away from Michael's gaze and stared into his own lap. 'She was the one who came up with the idea. Well, both of us did. She knew about it all along. I told her not to mention it to either of you.'

'Unbelievable.' Michael rolled his eyes. 'So, you trusted her more than you did us? When's the ferry leave?'

'At three. It's a cruise.'

Michael checked his watch. 'Just under two hours. What are we going to do in the meantime?'

'We've got to get there,' Danny said. 'The bus'll take fucking ages.'

'You want us to take a bus?'

'What about Mum?' Luke repeated. Danny suppressed the urge to clip him round the head again. 'Will she make it in time?'

'Of course she will, mate. They'll have found the keys by now and removed the collar. They'll interview her for a bit, make sure she's not involved with anything, maybe give her a once over by the medic or ambulance staff, and then they'll send her on her way. Our man in office will help expedite her experience.'

For a split moment, Danny believed his own lie.

'How do you know? What if they don't find the keys?'

Danny leant forward, placed his hand on Luke's shoulder and squeezed.

'I know you're worried about her, kid. But she'll be with us. Give the police some credit – the keys are piss-easy to find. I mean, Grandma Paula could find them, and she was almost as blind as you are,' Danny said with a smile.

'Remember when she'd try and make us a roast? Absolute fucking carnage, but she still knew where everything was, eh?'

Luke chuckled, bearing his white teeth. 'Yeah, I guess…'

One brother down, one more to go.

Danny turned his attention to him. 'Micky? You coming?'

Michael sighed. 'Not got much choice, have I? I'm having my fair share of this money regardless of where we end up.'

'And you'll get it. Down to the last penny.'

Danny waited until his brothers had started to undress themselves before he began. He unzipped the front of his overalls and rolled the top half over his shoulders. As his hands ran down his arm, he massaged the brown and yellow bruises on his skin. He pulled the overalls down his waist in the small confines of the back of the Audi and stuffed them into the footwell. Beneath his overalls he'd been wearing a pair of jeans and a hoodie. He reached into the pocket of his overalls, removed the final collar bomb key and slid it into his jean pocket. It rubbed against his skin, pinned next to his wallet.

'What are we doing with those?' Michael asked, pointing to the machine guns by Danny's lap.

'Those? Keep them here. Leave everything except for the bags.'

Danny opened the car door and slung the bags containing the jewellery over his shoulder. As he was about to close the door, he gave one last look at the red devil mask. It held many memories. It had been with him from their first heist to now. And it had served him well. He'd enjoyed witnessing the horror on the faces of those he was robbing. He was born into nothing, and he adored the anonymity that

227

it invoked – and now he was going to spend the rest of his life overseas, hidden further beneath that cloak of anonymity.

Luke slamming the driver's door shut brought him back to reality. He felt a hand on his shoulder. Then on his other. Luke and Michael were either side of him.

'Time to leave this world behind us, mate,' Michael said. 'For good.'

'We've got another one waiting on the other side of the Atlantic.'

Danny said his goodbyes and started off towards the nearest bus stop at the Hard Interchange, on the water. Danny and Candice had done their research beforehand. The X4 bus from Portsmouth to Southampton ran every half an hour.

CHAPTER 42

CAR PARK

Jake was situated on the side of the street by Victoria Park, one of Portsmouth's breathing lungs. He had been waiting for over twenty minutes for his colleague to arrive, and with every passing minute, his fear and apprehension that The Crimsons were getting further and further away from them multiplied. They were always one step ahead, just out of reach. To pass the time, Jake leant forward, resting his elbows on the steering wheel, and peered out at the majestic St John's Cathedral ahead of him. The gothic building was a clay red construction made entirely of brick, and the two spires at the head of the cathedral reminded him of a meat fork used for barbecues. Jake wasn't one for religion – he was a believer in natural selection and the Big Bang – but he always managed to appreciate the architectural prowess of religious buildings. The most overwhelming one he had ever been to visit was St Peter's Basilica in the Vatican, closely followed by St Paul's in London. Other than that, he was resigned to looking at them on the Internet and social media whenever they appeared in his news feed.

A few minutes later, a police car pulled in behind him.

Bridger, Jake thought, opening the door while keeping his eyes on the rear-view mirror. Then he slipped out and scurried towards the saloon. At the same time, Bridger alighted his vehicle. As the two of them met in between the cars, a uniformed officer whom Jake didn't recognise stepped out from Bridger's and joined them.

'All right?' Bridger asked, nodding.

'All right,' Jake replied amicably. He was willing to be professional so long as Bridger was.

'Been waiting long?'

'Long enough.'

'Sorry. We had to come a long way. Traffic's a bitch right now as well.' Bridger hesitated. 'You heard from Pemberton?' He leant against the front wheel arch and looked as though he was itching for a cigarette – playing with his thumbs, putting his hand in his mouth.

Jake shook his head.

'She's on her way down now. She's bringing Candice with her.'

'Come again?'

'With the intention of finding the key,' Bridger finished. 'Her and one of the bomb squad guys are coming down here now. They've quarantined her in the back.'

'I don't know how I feel about that,' Jake said, moving closer to his stationary car.

'It doesn't matter how you feel about it,' Bridger said.

'Because you don't get a say. None of us do.'

Jake stormed off to his car and opened his driver's-side door.

'Where are you going?' Bridger asked, rushing to his side.

'Where do you think? We're not going to find The Crimsons by standing around waiting for them to come to us.' Jake sat in the car and, as he tried to pull the door shut, Bridger's arm stopped him.

'We're going together,' Bridger said, pushing the door out of Jake's reach. 'Guv's orders. I don't like it any more than you. Now leave this here and get in the back of my car.'

Jake's frustration multiplied. *I don't need babysitting.* He gritted his teeth.

'Orders are orders,' Bridger added. Jake could see the satisfaction the senior officer was getting from ordering him around, and it was beginning to antagonise him even more.

Jake conceded defeat, removed the keys from the ignition and stepped out of the car. He followed Bridger to his vehicle and sat in the back.

'Where to?' he asked.

Before either the officer in the front or Bridger had a chance to respond, the radio on the dashboard sounded, taking Jake by surprise.

'Echo Bravo four-five, Echo Bravo four-five from Lima Golf, over.'

Bridger reached for the radio and held it against his lips. 'Lima Golf, Lima Golf, this is Echo Bravo four-five, go ahead, over.'

'Echo Bravo, we've got a positive ANPR hit on the registration for the stolen Audi. Last ping was less than

231

twenty minutes ago. The car was last seen situated in the Harbour Car Park, Havant Street, Papa-Oscar-one, three-Echo-Alpha. Are you able to attend with armed support? Over,' said the robotic-sounding individual on the other end of the line.

'Lima Golf, we're on the way. Will report back when we arrive, over.'

'Echo Bravo, received, thank you, over.'

CHAPTER 43

DISEMBARK

The bus pulled in front of them sharply, pistons hissing and brakes shrieking. The momentum caused by the sudden halt propelled the other passengers forward in their seats. Danny, Luke and Michael stood in a line waiting for the X4 from Portsmouth Harbour to Southampton Port via Fareham. They were at the back of the queue, allowing the elderly couples and young families to board first. The less attention they could draw to themselves in this pivotal final stage of their operation, the better. Danny didn't like to think what a life behind bars would look like. Freddy had told him as much in the letters he'd received from his former leader, but he knew they only scratched the surface; Luke also read those letters, and it was their bond that forced Freddy to play down the brutal realities of prison life. And from what Danny had heard, it made him even more determined to succeed and flee the country.

It was Danny's turn to board the bus, and as he stepped up onto the vehicle, he felt as though all eyes were on him. It suddenly made him very conscious of his surroundings, as though everyone inside the bus was an undercover police officer, and they were all just chomping at the bit to apprehend him. Danny dismissed the thought and joined his brothers on the seats towards the back of the bus. As he wandered up the aisle, his bag jostled against the sides of chairs and other passengers' shoulders. Panic struck him as the jingles of the diamonds and other pieces of jewellery inside the bag turned a few heads his way. But then he remembered that no one knew who they were, nobody knew their faces, nobody had seen them before. Danny rushed to the seat and sat beside Luke, with Michael on the other side of the aisle.

As soon as the bus pulled off, Danny's shoulders relaxed. He knew the bus timetable off by heart; as part of their preparations, he'd tested the running time of the journey: ninety minutes. Which left them with just half an hour to get their things together and board the boat. It was cutting it fine, but everything had been calculated to the final moments. They couldn't afford for any mistakes.

As Danny sat there wistfully staring at the yellow metal pole in front of him, his thoughts turned to Candice, and how every part of him was grateful that she wasn't there. For all he cared, she could be several thousand miles away and he wouldn't lose any of sleep over it. Or, even better, she could be six feet under… where she deserved to be.

In the first quarter of an hour, the majority of the passengers on board disembarked before they'd even left

Portsmouth, and as they merged onto the wider lanes heading out of the city, and as the driver began to open up the throttle, Danny felt more at ease. They were inconspicuous, just a group of lads hitching a bus ride. Nothing to look at or pay attention to.

Except something concerned him.

Luke.

His brother's attention was focused on the window and had been ever since they'd set off. His face was ashen and pensive.

Danny nudged him earnestly.

'You good?' he whispered.

Keeping his gaze fixed on the window, Luke replied, 'I'm worried about her.' His voice was so low that it was almost inaudible.

'I told you she'd be fine. With any luck, mate, she'll probably be waiting for us by the time we arrive, you get me?'

Luke said nothing. Danny took the moment to observe his brother and marvel at how much he had grown – physically, mentally and emotionally. At how much he had become an adult within the space of a few years. And at how much he loved him. The man beside him had, in recent months, become exactly that. A man. He had matured and begun to show some independence, something he'd never been able to do when Freddy was in control of them.

'You've done well today, Luke,' Danny said. 'Dad would have been proud.'

'Dad?' Luke said, his voice turning agitated. 'What do you mean, "dad"? Dad wouldn't have been proud even if he knew what we were up to.'

'What makes you say that? Whenever he was back from serving, he always put you first.' Danny kept his voice low, lest any other passengers overhear and take it upon themselves to listen in. 'What else has Candice been telling you about him?'

Luke swallowed before responding. 'She told me he was never there. He left when I was three. Flew off to Afghanistan to be with some Arab woman.'

Danny chuckled in disbelief. It was laughable, the lengths that Candice would go to in order to deceive Luke and win him over. 'You're fucking joking, right? You've got to be kidding me. How can you turn around and say that Michael and I have lied to you all your life?'

'I'm not—'

'That's exactly what you're saying. You're believing the woman who claims to be your mother – the woman you've met fewer times than the number of fingers on your hand. She's known you for two seconds – of course she's going to feed you stories you want to hear. And you lapped it up, didn't you?'

Danny turned to face Michael beside him. 'Are you hearing this?'

'What's that?'

Danny scoffed. 'This idiot believes the things that woman's been telling him about our dad. He listens to her stories over ours. She has no clue what she's talking about. If he was here to defend himself, he'd—'

'But he's not here, is he? Do you know where he is? I don't?' Luke snapped. 'He hasn't been there all my life.'

'He's more than half the man she claims him to be though.'

Around them, heads started to turn in their direction; he was aware they were raising their voices, but now he also realised that they were also raising suspicion.

Luke reached into his pocket, produced his wallet and removed a small photo. On it was a heavily pixelated image of a dark-haired man with a thick, shaggy beard. His eyes were as dark as his hair, and they were cavernous, never-ending.

Danny hardly recognised the man in the photo.

'What's this?' Danny snatched the picture from Luke and inspected it. 'This ain't him.'

'Yes, it is. Mum gave it to me. It was the last photo she ever had of him.'

'This man's a pussy. Look at him with his stud earring. This isn't him. Ours was a hero. A *fucking* hero.' Danny clenched his hand into a fist, scrunched the photo in his grip and dropped it. Then he removed his wallet from his pocket. As he pulled it out, the fourth key tumbled out and landed on the floor by his feet. At that moment, the coach seemed to go silent, and the unmistakable sound of a metal key bouncing on the plastic floor deafened them.

Danny reached his arm out, but Luke beat him to it.

'What is…' Luke began as he inspected the key. 'No…'

'Luke—'

'No!'

'Luke, listen—'

'No!' Luke shook his head viciously, and his voice turned deep, almost demonic. 'No! No! No!'

Luke shoved Danny in the chest. The sudden and brute force winded him.

'No!' Luke screamed.

237

By now, others in the coach had turned round and were glaring at them both.

'What's going on?' Michael asked, leaning across the aisle.

'Nothing,' Danny said. He tried to placate Luke by placing an arm around his body and concealing the key with his other hand, but both efforts were pointless. Luke had no intention of calming down – not after what he had just realised.

'Luke,' Michael said, 'Luke – listen to me! Shut up and listen.' Michael grabbed Luke by the wrist and, almost instantly, the youngest brother froze. 'You're causing a scene, and you better fucking stop it right now. What's the matter with you?'

Luke shook off both Danny and Michael and brandished the key in the air. The sunlight from outside the bus reflected off the key's darkened surface.

Before Danny could say anything, Michael spoke first. 'Is that what I think it is?'

'Yes,' Luke said, nodding. 'This cunt betrayed us. He betrayed Candice. He's left her there to die.'

'Oh my God,' Michael said. 'You told us you'd left it on the airfield—'

Danny snatched the key from Luke and locked it in his grip. 'Boys—'

'You lied to us. You said she was going to join us at the port, but you knew all along that was never going to happen, didn't you?' Michael said.

'Listen—'

'No. *You* listen,' Luke said, shoving his finger in front of Danny's face. He hissed as he spoke. 'Do you know what you've done? You've killed your own mum.'

'She was already dead to me,' Danny replied, pocketing the key in his jeans.

'But she wasn't to me. And she wasn't to Micky. We were going to restart our lives together, make up for all the time we'd lost, and you've taken that away from us. You selfish bastard.' Luke's eyes turned black with hatred.

'What else have you lied about? What else aren't you telling us, Dan?' Michael said, bringing his voice down to a hush.

'Nothing—'

'Bullshit!' Luke blurted out. 'You're a fucking liar and you always have been.'

As soon as Luke finished, the bus skidded to a halt and dipped to the front left. The three brothers stopped and looked ahead. There was no one standing at the front of the vehicle, waiting to disembark.

'Off! The lot of you, off!' the bus driver called back. He stared at them in the rear-view mirror and pointed to the doors as they opened with an eerie hiss.

Nobody said anything, and Danny felt all eyes boring into him.

'I said get off!' the bus driver barked.

'It's fine. Honestly. We won't do anything. We've stopped.'

'This bus isn't going anywhere until at least one of you gets off. Otherwise I'm calling the police.'

Both Michael and Luke glared at him. He knew their intentions, but he wasn't going to concede defeat that easily. He had hundreds of thousands of pounds' worth of jewellery in his bag that he wanted to smuggle out of the country – and more waiting for him at the port. There was no way he was going to miss that opportunity.

As Danny opened his mouth to argue back, Michael hefted his share of the loot from the seat beside him and stood. He stepped into the aisle and stopped beside Danny's knee; Danny clenched his bag between his legs.

'Come on, Luke. Let's get out of here,' Michael said.

'No. Stay here, we—'

Luke leapt up from the seat and barged into Danny's legs, trying to pass through.

'No,' Danny said. 'I won't let you go. Luke – you have to stay here.'

Luke eventually shuffled past and joined Michael's side. 'No, Danny, I don't. I don't have to do anything you tell me. I don't have to listen to you anymore. I've had enough of you. I wish you weren't my brother.'

'What are you going to do now, eh? You can't do anything? You can't go anywhere. I'm the one with the tickets.'

'So long as we're without you, we'll be fine no matter where we are. I'm sorry it's come to this, Dan,' Michael said.

Without saying anything else, Michael and Luke turned and strode off the bus, keeping their backs to him as the driver pulled away.

CHAPTER 44

ASSUMPTIONS

Bridger brought the car to a stop twenty yards from the Harbour Car Park. With them was a convoy of armed support in the back of a van. In the centre of the car park was the stolen Audi. The front bumper was smashed; one of the headlights was missing, the metal bent; and the bonnet had crumpled under impact. The car was written off, and the passenger-side door had been left open.

'They must have left in a hurry,' Bridger said as he climbed out of the vehicle.

Jake and Smithers followed, and then all three stopped by the front of the car as they watched the armed support alight from the van. There, they received instructions to remain where they were while the firearms team approached the abandoned Audi for any signs of life or threat. It was clear to all of them that they were under Hampshire Police's control now.

A minute later, Jake, Bridger and Smithers were given the all-clear.

Before they were allowed to investigate the Audi for themselves, they changed into their forensic suits. Bridger was the first to the car. He rounded the front and stopped by the opened passenger door.

'What can you see?' Jake asked as he edged closer to the vehicle.

Bridger reached in, out of Jake's sight, and removed something. At first, he couldn't see what it was, but then, as Bridger shuffled around the vehicle, the object came into view.

'The mask,' Jake whispered. In Bridger's hand was the insidious mask that had been a source of his own nightmares for weeks following The Crimsons' last heist in Oxford. It invoked fear and horror in him every time he saw it.

'I think we can finally confirm it's The Crimsons,' Bridger said.

'You mean you think *you* can finally confirm it's The Crimsons. The rest of us have known all along.'

Bridger ignored Jake and continued. 'We're close. We can't be too far behind.'

Jake took another step closer to the vehicle and looked through the window. Bullet casings were scattered along the floor, and a few jewels and crystals were buried in the seams of the seats from where they'd fallen out of their bags.

'Do you know if the officer they shot is OK?' Jake asked.

'Sedated,' Smithers said by Jake's side. 'Heavily sedated. They caught him in the side of neck, but someone got pressure on it quickly, helped him until the ambulance showed up – he was lucky.'

As soon as he finished speaking, a flurry of liveried police cars skidded to a halt on the outskirts of the perimeter that had been set up. It was another patrol from Hampshire Police. Joining them, from the back, was an unmarked car. Two officers disembarked and patrolled towards them.

'What's going on here?' one of the uniformed officers asked them. From the way he spoke and the presence he held over the rest of the team, it was clear to Jake that he was the officer in command.

'DS Bridger. Surrey Police,' Bridger replied.

'We have no need for you here, Sergeant. My team and I can handle this. Let them do their jobs. If I need you, I'll catch up with you in a minute.'

Bridger nodded and smiled graciously in defeat. From the short amount of time that Jake had spent with Bridger, he knew that that was going to hurt his senior's ego, even if it was the procedure to follow Hampshire Police's orders from here on.

Deciding that he'd had enough of arguing for an afternoon, Jake stepped to the side and started back to Bridger's car. As he reached the passenger-side, his mobile rang.

'Hello?'

'Jake.' It was Danika. 'I was looking into the tickets for the ferry in Portsmouth. They're all purchased under their Cipriano name. All through the same credit card. They were all registered to the same address in Guildford, near the university – we've organised a team from the office to search the address.'

'Where were they going?'

243

'Spain.'

'Spain?'

'Spain.'

'Bloody hell. When's the ferry leave?'

'It's scheduled to leave at 14:00.'

Jake checked his watch – 13:11 p.m.

'I need another favour,' he said. 'CCTV from the Harbour Car Park and the surrounding area. The brothers are most likely on foot. They'll be much easier to track, so long as they stay like that. Find out which way they're heading, and where they are. Also – are their faces on the news yet?'

'I don't think so,' Danika replied.

'Social media? The internet?'

'I don't think so.'

'Who's the media liaison officer? They should have taken care of that by now. Their faces should be all over the television, internet, social media – they should even be on the sides of buses!'

'I'll speak with DI Murphy. I will see what he can do.'

'Hero,' Jake said before hanging up.

As he lowered the phone, he tried to focus on what was happening in front of him. At the forensics team burying themselves in the seams of the Audi's seats as they searched for evidence. At the flurry of pedestrian activity to Jake's left. At the police officers that were struggling to keep the general public at bay. But there was something niggling at the back of his mind. Like why would The Crimsons leave the car in plain sight and with no obvious effort made to conceal the damages sustained to it? Why would they book tickets under their own name and not the alias like Freddy had advised? Had Freddy been pulling him along or was he telling Jake the truth?

Bridger joined his side.

'You know when something's not quite sitting right with you?' Jake asked him.

'You mean like after you've had a curry?'

Jake smirked. 'Not exactly. But when your intuition starts flagging a few things.'

'It's been known to happen. What are you thinking?'

'That it doesn't add up,' Jake said. 'DC Oblak called and said they had tickets booked to Spain under their original names…'

'What's DC Oblak telling you that for? That information should be coming from someone else.'

Jake shrugged, not meaning to drop Danika in it. 'I guess she's got her orders just the same as us.'

Bridger pursed his lips and changed the weight onto his other foot. 'What were you saying about… about the booking…?'

'When I spoke with Freddy, he told me to look out for their other name. He said it was likely they would have booked tickets under a name nobody knew they had,' Jake explained.

'What's that?' Bridger asked, putting his hands in his pockets.

'Harrington.'

'Candice's maiden name?'

Jake nodded.

'You think they've booked tickets for the same cruise but just under different names?'

Jake shook his head. 'That would just be stupid.' He paused a beat. 'They're either on a later boat today, or an entirely different one altogether... Maybe even at a different port.'

And then it clicked.

'Jesus Christ,' he said, 'they're going to Southampton Port instead.'

CHAPTER 45

X4

'We think it's a decoy, ma'am,' Bridger said as he tore out of the car park, heading up Queen Street and turning onto the A3. He was on the phone with Pemberton through loudspeaker, who was only a few miles away from Portsmouth.

'What do you mean?' she asked.

'Tanner believes they've booked the ferry tickets from Portsmouth as a decoy. He believes they're really going to Southampton.'

'What evidence do we have?' Pemberton asked.

Jake had taken control in the front seat and relegated Smithers to the back. Both Jake and Bridger looked at one another awkwardly.

'It's a working theory at the moment, ma'am,' Bridger explained.

'Speculation isn't going to catch these guys, Elliot. You can't just go gallivanting across the country in the hope that they might be there. What if you were right and Tanner is leading us further away from the Cipriano brothers?'

That was it. Jake was done. He'd had enough of being belittled and undermined. He was trying his hardest to find the brothers, and their lack of faith in his abilities and integrity infuriated him.

Bridger opened his mouth but was cut off by Jake.

'With all due respect, ma'am, from the very beginning you've asked for my advice. I have reasonable grounds to believe that's where they're heading. Hampshire Police have sent several officers to search the Portsmouth ferry we originally believed they were taking, so if they do show up there – and I turn out to be wrong – then they will be caught. I've asked DC Oblak to find any ticket references that have been booked under the name Harrington.'

A long moment of silence played out in the car as they awaited a response.

'Candice never mentioned anything about Southampton…' Pemberton said.

'Either she's still protecting them and not telling you about it, or she doesn't know that it could be a part of their plan.'

'She's got a collar bomb strapped to her neck – she's not going to try and cover for them now, Jake.'

'Then Danny might not have told her the full story. If he's capable of hiding the key from her, then he won't be stupid enough to hop on a ferry at Portsmouth where he knows we'll be waiting for him. Danny hates Candice. This is just his way of getting revenge.'

248

'What makes you so sure?' Pemberton asked.

'Freddy told me. Candice walked out on the three of them when they were young, and he never forgave her for it.'

Eventually, after another long pause, Pemberton sighed heavily. 'You'd better be right, Jake.'

'I hope I am,' Jake replied. 'There's also something else you should know. She has a storage unit there too. She's been paying for it for about a year. I think that's where they've been keeping their takings from the previous robberies, and now they're going to pick it up.'

'How do you know?' Pemberton asked.

'Danika, ma'am. She's been working behind the scenes.'

'Why did no one tell me this?'

'I completely forgot about it until now. But I'd have thought DI Murphy would have mentioned it to you, ma'am. Danika told me that she was reporting to him while you're out of the office.'

'Leave that with me. We'll meet you in Southampton. Keep me updated.'

She hung up and, again, the car was filled with silence. This time Jake enjoyed it. It allowed him to be in his own headspace. Pemberton was finally siding with him again, trusting him enough to follow his advice. He hoped it would stay like that for the rest of the day.

Bridger slowed as he pulled up to a set of red traffic lights when the radio bleated.

'Echo Bravo four-five, Echo Bravo four-five, this is Lima Golf, over,' it said.

'This is Liam Golf, reading you, over.'

'Echo Bravo four-five, we're receiving reports of an

altercation on board a bus in the Fareham area from the driver. Reports indicate three IC1 males matching the descriptions of Luke, Danny and Michael Cipriano. All three individuals were seen carrying large black gym bags at Fareham bus depot. Armed officers are en route. Could you check it out and support?'

'Which bus was it?' Jake asked, feeling the palms of his hands turn sweaty.

'The X4, headed to Southampton from Portsmouth.'

'I don't fucking believe it,' Bridger said, turning to Jake. 'You were right.'

CHAPTER 46

DEPOT 7

After receiving the news from HQ, Bridger raced onto the M27 and blitzed through to Fareham with the armed units driving in his wake. Not before long, three lanes blended into two as they pulled off onto the A27, heading south at the beginning of Portsmouth Harbour. Running alongside them, on the left-hand side, was a railway line, and beyond that was Cams Hall Estate Golf Club on the other side of the water. Fluorescent green bounced into the sky, and Jake struggled to keep his eyes from it. He had already been to one golf course today, and he hoped that, should he visit another, it would be under entirely different circumstances. The game was being eternally ruined for him.

As they drove deeper into town, Bridger pulled off the A road and headed towards Fareham bus depot, a few hundred yards from the shopping centre. They parked up on the other side of the road.

Jake, Bridger and Smithers disembarked the vehicle simultaneously, and met the armed officer in charge of the unit that had been following him.

'Where were they last seen?' PS Cavanagh asked.

Bridger pointed to the bus depot over a hundred yards away. 'About ten minutes ago.'

'OK,' PS Cavanagh said. 'Wait here. My team and I will scout it out. Wait for our orders.'

Bridger nodded in acceptance and the four of them departed in different directions. Jake, Bridger and Smithers headed back to the car while PS Cavanagh and the rest of his team skulked across the pavement towards the depot in formation, bodies poised, weapons raised.

Jake rolled down the window to get a better view.

'You reckon they're still here?' Bridger asked beside him.

'Could be anywhere,' Jake replied, keeping his gazed fixed on the officers as they approached the depot.

The bus depot was long and stretched far back. A row of First buses were waiting in a line. As the firearms team arrived, a coach reversed and drove past them. Jake's heart leapt and his eyes scanned the passengers as the vehicle passed by the car. Nothing. On the right-hand side of the depot was the bus shelter, where the passengers were waiting for their next departure. As the armed officers strode towards them, the passengers jumped out of their way.

But, a few seconds later, the firearms team disappeared out of sight, hidden behind the row of busses. Jake drummed his feet on the footwell and tapped his finger on his leg as he waited impatiently. It was one of the tensest moments of the day, and he was afraid of what would happen next. A myriad of thoughts raced through his mind. Where were they? What were they doing? What had the brothers been arguing about that forced them to step off the bus?

Before Jake was able to focus anymore on it, screams and shouts erupted from within the bus depot. Jake opened the car door and started towards the commotion.

'Jake!' Bridger called him back. 'Jake!

And then he saw them.

In the distance, Michael Cipriano forced one of the armed officers to the ground, kicking his weapon away across the concrete. Behind him, Luke Cipriano – smaller, skinnier – sprinted from beneath the bus, heading towards the depot's exit.

Jake raced towards them, the muscles in his legs pumping the adrenaline through his body. Not before long, the soles of his feet began to ache, and sent bolts of pain up and down his legs with every step. Behind him, he heard the sounds of more footsteps. Jake chanced a glance backwards; Smithers was bounding after him, joining the chase.

Both Michael and Luke were lumbered with their gym bags, swinging uncontrollably as they ran, bashing into their legs, hips and back. It was only a small advantage, but it gave Jake and Smithers one, nonetheless.

Ten yards separated them as Luke reached the end of the depot and made a sharp right, heading onto the main road.

Eight.

Five.

And then Jake felt a kick against his legs, buckling him. The world span upside down and inside out in a carousel of grey as Jake soared through the air and clattered onto the concrete. He landed heavily on his shoulder and yelled out in pain.

Just as Jake was about to pick himself up, Michael Cipriano leapt over him. His trailing leg caught Jake in the ribs and knocked him down again.

'Stop!' Smithers called beside him.

Jake craned his neck and saw the police officer charging after Michael, reaching for his radio and shouting into it. To Jake's left, trailing behind, was Bridger, followed by the armed officers. Their shouts and cries were no use. Michael and Luke had no intention of stopping. They were too far ahead.

But then Jake heard another shout. He snapped his neck towards Smithers and saw the man tackle Michael Cipriano to the ground, their bodies rolling together in one. Jake staggered to his feet and hobbled after them, ignoring the pain in his shoulder and palms. As he arrived, both men were panting heavily. Michael was pinned to his front and Smithers was atop him, wrapping his arms behind his back, pressing into him with his knee.

'Run, Luke! Run!' Michael bellowed with the side of his face pressed against the concrete.

Jake stuttered to a halt beside Michael, and as he helped lift the man to his feet, the armed officers tore past them, their legs and arms pumping hard. They disappeared down a residential road to their right, but it was pointless. Luke was out of sight. He'd evaded them and there was no way they were going to find him on foot.

A second later, Bridger arrived, breathless. He placed his hands on his knees and bent double, gasping.

'Good work, boys,' he said in between breaths.

Jake appreciated the sentiment. It was the nicest thing Bridger had said to him all day, even if he hadn't been the one responsible for capturing Michael in the first place.

'Michael Cipriano,' Jake said, as Smithers tightened the handcuffs around his wrists, 'I am arresting you for murder, armed robbery, assault and kidnap. You do not have to say anything. But it may harm your defence if you do not mention when questioned something which you later rely on in court. Anything you do say may be given in evidence.'

After Jake finished telling him his rights, the armed officers returned, flustered, yet their breathing remained the same as when Jake had first met them.

'Gone,' PS Cavanagh said, 'but he's got to be around here somewhere. He must have vaulted the walls.'

'OK,' Bridger replied after finally catching his breath. He moved over towards Jake and Michael. 'Right now, I want to speak with this one. Let's get him booked in.'

| PART 5 |

CHAPTER 47

CLEAN SLATE

'Rupert Haversham. He's my solicitor. I want my solicitor,' Michael Cipriano said with a wry smile.

'Tough. You're not getting one.' Bridger rested his arms against the edge of the table.

'On what grounds?' Michael protested. 'I know my rights.'

'You want the specifics? All right then. Code C 6.6 and Annex B. The police may proceed with an interview in the absence of a solicitor if an officer has reasonable grounds that failure to do so will lead to interference with, or harm to, evidence connected with an indictable offence, lead to alerting other people suspected of having committed an indictable offence but which they have not yet been arrested for, or if they have reasonable grounds to believe it will hinder the recovery of property obtained in consequence of the commission of such an offence. So I'd say that covers you straight off the bat, doesn't it? We've got all three' – Bridger held his hand in the air and displayed his thumb, forefinger and middle finger in front of Michael's face – 'haven't we? We've got the evidence connecting you to the crime… We've got your brothers being alerted to what's happened to you… and we've got the jewels and money that your brothers have run away with that are still at large.'

The smirk on Michael's face grew even bigger. 'How many nights did you lose memorising that word for word?'

'More than you've spent in a nice warm bed.'

'There's just one thing you've forgotten to mention, Detective *Sergeant* Bridger, which is that the law also states that the officer making such a decision must be of the rank of superintendent or above. I don't see those credentials in your title anywhere. Nor your colleague here.' Michael flicked his head towards Jake.

'How many nights did you spend memorising that particular part of the code?' Bridger retorted.

'One actually.'

'I've got it cleared with the powers that be,' Bridger replied.

Had he? It was the first Jake had heard of it.

'You don't have to worry about me doing my job properly,' Bridger continued. 'So why don't you just tell us everything you know?'

Michael, with an air of defiance, leant back in his chair and folded his arms. The three of them were locked inside the interview room in Fareham Police Station a few hundred yards from the bus station where Michael had been arrested. Bridger had managed to pull a few strings and called in a favour to get them into the interview room as soon as the procedure allowed.

A few seconds of silence passed. Jake's steady breathing pounded in his ears. This was his first interview where he was unprepared. Usually, he was allowed time to prepare and present the evidence and line of questioning against the defendant. But now he didn't have that luxury and didn't want his inexperience to hinder the proceedings in any way. It was down to Bridger now, and after that small exchange between Michael and Bridger, Jake admired him much more than he had done half an hour ago. He was in control of the interview, and Jake was happy to keep it that way... unless, of course, he saw an opportunity for him to strike. And then he'd let his intuition take over.

'It's simple,' Bridger continued after Michael's silence. 'If you want it to be.'

'Leave my brothers out of this.'

'Where are they?' Bridger asked, snapping to the point.

'Gone.'

'Where?'

'Neverland.'

'With Captain Hook?'

'Tinkerbell,' Michael corrected. 'You can always rely on Danny to sprinkle some magic dust on everything and make it better.'

'And you believe that, do you?' The words came out of Jake's mouth before he had a chance to process them. It looked like he'd taken his opportunity to strike without realising it. 'You think he's got the special powder to fix this situation you're in?'

Michael shrugged.

'He knows people—'

'So do I. We meet a lot of people in our line of work,' Jake said sarcastically.

'I'm willing to bet Danny knows the same people you do. If not more. And if not better.' The same wry smile grew on Michael's face again, this time filling Jake with incipient rage. 'Shocking, isn't it? That there's still bent coppers looking for the next pay cheque.'

'I imagine every copper looks for the next pay cheque.'

'You'll never find him,' Michael said, wiping his nose.

'Just the one brother? You have two.'

'I don't need reminding.'

Jake straightened his tie and flattened it against his shirt.

'So, what happened with you guys?' he asked. 'How come you separated?'

Michael remained silent.

'Tell us about Luke,' Bridger said, budging his way back into the conversation. 'Where is he?'

'Alone and scared, no doubt,' Jake added.

Michael's breathing increased. The steady rise and fall of his chest turned into a heaving balloon that was nearing its limit.

'Luke's fine,' Michael said eventually, avoiding their gaze for the first time. 'He'll be fine.'

'You were the one looking after him, weren't you?' Jake asked, tilting his head to the side. 'You were the middle child. No mum. No dad. You were the one getting him ready for school. Feeding him. Making his breakfasts, lunches, dinners. Making sure he didn't miss the bus or turn up late. But Danny's role was different – Danny protected Luke when there was any sign of danger, and he left you lurking in the background. Luke never appreciated your help. At least, he never told you he did. So, Danny became the big brother that would always protect Luke, the one he looked up to, and you were cast to the side.'

'Do you have brothers or sisters, detective?' Michael asked, keeping his arms folded. A fire of aggression smouldered behind the curtain of his eyes, ready and waiting to burn the stage down and unleash hell.

Jake nodded. 'Younger brother. Older sister.'

'Similar to me. Do you love them?'

'For the most part,' Jake said, his thoughts turning to his siblings, and how they had grown distant in recent years.

'Have you ever taught them anything?'

Jake paused a moment to think. 'I've taught them many things.'

'Like what?'

'Respect one another. Work hard. Accomplish anything you want. I'd say that qualifies me as a good brother.'

Michael leant forward, wrapping his fingers round the edge of the desk.

'Have you ever taught your brother how to steal so he doesn't starve that night? Have you ever taught him how to look out for number one? Have you ever told him never to let anyone else tread all over him? Have you ever told him that, if anything happens to him, he must fight, and he must fight, and he must fight until the other person gets knocked down and never gets back up again?'

Jake hesitated. 'I can't say we ever needed to have that conversation.'

'Well, we did. Luke and I. I taught him to punch back twice as hard as he got. So don't underestimate him. He's smart. Always was. The brightest out of all of us—'

'Then why didn't you keep him at school?'

'Danny decided to get involved. He always told Luke he needed to stay with us and continue what we were doing, so Luke was always by our sides. He never left them. He would always wait to be told exactly what to do. He lost his independence. That's Danny's fault. Danny made him that way.'

Jake nodded, absorbing everything Michael told him. 'So, he's going to be left all alone, with no one to help?'

Michael shrugged.

'Your actions now will determine what happens next,' Bridger said in an authoritative yet calm voice. 'The past is where it needs to be: left behind. We've all got things we'd like to bury, but right now you should be concerned about your future. Tell us where your brothers are, and things can be made easier for you.'

Michael looked at his lap, exhaled deeply and then lifted his head. 'You know, I read something once. I can't remember where from. Might have been from a book somewhere. But there was one sentence that jumped out at me. It said: "All men have one entrance into life, and the like going out." What do you think that means?'

Jake glanced over at Bridger, whose expression was as confused as Jake felt.

'That you're going to give yourself up for your brothers?'

'It means that I'm not going to give you what you want unless I get what I want.'

Jake shook his head in disbelief. 'I don't see the correlation, but I'm starting to think maybe you're the smart one. What is it that you want?'

'I was born with one brother, and I'm going to end it with one. I'll give you Danny if you let Luke go. He's had nothing to do with any of this. Detective,' he said, addressing Jake directly, 'this is my act of retribution – I'm wiping Luke's slate clean instead of mine.'

'You realise it doesn't work that way?' Bridger added, checking his watch.

'Yes, but you haven't got long. Time is of the essence for you lot. You need me, whether you like it or not. Otherwise this has been a complete waste of time.'

Jake smirked. 'You're loving this, aren't you? Middle child… sidelined by the elder and younger brother. Craving the attention you never had. We don't need you as much as you think we do. We'll find Danny, and we'll find Luke – and when we do, none of you will remember what life was like before prison.' He hesitated a moment. 'Do you remember Freddy?'

Michael's pupils dilated, like giant black holes swallowing the rest of his eyes.

'I met with him earlier. He was thrilled to see me. He said that he'd tried to make contact with you boys, but he'd heard nothing back. And do you know the most disheartening thing he said to me? He said, more than anything else, he was disappointed in you. *You*, Michael. He expected more from you. I think he even likes me more than he does you and your brothers. But imagine – a few years down the line, you're in prison. You attempt to reach Luke, and he doesn't respond. He's forgotten about you. Nothing but a stain in his memory that he regrets, trying to make his life better without you. If you tell us now what we want to know, we can work something out for you. We can work on

264

something suitable. Perhaps the two of you could share a cell.'

Michael descended into a deep state of reflection. He lowered his head and twiddled his thumbs. After what felt like a long time, he opened his mouth.

'Southampton Port. He'll be there by now. If I could tell you where Luke was, I would. But you saw him – he ran off, so he could be anywhere by now.'

'It's fine,' Jake said, rising out of his chair and straightening his tie. 'We already know where Danny is – you just confirmed it for us. And now we've got a pretty good idea of where Luke is going to be as well.'

CHAPTER 48

GOOD SAMARITAN

Luke's body shook. The sound of his heart beating in his ears was like a subwoofer. *Dumf. Dumf. Dumf.* His breathing was wheezy, the result of too many cigarettes and a lack of exercise. He was bent double, resting his palms on his knees. He didn't know where he was, other than that he was hiding behind a tree and a car. He had sprinted as hard as he could after he saw Michael get arrested. He had wanted to stay, fight, defend his older brother. But he knew that would have been worse for them both. Michael was gone, and he needed to accept that. He just wished he'd had a proper chance to say goodbye.

Stop it. You're being a twat! Luke chided himself for thinking such pessimistic and defeatist points. He had been taught better than that. *Never give up. Never let the other team win. Never let them get inside your head.*

The sound of police sirens echoed around the city in the distance. The noise of helicopter blades whirring overhead buzzed in his ears. He was just over a mile away from the bus depot, and as he waited for his body to restore its vastly depleted oxygen levels, he heard a car speeding along the road. He caught sight of it: a police car, replete with reflective stickers and indicia. Panicking, he vaulted a nearby wall and ducked behind it. He closed his eyes as the police car sped past him. His chest heaved, and as the excitement and adrenaline dissipated in his blood, he opened his eyes again.

He was fucked. Alone, lost and without any means of getting out of the country.

If he was going to succeed, he was going to need help. And fast.

Still keeping himself behind somebody's front wall, he reached into his pocket and produced his phone. He dropped it onto the grass and swore aloud. His body was still shaking. He picked it up, scrolled along the address book and dialled Danny's number.

As he held the phone to his ear, the owner of the property he was outside opened the door and stepped away from the porch.

'Who are you?' he asked. He was elderly and was wearing a woollen jumper and checked shirt that had buttons on the collar. On his feet he wore a pair of slippers. 'What are you doing in my garden?'

The phone answered, but Luke ignored it. For a brief moment he was frozen, lost for words. As reality began to settle in again, he realised where he was.

'Please,' he said, ignoring Danny who was shouting in

267

his ear through the phone. 'Please – you have to help me. My girlfriend. She's looking for me.'

Luke scrambled to his feet and let the bag of jewellery drag behind him on the grass.

'Why—'

'She hits me.' Luke rushed to the man's side, stumbling as he went. He tripped on a small step and caught the man's arm, pulling the sleeve of his wrist. 'She beats me. Sometimes it's in the evening when she gets home. Sometimes it's in the morning before she leaves for work. But today she left the house unlocked. I packed my bag' – Luke gesticulated to the bag – 'and I got out of there. I need to leave the city before she finds me. You have to help me – please!'

The man peered over Luke's shoulder and glanced into the street. Luke took the opportunity to climb the man's body and cling to his collar.

'Wh— I—'

'Please, man! You honestly don't know how bad it gets. The bruises don't go away. And they're in places you'll never see. Please, man. You've got to help me.'

The man hesitated before responding. 'How… how can I help?'

Bingo.

'Hide me,' Luke said, stifling a victorious smile. 'Inside. She won't find me in there. You have to help me.' Luke pulled up his sleeve and revealed a thick scar he had on his arm from a bicycle accident when he was young. The skin was raised and coloured a lighter of shade of pink compared to the rest of his forearm. 'This is what she's capable of. And if she finds me, she'll do it again. If not worse. She… she…'

268

Luke scratched the side of his head. 'She likes to use her hair straighteners.'

The man's face contorted as he fought with himself. His brow furrowed and then the discontent in his expression drained.

'Come on. I'd better get you inside. I'll get the kettle boiled.'

Luke's body tingled with a sensation he hadn't felt before. Satisfaction. Pride. He had succeeded in doing something for himself without the help of either of his brothers. And he didn't even feel guilty about deceiving this old man.

The man spun on the spot and entered the house. Luke followed, closing the door behind him; as he did so, another police car sped past. Luke slammed the door shut and held his breath. He listened for any signs that suggested the driver had seen him and stopped and was on his way to arrest him. But there was nothing.

'Sugar?' a voice called, distracting him.

Luke released the door handle, the colour returning to his knuckles, and faced the kitchen at the end of the corridor. The sound of the kettle boiling wafted through the hallway.

'One,' Luke said. 'Thanks.'

He took a moment to absorb his surroundings. The first thing he noticed was that it smelt. Horrible. As if it hadn't been cleaned in a few days, and that a dog had shared its last breath there too. To the right of the hallway was a living room. There was a single armchair in the middle of the room, directly facing the television. Beside the chair was a coffee table with a lamp on it and a collection of fishing magazines.

'You can sit in my chair, if you like.' The man's voice startled Luke. He stood in the kitchen doorway with two mugs full of tea, wisps of steam dancing from the top. He started towards Luke and entered the living room. 'You might struggle to get back up though. It's one of the most comfortable things I've ever been in.'

Luke pulled himself out of his mind and back to reality. Now that he was in the security of the man's house, he could start to plan his next move.

'Yeah. Thanks.' Luke reached into his pocket and pulled out his burner phone again. 'Do you mind if I make a call?'

'Not at all.'

By the time the man finished speaking, Luke was already talking into the phone with Danny.

'You've come crawling back, have you?' Danny said. In the distance, Luke heard the sound of car engines revving.

'Shut up,' Luke replied. The man shuffled past him in the living room doorway and Luke entered the room. He kept his voice low. 'There's an issue. Micky's been arrested. The cops found us by the bus depot. Two of them got him, but I managed to get away.'

'You're shitting me?' Danny said. 'Where are you now?'

'Emily is abusing me again.'

Luke had only ever had to use the cover once before, after their first heist in Newcastle. And it had been a success then too. It had been Danny's idea originally, to lie and confuse susceptible people into allowing them access to their home. Emily was the name they'd used back then, and it had stuck as a code word for the situation.

'Does he believe you?' Danny asked.

Luke cautiously glanced beside him. The man had set the

cups of tea on the coffee table and then wandered out of the room. As Luke returned his attention to Danny, something caught his eye. The television in front of him. ITV News was playing, and the first thing Luke noticed was Danny's mugshot, taken years ago from when he'd been arrested for possession of drugs. And then Michael's appeared. They were much younger in them, but there would be no mistaking them now.

Luke's eyes widened and his lips parted. 'Shit,' he whispered. 'Our faces… they're… they're all over TV.' Luke scrambled beside him for the television remote. He found it on the coffee table and switched the channel.

'You need to get out of there.'

Breathing a heavy sigh of relief, Luke asked, 'Where are you?'

'Southampton.'

'Already?'

'I dipped early. Bus driver was scowling at me. Didn't want the police to catch me on board it so I got myself a cab the rest of the way. Paid him extra to floor it.'

As Luke opened his mouth to speak, the sound of feet shuffling on carpet distracted him. The man was standing in the door frame of the living room, holding a small plate of biscuits.

'Everything OK?' he asked.

'Y-Yes,' Luke said, removing the phone and looking at it. 'It's my brother. He can help me. I n-need to get to him.'

'Where is he?' the man asked.

'Southampton.'

The man lifted a finger in the air. 'I can call you a cab.'

'No!' Luke said, shocking the man. He took himself by

271

surprise, and instantly regretted shouting so abruptly. 'You.'

'Excuse me?'

'You. You can take me. I'll pay. I have money. Lots of it. Look.' Luke swung the bag by his side, opened it and grabbed a wad of money, waving it in front of him. 'You're the only person I can trust right now.'

The old man hesitated for what felt like an age.

'It's not about—'

'Please, I wouldn't ask unless I was desperate…'

'I…'

'Please,' Luke begged, clasping his hands together. He sniffled, hoping it would bring a forced tear to his eye.

'Let me grab my keys.'

CHAPTER 49

THUMB

Danny slung the bag over his shoulder. The arrogant cabbie who had seemed to be in too much of a hurry to care about his safety had dropped him off right in the heart of Southampton, and Danny had been forced to walk the remainder of the journey. He was standing beside a roundabout, and ahead of him was a multitude of signs directing him towards the port where, soon, he and Luke and Louise would board the boat.

All he had to do now was wait.

Danny checked his watch.

Still another hour until the ferry left.

Still another thirty minutes until Luke arrived.

But where was Louise? She was supposed to be here already. They had agreed a meet at this exact location – just a few hundred yards away from the cruise ship.

Danny checked his watch again, as though it would speed up the ten seconds that had just passed.

He didn't want to upset her.

As he lowered his wrist, his phone vibrated once. He read the message and swivelled on the spot.

Behind him, two metres away, was the most beautiful woman he'd ever seen.

Louise. His Louise.

'Hello, stranger,' she said. She waltzed up to him and dangled from his neck. Her face and neck were covered in make-up that made her look as orange as the sun, and the layers of fake tan she'd applied stood in stark contrast to the blue hoodie that hung from her shoulders.

'Are you OK?' he asked, letting go of her. 'Nothing's happened to you has it? I was worried about you. I have been all day.'

'I'm fine.'

'Did everything go all right? The key? The unit?' he said before kissing her. As he released her, she licked her lips, flashing that delicious red tongue of hers that he'd grown to love.

'Relax. Everything's fine. The suitcases are in my car. It's all there. I just can't believe you made me dress up as a fucking golfer. I've never felt so uncomfortable.'

Danny smirked. 'I've been worried sick. I thought they might have got you. I didn't think you were going to show,'

'And miss out on my chance to get my share of everything? You really don't know me at all. Where's everyone else?'

'It's all gone to shit. We got separated. Michael's been arrested. Luke's stuck in Fareham.'

'More money for us,' Louise said, winking at him.

Danny shook his head dismissively. It was an instinctive reaction – paternal, brotherly – but one that he immediately regretted. His eyes widened and he stared at Louise. Then he lifted his arms in the air defensively, surrendering to what was about to come.

Louise said, 'Excuse me?'

'I... Luke... I didn't mean anything by it. Don't—'

Louise thrust her hand towards his midriff and, using her thumb, buried it beneath his rib cage and into his diaphragm, cutting him off instantly. A sharp stab of pain squeezed the top of his body. He exhaled sharply, breathing through the discomfort.

'Don't talk to me like that,' she hissed. 'What have I told you?'

'S-S-Sorry,' Danny struggled, the pain too much for him.

'If Luke isn't here by the time we board, that money's mine. You understand?'

Danny nodded. 'Yes, Louise. I under-understand.'

'Good. Where's Candice?'

Danny looked down at the ground. 'She won't be joining us.'

'She's dead?'

Danny's gaze rose to meet hers. 'No.'

'What happened to her?'

Danny told her. She pressed deeper into his diaphragm.

'You idiot. Do you know how much more complicated that makes things? I knew you hated her but not that much.'

'I didn't... I do, but...' He inhaled and regained his composure. 'Listen – you don't need to worry about her. She won't be troubling us anymore.'

Louise eased the pressure against his body. 'I can't believe she didn't approve of me.'

'Neither can I,' Danny replied, breathing slowly, hiding the discomfort in his voice. 'You know, before all of this started, she told me to stay away from you.'

'And what did you say?'

'I told her to go fuck herself. I ain't going nowhere.'

Louise prodded his body one final time for good measure and then removed her hand. 'Good. Because you know what will happen if you decide to go anywhere. What are we going to do now?'

Danny breathed then rubbed the part of his skin that would no doubt turn bruised within a few minutes.

'We wait,' he said. 'When Luke gets here, I want you out of sight.'

'He doesn't know I'm coming?'

Danny shook his head. 'And I'd like to keep it that way for as long as possible. That boy's been through enough today. And he's about to go through a lot more.'

CHAPTER 50

IDEA

Candice was petrified. The spike collar dangling from her neck grew increasingly heavy with each passing minute. Her neck ached. Her back ached. Her entire body ached. She just wanted to rip it from her and throw it against the wall, heedless of the outcome. She'd given up. In fact, she'd given up a long time ago. She had allowed her sons to betray and beat her. Danny, that sick son of a bitch. She'd known from the moment his finger had hovered over the trigger in the shop that something had been wrong – that something wasn't right about any of this. But not Luke – Lukey. He was the good one. The one who had believed all of the lies she'd fed him about their father. If anyone could save her from the black box of death, it would be him.

The cramped prison cell she was locked in jostled and swayed as the van pulled round bends and weaved its way through traffic, stopping and starting every now and again. There were no windows in the van, no slithers of light coming from the four walls, save for a tiny hole in the ceiling the same width as a paper straw. The cell was grimy, damp and smelt of piss, as if the previous occupant had no other choice but to soil themselves and nobody had bothered to clean it since. Well, she needed to go, but she wouldn't be subjected to such inhumane treatment.

A part of her wanted to scream. Cry. Bawl her eyes out until someone heard her. But she knew it would be pointless; she hadn't heard so much as a car horn from outside. She was alone, and that was the way she was going to die. She had admitted it to herself already. There was no point trying to fight it. The police were keeping her prisoner, and what was taking them so long? Why weren't they roaring along, breaking the speed limit, trying to catch up with Danny and Michael and Luke? Were they purposely trying to kill her?

The van started off again, startling her. She slipped off the small metal block that she had assumed was a chair and fell onto the cold, solid floor. She bumped her elbow and grazed her right arm as she fell, and then began to cry out. Her body recoiled and she smacked her head on the wall. A hair pin fell out and landed by her feet.

And then it finally clicked in her head. That tiny little thing was going to save her.

Candice crouched down to the floor, steadying herself with her knees and shoulders pressed against the walls, and picked the pin up using her hands behind her. She reworked the metal pin until it snapped in two. And then she remembered something that Danny had shown her when they were preparing for the heist. It was simple, but something that was only supposed to be used a last resort. This was it.

If she was going to break out of the handcuffs, she needed to dislocate her thumb. Left or right. Either or. Whichever one she favoured least. It didn't matter.

After a second's deliberation, she decided on the left. It was an easy decision to make.

Candice pressed her left thumb against the wall and leant into it, applying pressure on the bone. Pain swelled and throbbed in her hand, and on the count of three, she convinced herself to thrust her hips backwards to dislocate the joint.

One.

Two.

Three.

Candice screamed out in agony. Hard. Until her lungs hurt and she lost breath, almost dipping her toes into the deep lagoon of unconsciousness. Her cries only made it as far as the ceiling above her. As she came to, she panted through the pain. But now wasn't the time to focus on it. If she did, then she knew that she wouldn't have the courage to do the next part: slip her wrist through the cuff.

Gritting her teeth and tensing every muscle in her body to draw the pain away from her hand, Candice wriggled and writhed her hand until it narrowly slipped through the cuff. The metal dug into her flesh, leaving behind red indentations and drawing a little blood.

But she didn't care. The adrenaline drowned out the pain now.

She had her hand back.

She was free.

Using the forefinger and middle finger on her free hand, she slotted one of the pins into the cuffs and twisted, rotated, fumbling with them both. After a few more seconds, the pin slid inside the lock and the cuff on her right hand snapped open. She brought her hands to her front and rubbed where the cuff had been, the sensation and blood rapidly returned to her wrist. She repeated the same for the other hand as much as she could and, once again, tried to shake the collar bomb free, yanking it from her neck, pulling it from side to side, then apart like it was a stretchy toy. But it wouldn't budge. Her efforts were futile.

She screamed again. But this time she stopped almost as soon as she'd begun. She was acting erratically. Illogically. If she could get out of the handcuffs, then she could get out of the collar bomb. There was no point detonating the device and decapitating herself and removing whatever opportunity she had at saving herself, no matter how small it was.

She was going to save herself.

She *was* going to save herself, even if nobody else would.

And she had just had the perfect idea of how to go about it.

CHAPTER 51

PENDULUM

The old man was called Dennis. He was in his seventies and had been widowed for nearly three decades. After his wife died, Dennis had decided he would never date again. He thought it was a betrayal to his wife, whom he had spent more than half his life with. They were soulmates, and anyone new who entered his life would constantly remind him of the past. It wasn't fair on him, his wife, or the new person.

Luke and Dennis had been talking non-stop since they'd started the journey towards Southampton, and the further they travelled, the more Luke was warming to the old man. He reminded him of the grandfather he'd only met once or twice after the man had realised that the three of them existed. And Luke hoped that, when he got out of the car in Southampton, Dennis would just drive away and not ask any questions. That he would get himself out of the area before Luke bumped into Danny. There was the prevalent risk that their paths would cross, and there was no knowing how Danny would react.

Danny was a different man today. And Luke distrusted his volatility.

They entered Southampton city centre from the east, crossing the Itchen toll bridge, and continuing past Queen's Park at the south of the city. A few seconds later, they approached the Mayflower Roundabout. In the distance, Luke spotted the yellow and blue of an IKEA logo. He instructed Dennis to continue straight on at the roundabout and slip into the IKEA car park. It was multi-storey, and Luke and Danny had agreed via text message to meet on the fourth floor. As Dennis pulled the car to a stop, Luke exhaled, reached for his wallet and handed Dennis a twenty.

'For the car park,' he said, before he opened the bag by his feet and produced a wad of notes. The smell of old money wafted to his nostrils. 'And this is for your troubles.'

Dennis shook his head, swatting Luke's hand away with his. 'I don't want it. Keep it. I have no need for it... you might.'

A smile crept over Luke's face. 'It's OK, I've got enough. I want you to have it. Maybe you can treat yourself to something nice. That holiday you were talking about.'

'You're going to need it, wherever you're going. Please...'

Luke smiled and was about to say something when he noticed Danny standing with his back pressed against a wall. His head was low, and a hat was pulled over his eyes.

Luke opened the door, grabbed his things and stepped out.

'You'll be OK, won't you?' Dennis asked as Luke prepared to close the door.

'I'll be the best I've ever been,' Luke replied. 'Trust me.'

Dennis extended his hand. Luke reached and shook it. The old man's grip was fierce, a lifetime of manual labour and hard practical work hidden behind the muscles.

'I'll never forget you,' Luke said.

Dennis grinned. 'Likewise.'

With that, Luke shut the door gently, waved goodbye to Dennis and hurried over to Danny. His body surged with excitement. Luke didn't know what it was, but as soon as he locked eyes with Danny, he felt safe, he felt at home. As though the events of the past few hours hadn't happened. As though his older brother wasn't responsible for their mother's inevitable death. As though Danny hadn't shot and killed an innocent shop worker. Danny was the one in charge of the entire operation, and he had made it to Southampton without any issues. So maybe there was a method to his madness? There was only one way to find out.

'About fucking time,' Danny said.

Luke ignored him and embraced Danny's muscular body. When Danny reciprocated the hug, Luke eased into his brother's arms and felt the tension in his shoulders dissipate.

'Stop it,' Danny said, throwing Luke off. 'Making us look like a bunch of poofs. What took you so long?'

'I'm here, aren't I?'

Together they started off, heading down four flights of steps. The air inside the stairwell was cold and it was a welcome change from the stifling heat of the car park.

'Were you followed?' Danny asked as they descended the steps.

'No,' Luke said with assurance.

'Sure?'

'Do you trust me?'

They reached the bottom of the stairs and breached into the car park's entrance, at the base of the IKEA centre. A queue of traffic had formed by the ticket barriers, and car engines purred as they waited idly for the car in front to move. A wall of heat clapped him round the face, and he inhaled a large quantity of warm air that made him cough gently. And as they stepped out of the car park, Luke shielded his eyes from the blinding sunlight.

'Here,' Danny said, placing a pair of sunglasses on Luke's head. 'While I was waiting, I bought these for you. Help keep your ugly mug away from the CCTV.'

'Our mugshots need updating. Yours is from that time with Richard.'

'Richard who?'

'Richard Maddison.'

'I don't even want to think about that guy.' Danny slapped Luke on the back jovially. 'Come on, we've got a boat to catch.'

They came to a stop at a set of traffic lights. Danny pressed the button and they waited as cars tore past them, their brake lights nothing but a flashing blur. After a few seconds, the lights changed and they crossed the road. In the distance, dominating the skyline along the riverbed, was the cruise liner. Luke afforded himself the opportunity to appreciate its magnificence. It was one of the largest man-made structures he had ever seen, if not the largest.

He tried to open his mouth, but the words wouldn't come.

'Brilliant, eh?' Danny said. 'In a few hours we'll be out of this clusterfuck, ready to start new lives for ourselves, you get me?'

Luke could hear the excitement in Danny's voice. But something troubled him. Danny was too jovial. Too happy. As though he'd forgotten that their other brother had been arrested.

'What about Michael?' Luke asked.

'What about him? He's gone. There's nothing we can do for him. With any luck they'll lock him up with Freddy and the two of them can work on getting out at some point in the next twenty years.'

'Never. They'll never be locked up together.'

'Micky's a big boy. He can look after himself.'

'Just like that?'

'What?'

'Just like that, you're going to forget about him? As though he never existed.'

'Forget about him?' Danny said, coming to an abrupt halt. 'You're the one who left him behind. You're the one who let the cops arrest him.'

'He surrendered himself for me.'

'What a hero,' Danny said, rolling his eyes. He stormed off, leaving Luke to catch up.

As Luke followed, he noticed something irregular about Danny's ensemble.

'Dan,' he called after his brother.

Nothing. No response.

'Dan!'

'What?' Danny snapped on the half-turn.

'Where's your bag?'

285

Danny's expression dropped. His eyes widened. 'I…
er…'

'I don't believe it,' Luke said, stepping away from his
brother. 'She's here, isn't she?'

'Who?'

'Louise. She's here.'

'No. What— Why—'

'She's got all the stuff from the storage units, hasn't she? I
can see it on your face. That smile. I knew I recognised it.
You only smile like that when she's around. I thought you
said you two had broken up.'

Danny bit his nail.

'You lied. Again. You're pathetic.'

'You don't know what you're talking about, Luke. Don't
say something you'll later regret.'

Luke shook his head. 'No. That's it, Dan. I've had
enough. It's over. I thought coming here would be the best
thing, but I was wrong. I thought you'd be able to help. I
thought the two of us were going to get out of here. Not
three. Not her. She's a plague to our family, Dan. Don't you
see what she's done? You've done all of this for her. I hope
she was worth it, because you've just lost two brothers in the
process. And a mum.'

'She was not our mum! She never was,' Danny screamed.
They were still standing by the side of the road, oblivious to
the sea of traffic charging towards them from either side.

'She was more of a mum to us than all the other women
attempted to be.'

Danny pointed his finger in Luke's face. 'Do you know
what' – he reached inside his pocket and produced the final
key and threw it at Luke – 'you can keep this, if she means

that much to you. But I want you to know one thing: she wasn't the one who helped put food on the table. I was! Paying for your school lunches and everything else so you wouldn't go hungry. Not her, *me*.'

Luke froze. His mouth dangled like a pendulum. He left the key on the ground and fought every will in his body to pick it up. 'You're lying.'

'I always gave the money to Michael. I saw the relationship you two had. He taught you things I never could. You were always with him. I didn't want it to seem like I was buying your love.'

'Danny, I… I had no idea.'

'Why would you? Michael was happy to take the credit for it. He was happy…' Danny choked, regained himself, rubbed just beneath his ribcage and then continued. 'He knew how close we were. He knew you always looked up to me despite everything he did for you. But he wanted a piece of that. He wanted to share the same bond. We never told you because you were too young.'

'I was twelve. I was old enough to make my own decisions.'

'You were naïve. You still are.'

Luke stopped. He couldn't believe what he'd just heard. What he'd just been told. Everything in his life was a lie. And he had been deceived consistently. It needed to change. *He* needed to change; get his own life back. Make decisions on his own.

'For too long I've depended on you and Micky. I need to get out of here. I need to clear my head.' Luke bent down, picked up the key, adjusted the strap on his shoulder so it felt more comfortable, and then turned his back on Danny and started to walk away.

'Luke!' Danny called back, but Luke ignored him. 'Luke!'

He stopped, turned on a half-twist, and said, 'I hope you and Louise are happy together, Danny. Enjoy your new life.'

CHAPTER 52

GREEN LIGHT

Jake and Bridger were headed west, towards Southampton. It hadn't taken him long to work out where Luke Cipriano was headed. The young man was alone and in need of his brothers. He'd relied upon them his whole life — they'd protected him, raised him, shielded him from the outside world — and he needed to return to that security. And with Michael out of the picture, there was no doubt in Jake's mind that Luke was currently on his way to Danny where they'd be able to live their new lives together.

He just hoped they'd be able to make it there in time.

'You sure about this?' Bridger asked as he turned the car off the M271 and onto Redbridge Road a few miles from the centre of Southampton.

'Have I been wrong about anything else up to this point?' Jake responded, feeling confident.

He turned to face Bridger momentarily. There was something about him that troubled Jake. The interview with Michael. It had been unprofessional, and he was almost certain that it had been unlawful, even if Bridger did get the approval required for conducting the interview without Michael's solicitor present. But Jake had been a part of the problem also. He'd lost sight of what they were there for and what they should have been doing, and joined in on the tirade against Michael and his family instead. There would be repercussions, he was sure. But it wouldn't do to dwell on them now. He just needed to make sure he was able to cover himself when the time came.

'What's our ETA?' he asked, distracting himself. His eyes fell on the dash.

'Hampshire are in the middle of setting up the rendezvous point at the Mayflower Roundabout.' Bridger hesitated for a brief moment as he glanced at the clock in front of him. 'So I'd say we're two minutes out.'

Perfect. That gave Jake enough time to make a call. He removed his phone from his pocket and dialled Danika's number.

'Jake?' she began.

'Have you checked the bookings for Harrington at Southampton?' he asked, wanting to keep it nice and concise.

'Yes. Just pulled the reports now. I found four of them. Sean, Alex, Billy and Kate Harrington.'

'Their aliases…' Jake said, thinking aloud. 'Where's the cruise going?'

'Canary Islands. Scheduled to leave at three p.m.'

Jake checked his watch. 'That gives us just over half an

hour.'

Before Jake continued, they arrived at Mayflower Roundabout. Bridger banked the kerb and parked on a small patch of grass nearby an office block. It was devoid of any police presence, and cars continued to stream past them from four directions. To their right, towering above the office buildings was the cruise liner they were looking for, and to their left was a row of trees sitting in front of Mayflower Park.

Jake thanked Danika, hung up on her and then stepped out of the car.

'Where is everyone?'

The salt in the air licked his skin and stayed there, cemented in position by the chilled wind that buffeted his shoulders and legs.

'Seems they're late to the party,' Bridger replied, rounding the front of his vehicle.

Just as Jake was about to respond, the sound of sirens pierced the street, followed closely by the shrill pitches of horns and tyres squealing. Around them, an entourage of police vehicles pulled up to the roundabout from every direction, blocking off every stream of traffic. And then an unmarked police car skidded to a halt beside Jake. At once, the door opened and out stepped a uniformed officer. By the time Jake had registered who they were, Bridger was by his side.

'PS Hammond,' the middle-aged and balding man said. Hammond outstretched his hand and took Bridger's first. As they shook, Hammond glanced down and nodded at Bridger's watch. It was then that Jake realised he and Elliot were wearing the same timepiece. 'You gentlemen from

Surrey?' Hammond asked.

Bridger nodded.

'Glad to have you with us. We've got this under control for now, but if we need you for anything, I want you on hand to assist.'

Jake stepped in. 'Where is everyone? They should be here by now. There's a murderer on board that boat.'

Something switched inside Hammond. The uniformed officer advanced towards Jake, but before the situation was able to escalate any further, Bridger stepped in, jumping between the two of them.

'Sorry,' Bridger pleaded, the back of his arm pressing against Jake's chest. 'This is *Temporary* DC Tanner. He's new.'

Hammond peered round the side of Bridger's shoulder and pointed at Jake.

'You'd better know your place, son. You'll learn a few things quicker if you do it that way. Trust me.'

Jake retreated. 'We don't have time to be arguing.' He quickly checked his watch. 'We've got thirty minutes.'

'It's all under control,' Hammond said. He seemed to have calmed down almost as quickly as his temper had flared in the first place. 'Firearms teams are setting themselves up now. We're cordoning off the road. And everyone back at HQ is trying to alert the captain of what's happening. But until the firearms team arrive, I can't tell you much more.'

'Has Candice Strachan been cleared to enter?' Bridger asked.

'What do you mean?'

'Our governor, DCI Pemberton, is on her way down here now with Candice Strachan. She's got a collar strapped to her neck.'

'What's she doing that for?'

'Because the only people who can defuse it are inside that boat,' Jake interrupted. 'She's going to die if she doesn't get that key.'

Hammond sighed and placed his hands on his hips. 'I'll have to check whether it's been cleared. Might take some persuasion. Why can't bomb squad defuse it?'

Jake stared at Hammond, incredulous. Why was Hammond asking these questions? It have been the other way round. He should have been brought up to speed with intelligence. It was clear to see there was a disconnect between Hampshire Control and Hammond.

'It requires a key,' Jake said after a while of looking deeply into the man's face. 'Danny Cipriano, one of the offenders inside that boat, has it.'

'Has it been confirmed that Cipriano is on board?'

Shit. In the rush and excitement of it all, Jake had forgotten to ask Danika whether all the tickets she'd found had been collected and whether the brothers had set foot on deck. For all Jake knew, they could be anywhere, and Jake was putting all his eggs in one basket in the hope that they were all on that boat.

'We're not sure,' Bridger replied eventually. 'We have intelligence that suggests both Luke and Danny Cipriano are on board, but no confirmation.'

Hammond held his hand in the air, stepped away from the conversation and made a call. While they waited, Jake turned on the spot, cast his gaze around him and surveyed the area. He hadn't realised it, but in the short time that they'd been talking, the uniformed officers of Hampshire police had cordoned off all access points to the roundabout, blocking the road as far as the IKEA car park in the distance behind him.

But, as he stood there, waiting for the tactical firearms team to arrive, Jake couldn't but feel like it would all be a little too late.

A cough distracted him. It was Hammond.

'SFO has given the green light for Candice Strachan's arrival. She's good to attend.'

CHAPTER 53

SURRENDER

Luke was lost. Physically. Emotionally. Mentally. Everything he had ever thought about his brothers was a lie, a façade, an act. His entire life had been a tournament for them both to fight in. And he was the prize. They'd used him for their own narcissistic gain. He was most hurt by Michael. They had bonded the most during their childhoods. Almost been inseparable. Shopping together. Walking to school. Catching the bus. All while Danny was working somewhere, bringing in the money so that they could eat and drink that night. But Michael... he had been Luke's confidant, his closest companion, and it was only now that Luke realised it had never been reciprocated – Michael had never told him about anything that was really going on – and that there was an overwhelming disconnect between them.

In fact, there was a disconnect between the three of them.

In the space of a few hours, their entire family had crumbled. A mother and their sons split up in the wild, each left to fend for themselves. The metaphor disturbed Luke. He conjured images of blood and massacre and death… and eventually, a pride of lions being trapped by poachers. Surrounded by weapons. Forced to surrender.

Luke closed his eyes and banished the thoughts from his mind.

He found a nearby bench and sat on it, his head spinning. He removed the key from his pocket and played with it in his fingers. The rusted metal was tinted a shade of green and brown, yet it still managed to glimmer in the sunlight. Luke hoped it was a sign, but he didn't believe in that sort of thing. It was no use having it anyway. He had no idea where Candice was and no means of getting to her. He wished he'd taken Dennis's number; he could use a somewhat friendly face right now.

Snap out of it, you idiot, he told himself. *Stop being a twat.*

A siren sped past him, grabbing his attention. Luke's head shot upwards and he glimpsed a police car roaring down the street where it parked up beside another police car on a piece of grass in the distance. At the sight of the flashing lights, Luke's skin turned cold. The hunters were closing in around him.

And Danny.

A moment of epiphany slapped Luke across the face. It was a farce. It was all wrong. A mistake. The police would find his brother on the ship. Of course they would. Danny was stupid enough to be on there in the first place when they should have had a Plan C, something they'd never needed before. But Danny was too confident in his own plan, too

296

cocksure, too brazen. He had ignored almost all of Freddy's rules – the mantra they had all sworn by when their former leader was still with them. And for what? A stupid bitch who was going to steal all of his money anyway? Luke wished Louise had never entered their lives.

An anger from deep within him rose to his lungs. He wanted to scream, but he couldn't. His mouth wouldn't work.

He stared at the bag of money in front of him. Contemplating. With the amount he had, he could live any life he wanted. There wasn't much people wouldn't give to have that same luxury. And yet, here he was, pissing about with it, considering throwing it all away. His mind turned to the people who had been hurt in the process. The people who had *died* so that he could have the meaningless sheets of paper and diamonds sat before him. Luke thought of the employee who Danny had shot mercilessly, the Audi owner, the police officer, the families in their cars.

It was wrong. So wrong. They had gone too far. An entire city had suffered because of their evil – *Danny's* evil. And both he and Michael were complicit, even though they'd never pulled the trigger.

Luke's mind turned to Candice. And then he realised: the police were after *him*; they were only a few hundred yards away; they would know where Candice was; they would be able to save her. *He* would be able to save her. Even if it meant giving himself up to the police.

Luke squeezed his head in his hands and glanced towards the barricade of police vehicles in the distance.

A moment later, he'd made his decision.

It was better for everyone if he did it this way. Him.

297

Danny. Michael. The families of those that had suffered. Candice. Everyone.

Grabbing his bag, Luke slung it over his shoulder and started to shuffle towards the army of law enforcement that were setting up a cordon in the middle of the street.

CHAPTER 54

BARGAIN

It didn't take long for Hampshire Police to remove all seeds of doubt in Jake's mind about their efficiency and effectiveness during the operation. Within minutes, a plethora of police cars – both undercover and liveried – along with ambulances and fire engines had arrived at Mayflower Roundabout, with some of the vehicles spilling into the park on the other side of the treeline. They'd evacuated the area and sent the city in lockdown. And, as Jake folded his arms and rested them against his chest, impressed with what he saw, a black van waded its way through the stationary police vehicles and pulled up a few yards away from the roundabout. It was the armed response and tactical firearms units. Everyone in the area watched in high anticipation as the van came to a halt and four armed officers deftly disembarked from the back of the vehicle.

They fanned out, making their way slowly to the front of the van. Two of them approached Jake, Bridger and PS Hammond. Both of the armed officers were of similar height and build to one another, and their features were hidden behind helmets and masks.

'PS Riggs,' the man on the left said. 'I'm the Operational Firearms Commander.' Strapped over his shoulder was a SIG MCX 556 Carbine. Standard issue. He turned to his colleague, and said, 'And this is PC Radcliffe.'

PC Radcliffe gave a curt nod at the mention of his name and tilted his visor skywards, revealing a small scar above his eyebrow. On his bare wrist, he wore a scorpion tattoo stained into his skin.

Bridger introduced himself and Jake, leaving PS Hammond till last. All five men shook hands.

'What's the status?' Bridger asked.

'We've got sixteen plainclothes AFOs making their way on board now. They're going to conduct a thorough and methodical sweep of the boat, searching for the offenders.'

'Do they know what Danny and Luke look like?'

'They've been sent the visuals, yes.'

'Their mugshots?' It was Jake's turn to speak. 'That's not good enough.' Jake paused for a moment while an idea formed in his mind. He needed to get on that boat. He needed to put an end to it – partly for his own vanity, but partly because he didn't want to see Danny and Luke escape again. 'I can confirm their identities,' he continued. 'I've seen them. You'll need to get me on board. The last thing we want is to shoot or arrest innocent people and alert them to our presence.'

Just as PS Riggs was about to respond, the roundabout

filled with screams and shouts emanating behind him. Jake spun on the spot and turned to face the source of the commotion. Fifty yards away, on the wrong side of the police cordon, was a figure sauntering towards them, carrying a bag in his hands that jolted and swayed with each step. Jake's eyes widened. He sidestepped closer to Bridger's car.

'Is that...?' Bridger asked.

'Yes,' Jake replied, unable to tear his gaze from the man approaching them.

'Which one?'

Jake squinted to get a better view of the person's face, and as the man came closer, he recognised the young features. The red cheeks. The blonde hair.

'Luke.'

At the mention of one of the Cipriano brothers' names, PS Riggs cried out, barking orders to the authorised firearms officers. PC Radcliffe and the rest of the armed officers raised their weapons and sprinted towards Luke.

Screams of 'Armed police!' pierced the air.

'Wait!' Jake said, rushing behind the officers. Twenty yards away, Luke came to a stop and dropped the bag by his side. He was surrounded by tarmac on both sides. Behind him was the police cordon, and in front of him were five armed officers aiming their submachine guns at him. There was nowhere for him to go.

Tentatively, keeping his hands raised in the air, Jake crossed the threshold into the line of fire and entered his very own No Man's Land.

'Hold your fire!' he screamed, his voice breaking mid-sentence.

He knew that what he was doing was risky and breaking

several procedures, but he needed to step in. Something wasn't right. And it was his job to get to the bottom of it.

After a few seconds of uncertainty and silence, PS Riggs ordered the officers to stand down. They lowered their weapons slowly.

Jake took a deep breath before beginning.

'What are you doing here, Luke?'

The young man kept his head low and his arms raised, but there was no response.

'Where's Danny?'

Still nothing.

'Luke – we can help you.'

At that, Luke's head lifted.

'Michael's safe, Luke. He didn't get hurt. He's being looked after,' Jake said.

Luke lowered his arms.

'You need to keep them above your head, mate, otherwise these guys have got their instructions.'

Luke did as he was told, although he looked as though he'd given up – as though he'd lost all the fight left within him.

'What's in the bag, Luke?' Jake asked, trying a different approach. It was then that he noticed the undisturbed silence around him. Even the traffic in the far-off distance, the gentle lapping of the waves, the rushing coastal wind, seemed to have muted.

'Money,' came the monosyllabic response.

'The money you stole from Candice?'

'We didn't steal it from Candice – she gave it to us. She *shared* it with us.' There was a hoarseness in Luke's voice, as though there was a barrage of tears that would come flooding out as soon as the gates opened. All Jake needed to do was open them.

'Yes. That's right. She gave it to you. She was your mother, wasn't she?'

'Is,' Luke corrected. '*Is* my mother. She ain't dead yet.' He raised his gaze and stared at Jake. They were of a similar age, yet both had led very different lives at the opposite ends of the spectrum. Luke had led a life of crime and constant oppression, whereas Jake's was normal, civilised. He had gone to school, university, and now here he was. There were opportunities available to Jake that Luke had never been considered for.

'She won't be alive for long, Luke. And you know it...' Jake brushed his tie and loosened his collar; it felt as though it was strangling him. 'She told us everything. About you. Michael. Danny. The device.' Jake hesitated. 'Help us, Luke. Help us arrest him. He'll be out of your life and you'll never have to see him again. If nothing else, do it for Candice. She's dead if you don't.'

Luke's expression changed to a steely, cold glare.

'How do I know I can trust you?'

'Do you remember Freddy?'

'Yeah.'

'Did you know he had a wife and kids?'

Luke nodded.

'Did you know he's been writing to them – he's been writing to you as well – and he's not heard a single word from them in return.' Jake swallowed, hoping he was convincing enough in his lie. 'Well, they're going to see him tomorrow. I spoke with them earlier. Freddy wouldn't talk to me unless I persuaded them to visit. Little Sammy is really

303

excited to see his daddy for the first time. If I can get them to visit him, then I promise you that you can—'

'Where's my mum? I need to see her. I want to see her.'

'And you will. She's on her way down now. All I need you to do is make a call to your brother, and then she'll be allowed to come out. So long as you agree to give us what we want.'

'I'm not helping until I see her.'

Jake pursed his lips and shrugged.

'Then we'll just have to wait.'

CHAPTER 55

RADCLIFFE

A few minutes of silence passed. Luke remained where he was, staring up at the sky, kept still by the numerous SIGs trained on him. Deeming it safe to do so, Jake wandered back to Bridger, Riggs and Hammond.

'You think he'll do it?' Bridger asked as Jake returned.

'He'll have to if he wants Candice to live. It's his only option.'

Bridger patted Jake on the back. 'Well played.'

It was a hollow victory. He hated lying to people, but he also hated what The Crimsons had done, and how much devastation they had caused, not only to people's property but to their livelihoods. Their behaviour was inexcusable and all three of them deserved whatever punishment the law practiced on them.

'I just wish Pemberton would hurry up. Every minute

wasted is another minute Danny could escape,' Jake said.

'Don't worry,' Riggs said. 'The captain's been made aware and is currently holding fire. He's under instruction that, under no circumstances, is he to move the boat.'

'What? You're going to leave it waiting there?'

Riggs nodded.

Jake shook his head in disbelief. 'That's the wrong idea,' he began. 'Danny Cipriano is dangerous. His actions today have proven that he's irrational and willing to exercise any form of protection against himself and the ones he loves. But the longer you keep that boat idle, the more suspicious Danny's going to get. And the more he's going to retaliate. None of us have any idea what he might have been able to smuggle on board. If he can bring on several million pounds' worth of jewels, then he can bring on some firepower.' Jake swallowed before continuing. 'Tell him to wait until I go on board. I'll be able to identify the right man.'

'We'll get you on board now then,' Riggs said.

'I've got to deal with this first,' Jake replied, gesturing to Luke in the distance.

'How long's that—'

Jake's phone started ringing. He silenced Riggs with a wave of the hand and answered the call.

'Hello?'

'Jake,' Danika began. 'I've spoken with the cruise company. Nobody under the name Harrington has boarded the ship. All four tickets are still awaiting collection.'

'What do you mean?' he asked.

'None of the brothers have got on the boat.'

'Fuck,' Jake said loudly. His fears had been confirmed. Was this another decoy? Was Danny already on his way to another part of the country to escape their clutches again?

Jake thanked Danika for the update and hung up.

'What is it?' Bridger asked as soon as he'd finished the call.

'Harrington. The tickets. They've not been checked in.' Jake advanced towards Luke without giving Bridger a chance to reply. 'Where is Danny, Luke? He never used the Harrington ticket.'

'I don't know,' Luke said, raising his hands higher in surrender.

'Why isn't he on board the ferry?'

'I don't know. I thought he was.'

'Did he tell you where he was going?'

'No.'

'Where is he?'

'I don't know!' Luke gesticulated wildly. 'I don't know, all right? I don't know where he is.' He turned his attention to the white markings in the middle of the tarmac. 'He must have bought another ticket…'

'Another one?'

'Another one,' Luke repeated. 'For him and Louise.'

As soon as he finished speaking, a look of horror slapped Luke across the face, as if he'd just spoken out of line in the classroom and was awaiting his immediate punishment.

'Who's Louise, Luke?' Jake asked, cautiously closing the distance between them one step at a time.

Luke shook his head.

'Is she a sister?'

No.

'A friend?'

No.

'Girlfriend?'

Luke stopped shaking his head.

'What's her surname, Luke?'

Luke returned Jake's gaze.

'Where's my mum? I want to speak to her.'

'She's coming. Remember? I told you she was nearby.'

'You're lying. It's been too long.'

Where the fuck is Pemberton?

Almost as if on cue, a white police van appeared over Luke's left shoulder. It snaked its way through the traffic and sped the short distance to the roundabout on the other side of the road. As it stopped, the weight of the vehicle tested the suspension, bowing the car forward.

Luke's head darted towards the van. 'Mum!' he shouted, and then sprinted towards the vehicle. At once, he was prohibited by the wall of armed officers who were quicker to react than Jake. They charged at Luke, keeping their bodies low and their weapons trained on him.

'Get down on the ground! Now!'

Luke ignored them, and as he reached the central island that separated the two streams of traffic, a door opened on the side of the vehicle and Candice Strachan fell out. At the same time, Pemberton alighted the vehicle and rushed to Candice's side, holding the woman's arms behind her back. The sight of her son was too much for Candice – she broke free from Pemberton's restraint and bolted towards him.

'Luke!' she screamed as they collided with one another. Jake was harrowed by the sight of the collar bomb still attached to her neck and a lump swelled in his throat as they clattered together, fearing that the slightest jolt would detonate it and decapitate her right in front of him.

308

'Get down on the ground now!' the armed officers continued to shout, gradually encircling the two. Their cries echoed around the area.

Jake's senses heightened. His body turned taut. Tensions were rising, and it put him on edge. If someone wasn't careful, Luke or Candice could be at the receiving end of a bullet.

He intervened, tearing through the throng of armed officers. He grappled Luke, clutching the man by the scruff of his collar. In the process, Jake knocked the bag strap from Luke's shoulder and the money and jewels and other precious items inside landed with a terrible crash.

'Luke,' Jake said, shouting into the young man's ear, holding both of them apart, 'if you don't stop right now, you won't ever get to see her again. Is that what you want?'

Luke didn't respond.

'Tell us what we need to know, Luke. Danny… where is he?'

'Let me speak to her please.'

'Not until you answer my question.'

'No. *Please.*'

Jake sighed, looked at Candice who had her hands cuffed behind her back, and then returned his gaze to Luke.

'Give me one second. I'll see what I can do.'

Before leaving Luke behind, Jake gestured for the officer accompanying Pemberton to come over. The man hurried over to him, hooked his arm beneath Candice's and carried her away. Once there was a large enough distance between the two of them, Jake turned his back on Luke and strode across to Pemberton.

'What the hell is going on, Jake?' Pemberton said, pulling

him aside, out of earshot from Candice who was beside the police van.

'Luke won't tell us where Danny is until he's spoken to her. Danny never boarded the boat.'

Pemberton glanced back at Luke in the centre of the raised surface. 'I knew coming here was a mistake. And you think he knows where his brother is?'

'There's only one way to find out.'

'Can they be trusted?'

'Like I said…'

Pemberton sighed and looked down at the floor. She planted her hands on her hips and placed all her weight on one foot, but as she opened her mouth to continue, Bridger appeared, his breathing slightly exasperated from the short run between his car and the van.

'How long until the boat leaves?' Pemberton asked. 'Just in case Danny is on there and we just don't know about it.'

Jake checked his watch – 2:42 p.m.

'We have enough time,' he replied.

'You sure?'

He nodded.

'What do you think, Bridger?' Pemberton twisted her body to face Candice and Luke before turning back to face the detective sergeant. By now, a sea of police officers had surrounded Luke in almost every direction.

'I say we do it. But someone needs to stay with him. We can't just let them stand there, sharing their own little secrets,' Bridger said.

'We can't let anyone get anywhere near the collar device either. It's too—'

'I'll do it,' Jake said, keeping his eyes trained on Luke. He

310

ignored Pemberton and Bridger's muted stares.

'Jake, I can't allow—'

'I'll do it.' He hoped the confidence in his voice was enough to convince Pemberton that he wasn't about to budge from his decision.

'You're going to need a wire or something,' Bridger added, slapping Jake on the back. 'I'll source you one.'

As Bridger turned on the spot, preparing himself to go, Jake held him back.

'It's fine,' he said. 'I'll give them a radio.'

'What?'

'If they want to talk, they have to play by our rules.'

Saying nothing more, Jake reached for the radio on his hip, gripping it tightly. He steadied his breathing with long, deep breaths, and then he walked, turning down the transmission volume at the top of the device to prevent any feedback and cross-communication over the channels. To his left, he glimpsed the armed officers adjusting their grips on their SIGs, and to his right, he noticed Candice shuffling closer towards Luke. Less than five seconds later, he was standing in front of Luke, with the radio concealed in the sleeve of his left arm.

'What's going on?' Luke asked. The young man looked straight over Jake's shoulders.

Jake replied, 'Lift your arms in the air.'

Luke did as he was told.

'Keep them there until I tell you otherwise,' Jake replied. As he spoke, he turned his body at an angle and clipped the radio to the back of Luke's jeans so that it was out of Candice's line of sight. 'If you touch this,' he said, giving a slight tug on Luke's jeans strap, 'then you lose your privileges. You've got two minutes. That's all I could manage. And then you tell us everything. Nod if you understand.'

Slowly, tentatively, Luke nodded.

Jake breathed a sigh of relief as he stepped to the side and returned to Pemberton and Bridger, maintaining his body angle so that he faced both Luke and Candice.

Once Jake was by Pemberton's side, she gave the all-clear, and the officer guarding Candice released his grip on her. As soon as the man's hands were in the air, Candice bolted. She leapt across the concrete and up the small kerb. In an instant, she was on top of him. Luke lowered his arms and embraced her. They squeezed one another, despite the big block of metal impeding them. For that split moment, it reminded Jake of his relationship with his own mum. Their bond had never been close before his dad died when he was fifteen, but since then, they'd been almost inseparable. He appreciated her more now than he ever had done, and he was paying her back by allowing her to spend as much time as she wanted with Maisie.

After a few seconds, Luke and Candice released one another, and they began talking. Bridger nudged Jake in the shoulder, and he leant closer to them; in the time that he'd been gone, Bridger had managed to source another radio. Together the three of them listened in to their conversation.

'Where is he?' Candice asked in a whisper.

'On the boat,' Luke said slowly. 'With Louise. I was going to get on with him but then I realised she was here. They must have bought another set of tickets for the two of them under her name.'

'That fucking conniving, arsehole... bastard!' Candice

312

breathed heavily, exasperated.

'Mum. Mum! It's going to be all right.'

'How?'

'I've got the—'

'I just… I can't… I can't believe him…' Candice hesitated for a moment. 'My handcuffs,' she said eventually, 'they're unlocked. I'm going to find him and I'm going to fucking kill him.'

The words struck fear into Jake. Danny. Louise. Tickets. Handcuffs. Unlocked. Jake shot a look at Pemberton.

'Oh fuck,' she mouthed, her words silent.

'But wait, Mum,' Luke began, 'Mum, I have the—'

But before he was able to finish his sentence, Candice shook her hands free from the cuffs and swung herself behind Luke's neck, wrapping her arm around his throat. Jake and the rest of the team watched on in horror. He was trained extensively to react to even the minutiae in any given situation, but in that moment, nothing happened. It was as if all the hours he'd spent exercising and doing psychometric tests at home were for nothing. His body was held back by an impenetrable force.

'Let go of the hostage!' one of the armed officers shouted. 'Lift your hands in the air.'

Candice chose not to comply.

'Candice!' Pemberton called as she stepped closer to the action. 'Candice, for heaven's sake, put your son down. Nobody has to get hurt.'

Candice shook her head. 'You don't understand, do you? He left me to die. I'm done playing games with him. He won't get away with this.'

'We can all find Danny together!'

313

Candice edged backward, moving closer to the other side of the road, closer to the cruise ship, pulling Luke along with her. The armed officers matched her step for step.

'Stay back!' she screamed.

'Please,' Luke added, 'do as she says. I don't want anyone to get hurt.'

'That's the last thing we want as well,' Jake said, finding the courage from somewhere within him to speak up. Next he moved nearer to Pemberton and maintained her pace as soon as he was by her side.

For the next thirty metres, they followed Candice and Luke across a small expanse of grass, until they stopped between two oak trees. Now they were on the other side of the police cordon, and there was nothing between them and the ship two hundred yards down the road. Jake scanned the horizon, searching for anything that could stop them. He found his answer in the form of PS Riggs. The man was speaking fervently with his hand pressed against the side of his head. Jake's eyes moved to the rest of the armed officers. One of them spoke calmly, his voice inaudible.

Radcliffe.

Jake's gaze darted back to Candice. The woman snapped her head from side to side, checking the distance between her and the boat, her hair whipping in Luke's face.

And then she bolted, nudging Luke in the back. The young man stumbled forward but quickly regained himself and sprinted after her.

Pemberton cried after them.

Bridger cried after them.

Jake cried after them.

The armed officers cried after them.

They were fifty yards away, rapidly increasing that distance with every step.

And then a bullet rang out, followed closely by absolute silence.

| PART 1 |

CHAPTER 56

BLACK HOPE

Luke Cipriano's mouth felt dry. He wanted to vomit. He wanted the ground to swallow him up – the patch of grass where his hands were. Anything. Just so long as he didn't have to live in this horrifying, paralysing, painful moment. The bullet had torn through his stomach and wrapped itself around his organs, crippling him, and as he tried to clamber himself to his feet, the world span in a carousel of green and blue. A few feet away, Candice was standing in front of him, her body twisting and morphing as he dipped in and out of consciousness.

The pain was immense. A sensation unlike any other he'd experienced. At first, it started in the front as the bullet exploded from his stomach, and then it moved to his back, before eventually consuming his whole body. As the blood rapidly drained from his system, he became deaf to all sounds around him. The sound of engines ticking over. Water lapping against the ferry and sea walls. The screams and shouts from the armed officers for them to remain still. The police sirens bleating in the background. The general hubbub of the city way off in the distance. All of it was replaced by the sound of his heart straining as it gradually weakened and struggled to keep him alive.

Before he was able to move any further, Candice leapt down by his side and rolled him onto his back. She supported his head while her eyes danced between his stomach and his face. She babbled and muttered incoherently to herself. Luke tilted his head forwards and inspected the damage the bullet had caused. A flower of crimson had formed on his stomach and was gushing down the sides of his waist, forming a puddle on the grass. He tried to breathe but it was weak. He coughed and spluttered, the pain rising up and down his body like pistons.

At that moment, he should have been feeling scared, afraid. But he didn't. Instead, he felt calm. He was safe. He was with Candice. Everything was fine. She was going to look after him. She was going to care for him.

'M-M-Mum,' he said, blinking away the pain.

Candice squeezed his hand and looked into his eyes solemnly.

'I'm sorry,' she said, babbling, her voice barely a whisper. 'I should have... I should have been there... I'm sorry I ever left you.'

Luke's eyes closed as he danced with death. From somewhere deep within him, he found the strength to open them. There was a job he still needed to do.

'The key,' Luke whispered, choking on his own blood

between breaths and spitting it onto his collar bone.

Slowly, with as much strength as he could summon, he pointed to his trouser pocket. Without needing to be told twice, Candice rummaged through the contents and retrieved the key, quickly soiling it in his blood. She held it triumphantly in the air.

'Use it…' Luke tried. 'Free… Live…'

He gagged and spluttered as his body convulsed. He didn't know how long he had left, but he wanted to be able to see her survive. He wanted to be able to watch her remove the collar bomb and use it as a final middle finger aimed towards Danny.

Candice's hands shook as she held the key. Running her fingers along the base of the metal box of the collar bomb, she found the fourth lock and inserted the key. Luke held his breath as he watched her rotate it. His body froze as the lock snapped into place.

And then there was complete silence. The air around them stopped, and the only thing he could hear was his raspy breathing as he waited for the mechanism on the neck to detach itself.

It didn't.

Luke and Candice both glanced at the device, willing it to do something, anything. But when nothing happened, Candice screamed. She clawed at it, beat it, yanked it from her neck, punched it until the edges of the solid metal lacerated her skin and she started bleeding. She continued until her knuckles were covered in her own blood.

Luke watched on in horror. It hadn't worked. Danny had lied to him about the device. He had assured him – he had assured everyone – that the keys would diffuse the bomb.

But it had all been a lie. As soon as Danny had put that device around her neck, he had already slammed the final nail into her coffin, while he was readying himself to start his brand-new life with Louise. Tears filled Luke's eyes and streamed down his face as he lay there on his back. He reached his hand out for Candice to take it. She did. Her hand was moist and covered in blood, but he didn't care. So long as he got to hold her and be with her in his last few—

The ticking began. At first it was a few beeps: steady, rhythmic. But then within seconds, it intensified.

Beep-beep-beep.

Beepbeep-beepbeep.

Beepbeepbeepbeepbeepbeepbeepbeep.

Luke knew instantly what the noise meant. And so did Candice. But by that point it was too late.

The device detonated. All six blades plunged themselves into Candice's neck, rupturing and severing her arteries and muscles, breaking her spine and airway. Small jets of blood erupted from the incisions in her throat, raining down on Luke. Her eyes rolled into the back of her head and she collapsed to the floor. She was already dead by the time her head hit the grass.

Just like that, she was gone. It had been over so quickly, so instant.

Gasping, clinging onto what little life he had left, Luke rolled onto his side. They were facing one another. Candice's eyes were open, distant, yet, to Luke, it seemed like she was still there, like she was staring at him, ready to read him a story as she nurtured him into his permanent sleep. Luke reached out and stroked her face.

As he watched the colour run from her cheeks and the

blood trickle across her throat, anger swelled within him. All his life he'd tried to remember who his mother was. How she'd treated them when they were younger. What she'd looked like. How she'd behaved. What she'd done to provide for them. What she'd done with her life. In the few months that he'd been reunited with her, they'd tried to stitch together their relationship, set the foundations in place and build from there. But Luke was never going to get a chance to finish it. And now his final memory of her was tarnished with this image. Dead at the hands of the device. Covered in her own blood.

And it was all one person's fault. *Danny.*

His eldest brother. The one who had helped raise him was the one who had put him in this situation. How could he?

Luke tore his weakening mind from thoughts of Danny and consumed it with the memories that he and Candice had tried to build. As he lay there on the grass, staring into her eyes, a smile grew on the face.

And, before the world went black, he was just happy that he'd been fortunate enough to see her come back into his life.

CHAPTER 57

LINE OF DUTY

The tiny explosion sent a shockwave across the street. The image of Candice's neck rupturing into nothing played and replayed in his mind. And he knew that the images would remain charred there forever.

Jake turned his back on the scene and rushed behind the wheel arch of the nearest car. He vomited. Some of the liquid splashed onto his feet and legs. The acid stung his throat, chest, mouth and nose. He wiped his lips with the back of his hand and then rubbed the mess on his trouser leg. The taste lingered in his mouth and made him grimace. Spitting the remnants of the aftertaste onto the grass, he turned to face Luke and Candice's bodies, now strewn together like a piece of activist art.

By now, a team of paramedics had attended to their bodies and began checking for a pulse on Luke's neck.

Everyone in the area knew their efforts were futile, but Jake held a little hope. He was a human being, just like the rest of them, regardless of who he was and what he'd done. Nobody deserved to suffer a fate like that.

Jake forced himself to focus on something else: being smart. There was still a job to do – a final Cipriano brother to catch – and there was little time to do it.

An idea formed in his head.

He strode towards Riggs, with Bridger in tow.

'You need to get me on board that boat. Now,' he ordered.

For a moment, Riggs' face contorted as he considered what to do. Jake could see from the man's expression that he didn't want to be bossed about by someone who had nowhere near as much as experience as he did, but he also knew that Jake was on the right path. The threat to public life was dangerous so long as Danny was still on board the boat. With Jake on board, as well, he could help minimise the risk.

Eventually, Riggs nodded, raised his hand, and within a few seconds, two armed officers were by his side. He ordered them to strip down to their plainclothes, exchange their SIGs for Glock 17s, and then accompany Jake and Bridger.

'You need to put these on,' one of the AFOs said, holding up a body vest.

Jake's face beamed at the sight of it. He'd only ever worn one once, and it invoked in him a certain authority, a sense of power, a sense of invincibility. Stifling the smile away, he donned the vest and readied himself. But first, there was something he needed to do.

With Bridger and the armed officers behind him, he marched towards the paramedics and reached into his pocket. As he approached them, he removed his phone and opened the camera. He bent down closer to the bodies and began to take photographs of their remains, averting his gaze from the images on his screen as he took them.

Five photos later, he was finished.

'What are you doing?' Bridger asked, rushing over to his side. 'Have some respect...'

'I didn't want to have to do it.'

'It's all in the line of duty, eh?'

Jake ignored Bridger's remark, turned on the spot and started towards the boat, ducking beneath the overhanging branches of a nearby tree and breaching onto the road that led to the cruise liner.

The ramp that led to the cruise's deck was steeper than Jake expected, and he found his legs aching and his lungs out of air after a few steps. After the four of them reached the top, they were stopped by one of the stewards working on board the cruise ship. The woman in front of them asked to see their tickets. Instead, they flashed their warrant cards.

Jake pulled out his phone and displayed an image of Danny Cipriano's face. 'If you see anyone who looks like this, alert us. This man is incredibly dangerous. No one else is allowed on, and no one is allowed off. Do you understand?'

A look of fear struck the woman as she nodded, taking Jake's phone and committing the mugshot to memory. They thanked her and crossed the threshold into the boat, while the steward locked the gate, disabling access for anyone else.

As they entered the foyer, Jake stopped and turned to his

partner, ignoring the lavish decor around him; there was a job to do, and he wasn't going to be distracted by pretty artwork and furnishings. He touched his hip, searching for his radio, but then he realised where it was: still attached to Luke's jeans.

'We're going to have to do this on mobile,' he said.

'Fine by me,' Bridger said, brandishing his phone.

'What about you guys?' Jake asked, turning to face the AFOs with him. 'And the rest of the plainclothes officers we've got on board?'

'I can communicate with them on my radio,' Bridger replied.

Jake nodded. 'If you hear anything, let me know.'

'Aye aye, captain.'

Jake pointed to his left. 'Split up. You go that way. I'll go this. Don't get scared on me now, Elliot.'

Bridger's lips rose. 'That's what makes it so much more exciting.'

Then they disappeared in opposite directions.

Jake headed down a brightly lit corridor. Fluorescent lightbulbs hung overhead, blinding him. He hated boats. He was never good on them, though he'd only been on three before in his life. He always felt claustrophobic. Like the walls were closing in around him, an inch at a time. He hated the swaying from side to side, the constant motion. It sent his mind into a whirlpool of nausea and dizziness and made him want to vomit over the deck.

He steadied himself with his hands on the wall. He was sure the boat was moving, but deep down he knew it wasn't. His mind playing tricks on him again.

Jake ventured down the corridor and, at the end, arrived

at an even larger foyer than the one he'd seen when he entered. This one had a large, delicate chandelier dangling from the ceiling. It was almost as large as Jake's bedroom, and trumped Candice's chandelier tenfold.

At the reception desk a member of staff was attending to other clientele. Jake rushed over and barged in front of the next in line, flashing his ID.

'Excuse me,' he said. 'Sorry, but have you seen anyone that looks like this?'

Jake showed the man behind the computer the image of Danny. The man leant forward, squinted and then eased back to his natural position, shaking his head.

'OK,' Jake replied. 'If you see anything, call me on this number.' Jake grabbed a pen and paper from atop the desk and scribbled his contact information on it. Sliding the paper back, Jake thanked the man.

As he stepped away from the reception desk, his phone rang. It was Danika.

'Jake,' she said abruptly. 'I've done some digging and found out the name of Danny Cipriano's potential girlfriend. Louise Etherington. I've sent you an image of her. It's a mugshot taken from a previous arrest.'

'What for?'

'GBH. She almost beat another woman to death in a night club. And she's had a string of related incidences after that but never been convicted of anything. A previous boyfriend accused her of domestic violence, but he later rescinded his statement,' Danika explained.

Jake absorbed the information. 'You're a hero. I appreciate it.'

'Be careful,' Danika replied before she hung up.

Jake pieced together the information. Now some of it was beginning to make sense. Perhaps Danny wasn't the mastermind behind this. Perhaps it was Louise. Perhaps she was the manipulator who'd forced him into betraying his family and running away with her, ready to begin their new life with the money he'd stolen.

As Jake lowered his phone from his ear, he opened the email attachment Danika had sent him and showed the phone to the receptionist again. This time he didn't apologise as he barged in.

'This woman. What about her? You seen her?' Jake asked.

The man's pupils dilated. 'Yeah.'

'Where?'

'At least I think it's her.'

'When?'

The man's gaze flicked to the digital clock on his computer screen. He contemplated for what felt like an eternity before replying. 'About five minutes ago. Maybe more. She came to complain.'

'About what?'

'The delay. We've had a lot of frustrated clients. They've not been allowed in their rooms since they boarded.'

I don't care, Jake thought, careful not to voice his impatience.

'Which way did she go?'

The receptionist pointed to Jake's left, in the direction of a spiral staircase just to the side of the chandelier.

Jake strode towards the steps, forgetting to thank the staff member, and climbed the stairs. He came to a stop at the top. In front of him was another corridor; it looked almost identical to the first one. Fire Exit signs hung overhead

328

beside directions to different parts of the boat. It was then that an overwhelming sense of claustrophobia engulfed him. He realised how enormous and complex the maze of underground corridors was, and how tiny he was in comparison.

Up ahead, a cleaner, pushing a trolley, descended on the other side of the corridor. Jake snapped himself out of his thoughts and passed her. As he reached the end, he dialled Bridger's number.

'Louise Etherington. Danny's girlfriend. Possible sighting of her from the reception desk,' he said as soon as Bridger connected the call. 'Heading to seating area one on level two.'

A few seconds later, Jake was there. Although he had no idea where *there* was in relation to anyone – or anything – else. He just hoped Bridger was nearby. Large sofas and chairs were spread across the seating area, with tables and vending machines dotted around. Stands containing magazines and newspapers were situated at the four corners of the room. It reminded him of the time he'd been in the BA lounge once when he and his brother and sister had been upgraded for free. High-end. Lavish. Expensive.

Then, as Jake crossed the threshold into the area, he caught sight of Louise. She was wearing a thin blue jumper and a pair of jeans. By her side were several large duffel bags.

And, best of all, she was alone.

CHAPTER 58

BATHROOM BREAK

'Hey…' Danny spoke quietly. 'Can I go to the toilet?'

He hated that he sounded like a child, but he didn't want to embarrass himself any further by voicing the question loudly.

'Go,' Louise snapped at him, waving him away with her hand. 'Just don't be too long.'

'I won't, my love.' Danny stroked her arm; she flinched slightly, pulling away from him. 'Are you going to be all right?'

She glared at him, her gaze more piercing than knives. 'Do I look like a fucking child?' She reached her hand around his body, parked it under his armpit and pinched. Hard. Danny wanted to cry out, but he knew that was a bad idea. For his own sake, it was better to remain quiet and suck it up.

'I'll ask again: do I look like a fucking child? No. I didn't think so. So why do you insist on treating me like one?'

Danny opened his mouth to apologise but was interrupted by another harder pinch, this time a little higher, grabbing a clutch of hairs. He clenched his jaw, swallowing the pain. There was that fire in her eyes again. The one that always told him she was angry and that she needed to vent her frustrations on him. Sometimes it was a pinch. Sometimes it was a friction burn. Sometimes it was a whipping with his belt. Sometimes it was a punch. But it was always in the places nobody could see. The marks and bruises were his little secret, just like the way she treated him.

'Go to the toilet,' she said. 'You're a big boy.' And then she applied more pressure and twisted for good measure. His skin throbbed and he felt the onset of a bruise underneath.

She released her finger and a flood of pain narrowed in under his arm. It felt uncomfortable to move, and as he lifted his hand to soothe it, swapping the bag he held to his other hand, she grabbed him.

'No. You can leave that one there,' she snarled.

Danny did as he was told and hurried towards the bathroom, giving one last look at the bags of money and jewellery beside Louise as he entered. Inside, he rushed to the cubicle, slammed the door and locked it shut before leaning back against the door and letting out a heavy sigh. He was safe. Out of reach. She wouldn't dare venture into the men's toilets, that was for sure. But he knew that, if she had, she'd mean well. That she was looking out for his best interests, just like she always did. He had, in a way, deserved his punishment. He'd just insulted her dominance. He shouldn't have likened her to a child. It was wrong, and he'd paid the price for it.

Danny untied his belt buckle, loosened the buttons in his jeans and let his penis dangle in front of him. The cold air chilled him. The rash had been causing him issues all afternoon, but he hadn't been able to do anything about it. He wasn't allowed to touch it – Louise's orders. The rash that she'd given him was his fault. It was his fault he'd forced her to cheat on him and contract the virus. It was always his fault, and he agreed. He was a bad boyfriend. He did wrong things. He hurt her emotionally. He sometimes wounded her physically by accident. But he never meant any of it. None. And now he was on the final few days of treatment, and as soon as it was over, he could have sex with her again. It had been so long since he'd last touched her, held her, felt her.

He started pissing in the toilet, the lower half of his body tingling as the pressure on his bladder eased. Droplets of urine splashed on the seat and ricocheted onto the floor and his legs. After finishing, he pulled his pants over himself and buttoned his jeans, ignoring the wet patch that pressed against his leg, then unlocked the cubicle door and washed his hands, splashing soapy water across his face.

He peered up at himself and resented what he saw. Placing his hands in the sink, he hung his head low and exhaled deeply. He was exhausted – physically and mentally. Drained. But that was all about to change now. Everything. The Canary Islands with Louise. Where they could begin their new lives together. Where everything would stop. Where she'd promised the tormenting and the pain would continue no more.

A loud bang sounded in the end cubicle. Danny froze, his skin crawling. His pulse rose and his chest heaved. *What the fuck was that?* It had sounded exactly like the noise he'd heard a few minutes ago – the noise that had come from outside the ferry.

Dismissing it as an example of his overactive imagination, he returned his attention to the mirror and then looked at his watch. He'd been in there for a few minutes. Shit. Far too long for a piss. She would be timing him, he knew, and the beating would be even worse if he delayed any longer. Panicked, he wiped his hands on his shirt and trousers and rushed out of the bathroom.

The door flew open, and as he exited, he bashed into another man trying to enter. The man was twice his size and twice as wide. Danny apologised and pressed his back against the wall to allow the man to pass. He didn't want to admit it, but the blow had winded him slightly, and he gasped for breath.

But nothing could have prepared him for what he saw in the waiting room.

Louise – the love of his life, despite everything she had put him through – was gone. And so were his bags of money and jewels.

CHAPTER 59

LIGHTHOUSE

'Bridger…' Jake said quietly into his handset, holding the bottom of the phone millimetres from his lips.

'Go on,' Bridger replied as softly.

'Confirmed sighting of Louise. Seating area one, floor two. Heading down a corridor towards playroom two now. I'll approach. Danny must be somewhere nearby. She's got the bags of money with her.'

'Understood. I'm on my way now. ETA one minute.'

Jake lowered his arm and kept his phone pressed against his thigh. He continued deeper into the corridor, keeping twenty feet between him and Louise. At the end of the corridor, Louise arrived at a junction, stopped, looked overhead and then made her decision: left.

Jake followed, gliding along the carpet, making sure he made as little noise as possible. As he arrived at the junction, he crept up to the corner of the wall and peered round. In the short time it had taken Jake to catch up, she had almost doubled the distance between them.

She was suspicious.

Shit.

He pocketed his mobile – making sure to keep the call connected – and then formed an idea. Immediately opposite him, on the other side of the junction, carrying a handful of suitcases, was a steward and couple. They looked like newlyweds. Happy. Bubbly. Possibly on their honeymoon. Possibly on an escape from the mundanity of adult life. Jake didn't know, and right now he didn't care.

He hurried over to them, flashed his warrant card and grabbed the husband's backpack. Any protestations were stifled by the ID in his hand and Jake's finger pressed against his own lips.

'Stay here,' he whispered. 'I only need it for a second.'

He placed the backpack over his front, shielding the police body vest – and the police insignia on the front of it – from view. He didn't want to give Louise any chance to escape nor suspect him. Removing his phone from his pocket, he chased after Louise. By now she was at the end of the corridor and nearing another expanse of open space. Jake had to move quickly if he was going to catch her.

'Excuse me,' he called.

No response.

'Excuse me!' His voice carried up and down the brilliantly lit walls. He tried to place as much distress in his voice as possible.

The second cry for help worked. Louise came to an abrupt stop, turned and scowled at him. Jake closed the distance between them. Ten feet. Five. One. He stopped right in front of her, then paused, feigning exasperation.

'Do you work here?' he asked, pressing the backpack against his stomach, spreading the width of it across his body.

'No.'

'Oh.' Jake opened his phone and started to flick through the screens. 'I was wondering if you could help me? I'm a little bit lost. Would you...' Jake paused to open his camera roll. 'Would you be able to help me find someone please?'

'I told you I don't work here,' Louise said, her voice laden with disdain.

Jake continued regardless. 'Someone I'm looking for. I think you know him.'

He found the mugshot of Danny and then flipped the screen over. It didn't take long for the shock to register on Louise's face. Her eyes bulged and blood rushed to her cheeks.

In a flash, she bolted. But she was too slow for Jake. He grabbed her arm and pulled her back.

'Louise, don't do anything stupid.' She tried to shove him off, but his grip was too strong. 'Where is he? Where's Danny?'

Louise remained silent. She was stronger than he anticipated. She grabbed his arm and dug her nails deep into his skin, but Jake ignored the sharp, focused pain. There was menace in her face, a blazing fire hiding behind the eyes waiting to break free.

'Where is he?' Jake repeated.

'Fuck you.' She spat in his face. The phlegm landed in his eyes and disorientated him. He threw his free hand to his face and wiped away the spittle.

Jake fought every urge in his body to flip her to the ground and restrain her.

'I don't appreciate that,' he said, trying to keep a cool head. 'It will be easier for everyone involved if you tell me where he is. There's no way out of this. For either of you. Nowhere left to run.'

Louise's expression remained placid.

'Don't make me ask again.' Jake was losing his temper. 'Have you let him escape? Are you the decoy so he can run and hide?' As he said it, Louise's face changed. Her reaction was only the smallest of movements, but Jake was sure he'd seen it. A flicker of the eyebrow that confirmed his earlier suspicions.

'No,' he continued, 'of course you aren't. He doesn't even know you're gone, does he? You've just left him.' Jake looked down at the bags in front of him and grabbed one. 'And you've taken the money. His hard-earned money. But you couldn't have done this without him knowing, could you? You had to wait until he was out of sight and unaware before you took it, didn't you? So where is he, Louise?'

As Jake finished talking, Bridger arrived, out of breath and flustered.

'She's taken the money,' Jake said to him.

'Where is he?'

'Alone. He doesn't know it's gone missing. But I've got an idea where he might be. Wait here,' he said to Bridger.

Jake shoved Louise into his colleague's hands and started back the way he'd come. He'd seen a men's bathroom by the seating area. And there were only a couple of places where Danny Cipriano could have disappeared to. The shower. Or the bathroom. And if passengers weren't allowed in their rooms yet, that narrowed it down to the final possibility.

He rounded the corner, slowed to a walk and entered the seating area. There, standing in front of the door to the men's bathroom was Danny Cipriano. He was smaller than Jake remembered and for a moment, Jake just stood there, watching him. How he surveyed the room, his head moving from left to right like a lighthouse. How he wrapped his body tightly with his arms as if he was cold. How he tapped his feet on the floor, waiting impatiently for someone.

And then their eyes locked on one another. It was only a short moment, but it seemed as if everything else stood still – time, movement, his breathing, his reactions…

Before Jake could do anything, Danny Cipriano bolted.

CHAPTER 60

OVERBOARD

Jake sprinted after Danny. He followed him through another set of corridors, barging past holidaymakers and weaving his way in and out of laden suitcases. Danny was a few years older than Jake, and more physically able. His muscles appeared tauter, stronger and his legs were thicker, more powerful. It didn't take long for him to start pulling away and stretching the gap between them.

As they tore through clusters of people, Danny grabbed one of the passengers and pushed them to the ground. Forced to dodge the unsuspecting man, Jake hopped over him and stumbled as he landed awkwardly on the balls of his feet. His momentum carried him forward and he stumbled to the floor, barrel rolling. Landing on his shoulder, Jake clambered to his feet and continued the pursuit.

He chased Danny down another corridor and, as he came

to the end, saw him climbing a flight of steps.

'Danny!' Jake called. 'Stop where you are!'

Danny ignored him.

The chase continued to the top deck. Jake breached into natural light, the harsh and abrupt adjustment blinding him momentarily. The top deck was covered in wooden panels that stretched the length of the boat. Sun loungers, parasols and suitcases lay against the side of the boat, with some of the passengers already roasting their pale skin as they were forced to wait for their rooms to open. To Jake's left was a swimming pool with two slides at either end. Children were playing in it, using their underwear as swimming costumes. Ahead of him, Danny charged into an elderly couple, knocking the wife to the floor and the husband into the swimming pool.

Jake tore through the crowd once again, screaming, 'Police! Get out of the way!'

Bystanders panicked and dived to the side, affording Jake a clear path through. Danny made a sudden right turn and climbed another flight of stairs. He was on the outer top deck, and as Jake ascended the final step, Danny came to a stop. He'd reached a dead end.

There was a group of people clustered around one another. At the sight of them both, the group huddled closer in an attempt to protect themselves.

'Danny!' Jake shouted, almost bent double to catch his breath. 'It's over.'

Danny's head darted to the group of people and grabbed the nearest one. A young woman; mid-twenties, Jake assumed. Fair-haired, with a ponytail. Wearing denim shorts and a Harry Potter t-shirt.

She screamed as Danny's hands clasped around her neck. Her arms flailed at his face, but it was no use; he tightened his grip and began to suffocate her.

'Let her go, Danny,' Jake yelled, raising his arms in the air in surrender.

The young woman's screams faded and the air around them switched off, silent. Jake breathed heavily and regained his composure. Beside him, the family whimpered, still huddling together, still protecting each other.

As Jake composed himself, he became gradually aware that the boat was moving. Swaying from side to side. Forward and back. A wave of nausea and vertigo rolled over him until his head swam. 'Danny,' he said, blinking the dizziness away. 'Let her go.'

Danny said nothing.

'She hasn't done anything wrong, Danny,' Jake said. 'She's played no part in any of this.'

He remained silent.

'It's over. You got what you wanted. Now let her go.'

Danny tightened his grip on the girl's throat and pointed at him with the other. 'How do you know what I want?'

Jake considered a moment before responding. He had to be careful how much to share, and how much to keep to himself.

'Candice is dead, Danny. The device detonated. It killed her. That was what you wanted, wasn't it?'

Danny's hand flinched towards his right pocket, feeling for something. When he couldn't find it, his eyes widened.

'That bitch deserved to die! She deserved everything she got!' Balls of phlegm expelled from his mouth and landed on the wooden deck and the neck of his shirt.

Jake took a step closer, keeping his hands raised. 'You know, I spoke with Freddy earlier—'

'What?' Danny asked.

'Have you forgotten him already?'

Danny shook his head frantically. 'No. No, no, no. What were *you* doing talking to Freddy?'

'I was doing my job. I was hoping he'd be able to tell me where you guys were heading.'

'That stupid fucking bitch,' Danny whispered. 'She couldn't even get that right.'

Jake's eyebrow rose. 'What are you talking about, Dan?'

'That bitch, Candice. She told you to speak with him, didn't she? Didn't you think that was a bit odd, a bit out of the blue? Jesus Christ.' Danny shook his head again. 'She thought you were someone else. And I can't believe she fell for it. I can't believe she actually thought you were going to be able to get him out of prison and get him on the boat. She was even dumber than I thought.'

Jake paused, his mind racing. It would take him a moment to process what Danny had told him, but that was time he didn't have. He needed to put an end to this now.

Clearing his mind of thought, Jake continued. 'Freddy misses you. Apparently, he's been trying to get in touch. Quite a lot, in fact. But you never replied. He was like a father to you guys, and you couldn't just forget about him like that, could you? After everything he'd done for the three of you.'

Jake paused a beat and waited to gauge Danny's expression; the man's eyes closed briefly, and he avoided Jake's gaze. Jake wasn't sure of it, but he was nearly certain he'd seen Danny's grip loosen on the woman's throat.

He continued. 'Do you know what else he told me? He said you were different. All of you. This whole operation. It was unlike anything you'd ever done. He said there was something else going on. A driving force telling you to do it like this. Forcing you into it. "He's behaving differently. This isn't the Danny I know" – that's what he said to me...' Jake curled his fingers in quotation marks. It wasn't quite what Freddy had said but Danny wasn't to know that. 'And do you know what? I think he was right. You were forced into doing something you didn't want to do, and then you panicked. You were led to believe that causing as much death and destruction was the way forward, that it was the way to cement yourself in the history books. And do you know who'll get the credit for it? Louise. Not you—'

At the mention of Louise's name, Danny's face morphed into a scowl and he pointed at Jake again. As he did so, his sleeve pulled back and revealed a series of cuts and burn marks on his forearm and the back of his hand. Jake observed them. 'It's OK, mate. She's gone. She's not going to hurt you anymore. You won't ever have to see her again.'

'Where is she?' Danny said, his voice hoarse and weak. It sounded as though he had a catch in it, as though there was a flood of tears hiding behind a dam, waiting for a crack to form.

'She's been arrested, Dan. She's with my colleagues now.'

'I want to see her.'

'No.'

Danny's expression turned into a growl and he repositioned the girl closer against his body.

'I want to see her!'

'OK, OK,' Jake said, lifting his hands higher in the air. 'I can arrange that. I can arrange something. Don't worry. I'll let you see her. But only if you let the girl go. She wants to get back to her family... and then we can discuss.'

'What about Luke? Micky?'

This was the part Jake was dreading the most. He didn't know how volatile the man's response would be. *Only one way to find out.*

'Micky's fine, Dan. He's with us. He's safe.' Jake hesitated, feeling a lump grow in his own throat.

'And Luke? Please. Luke. Please tell me Luke is OK.' Danny took a step backward. Jake matched the step, maintaining the distance between them.

Jake fell silent and pursed his lips. He shook his head slowly. 'I'm sorry, Dan. They died together. The device killed Candice. And... Luke was shot by armed officers. He tried to protect her.'

Danny choked as he absorbed what Jake had told him. Then he moaned, his voice filled with pain and hurt and raw emotion. Jake felt sympathetic towards the older brother, despite everything he'd done.

'No,' Danny babbled, his mouth filling with saliva. He sniffed hard, fighting to keep the tears at bay. 'No... No. No, it can't— I don't believe— You're lying!' Danny spat as he enunciated the words.

'I wish I was,' Jake replied, reaching for his pocket slowly. 'But I'm not. I really wish I was.'

'How do I know I can believe you?'

'Because you can.'

'Prove it to me!'

'Are you sure?'

'I said prove it! Prove it to me now!'

Jake's hand lowered into his pocket and grabbed his phone.

'What are you doing?' Danny shouted as Jake began to remove the device.

'Just doing as you asked,' Jake replied. He pulled out his phone and loaded the graphic photo he had taken of Luke and Candice's mangled remains sprawled together. He waved the phone in the air. 'This is your proof, Danny.'

'Give it to me,' Danny called out. Around them, the air seemed to fall still, as if everyone's attention was focused solely on them. As if, in that moment, nothing else in the world mattered.

Reluctantly, Jake prepared himself to launch the phone across the deck. He swung his arm and released. The device soared through the air, and Danny tried to catch it with his free hand, but it bounced off his hand and fell to the floor.

Danny bent down to pick it up, pulling the girl down with him, his eyes widening as he stared at the image. His grip loosened on the girl and moved to his mouth; the young woman wasted no time and rushed towards her family. Once she was with them, the group sprinted away from the deck to safety. Now it was just the two of them. Jake and Danny. Jake and The Crimsons leader, just like it had been all those years ago.

'Luke…' Danny trailed off.

'Danny, listen to me,' Jake began, taking another step forward.

But it was too late. Danny had already made his decision: he dropped the phone, smashing it on the deck, and then sprinted to the side of the boat and vaulted into the English Channel.

Jake reacted instinctively. He tore after Danny. As he reached the barrier, he climbed over the top, ignored the petrifying chasm of blue beneath him and dived two hundred feet into the water.

CHAPTER 61

CLAUSTROPHOBIA

Jake's eyes ripped open as the rush of water assaulted his face. The force of the dive had sent him deep into the cold, the pressure squashing his head. He exhaled through his nose and swallowed to equalise, surrounded by a wall of black.

He searched the murky water for Danny, fearing the worst: that the man had been swept underneath the boat. That he had been knocked unconscious upon impact. That he had vanished completely.

Jake allowed the current to carry him, hoping that it would somehow lead him to Danny. As his natural buoyancy lifted him to the surface, he flailed his arms and legs about, trying to remain submerged. The body vest and clothes on his back weighed him down, but not enough.

And then it struck him. At first it was the intense

claustrophobia. Then the fear of imminent death, followed by the crushing pain in his chest. The same sensations he'd felt when he'd been swallowed by that avalanche during the snowboarding trip. Jake thrashed his arms violently, kicking out, now clawing for the surface, then opened his mouth in an attempt to scream for help. Water flooded in and he swallowed. He coughed, ingesting more salty water. He gasped for breath, choking, gagging, running out of oxygen. But there was none. There was only water, surrounding him from every angle.

Yet the surface was still so far away, just out of his reach.

Jake stared vacantly at the sunlight burning through the Channel, as the tide overhead rippled and distorted the light. Jake lowered his arms to his side, ready to let the water take him. And then he felt something behind him. At first he thought it was the boat running him over, trampling him, crushing him. But then he felt a pair of hands wrap around his chest. The hands removed the velcro from the body vest, threw it off him and then heaved him upwards. The pressure in his head released and a barrage of bubbles distorted his vision.

A few seconds later, he breached into the open. He gasped for air and spluttered and coughed water out of his lungs and mouth. Then he scrambled his legs and arms to keep him afloat. Breathing rapidly, he turned to face his rescuer.

There, with a piece of seaweed adorning his brow, was Danny. The man's head bobbled just above the surface and dipped below every now and then as the current pulled him this way and that. By now, the ferry had already passed them and was several hundred yards ahead. How long had he been under there? It had only been a few seconds, but it had felt like minutes, hours.

'Th-Th-Thank y-you,' Jake said, his body going into shock. He began to shiver as the freezing temperatures of the Channel numbed his skin. His teeth clattered. 'Why—Why did you s-s-save me? Why didn't y-you let me d-d-drown?'

It was then Jake realised how close he'd come to dying, and for that he would be grateful to Danny. Forever.

'Too many people have died today. I'm not adding another to the list,' Danny replied, spitting goblets of water back into the sea.

Jake thanked his saviour again and together they waited, both struggling to stay afloat, until less than a minute later a RIB made its way towards them. Their rescuers – consisting of the firearms unit that Riggs had deployed earlier – launched life rings into the water as they approached. Jake was the first to be saved. One of armed officers threw his weapon over his back, leant over the side of the RIB and hefted Jake onto the solid flooring of the boat. For a moment, Jake lay on his back, catching his breath, allowing the dark and depressing thoughts of suffocating under mountains of snow to pass from his mind.

He opened his eyes. Light flooded into them and he stared into the sky. In the top-right corner of his vision was a small cloud, thin, delicate, floating through the air.

The man who lifted him to safety suddenly came into view, a wide grin on his face.

'You took your time,' Jake said as the officer helped him to a seating position on the side of the boat. The officer placed a space blanket over Jake's body and handed him a bottle of water.

'We can drop you back in if you're going to be ungrateful about it,' the officer replied, sitting beside him.

'You couldn't pay me enough to get back in there,' Jake said.

'There's a price for everything, lad.'

The remaining officers loaded Danny Cipriano onto the boat and wrapped him in a space blanket of his own. The sun reflected off the aluminium sheet and dozens of shards of foiling danced in Jake's eyes as he stared at Danny being arrested and told his rights. There was no more fight in the man's eyes anymore.

He had lost, admitted defeat.

It was over.

And Jake had won.

CHAPTER 62

TRAFFIC

A few hours later, after they'd completed the post-incident procedures following the police shooting, Jake returned to the office. He had been given the once-over by the paramedics, fed some glucose in plastic sachets, warmed with a change of clothes and then sent on his way. For most of the hour-long journey back to Guildford, he, Bridger and Pemberton travelled in silence, the morbidity and suffering of the past few hours' events hanging over them like a heavy cloud. Jake's thoughts wandered as he stared out of the window. He had seen things he'd hoped he'd never have to. He had seen things nobody *should* have to. But he'd been responsible for putting an end to it. Louise and Danny had been caught and were on their way to the station, a few minutes behind them in another police car.

At 7:15 p.m., Bridger pulled into Surrey Police

Headquarters and killed the engine. The three of them exited the vehicle and entered the building, signing in at the reception desk. As Jake passed the civilian receptionist, he avoided the man's scowl. It was the same man from the morning, and judging by the disparaging look he shot Jake, he wanted to reprimand him for leaving the polystyrene cup on the table earlier.

Jake followed Pemberton and Bridger through the double doors to the side of the registration desk and into the lift. The doors closed and they waited; they didn't even have monotonous lift music to disrupt the silence. Jake felt relief as the doors slid open and the three of them stepped into Major Crime.

As soon as the team noticed their presence, they stopped what they were doing and rose to their feet, clapping. Someone in the background whistled. Jake slowed as Bridger and Pemberton entered the room, separating himself from them. It wasn't his place to accept the praise. He was just training to become a detective. The DCI and DS were the senior rank – they were the ones responsible for the success of the operation, they were the figureheads, they were the ones who should take the credit. Instead he was just going to act as the embodiment of being humble in victory.

As Pemberton and Bridger moved deeper into the room, members of Major Crime Team rose out of their seats and continued to congratulate them, patting them on the back and shaking their hands. Meanwhile, Jake stepped to the side and searched for Danika. His friend. His colleague. His closest ally.

He found her at the back of the room where he'd left her. She was on her feet, applauding.

'You all right?' he asked, wandering up to her.

Danika's eyes widened.

'You're alive!' She threw her arms around him and embraced him.

Chuckling awkwardly, Jake said, 'It wasn't that bad.'

He let go of her and moved beside her, so they were both facing the small crowd that had formed at the middle of the room. 'I mean, I couldn't have done it without you, mate. You really helped me out there. For a while it felt like everyone was ganging up on me. Bridger. Pemberton. They actually thought I might be working with The Crimsons.'

Danika said nothing. A moment of silence fell on both of them. Jake welcomed it. With her, it felt easy, natural.

'Yeah... I... Er...'

Jake turned to her. 'You didn't believe it as well, did you?'

She touched him on the shoulder. 'No, of course not. I was just...'

'What?'

'I'm sorry if it sounded like I didn't want to help at times. I did. Trust me. But DI Murphy wanted all the information for everything I was working on. I didn't want to upset him, considering we're both here for the long haul. I was just a bit jealous that you got to do it all. I wanted to get in on some of the action, no?'

'It's fine. You had to do what you had to do.' Jake nodded to Bridger and Pemberton, who were talking to the rest of the team, their conversations inaudible from where Jake and Danika were standing. 'You don't hear them complaining.'

'Without you they wouldn't have even found the brothers, let alone find out about Candice.'

353

Jake looked up at her. 'That was all you on that one.'

'Another day in the office,' she joked. They both chuckled, interjecting some humour and escape from the realities of the day. It was needed. 'What happens now?' she asked.

'Danny and Louise are being signed in with the custody officer while Michael makes his way up from Fareham. Then I suppose we'll interview all of them. Not that there will be much to discuss. It just depends on whether Michael is willing to talk.'

'What about Danny?' Danika asked as the crowd in the middle of the room began to disperse.

'He's going to give a full statement.'

As Jake finished, the doors to Major Crime opened and a man Jake vaguely recognised entered. His head was long and narrow, as if someone had pinched the sides of it and let the excess skin and bone and brain matter stretch. The officer spoke with Pemberton at the centre of the cluster of people. After they'd finished, her eyes searched the room until they fell on Jake.

'Tanner,' she called. 'With me. Danny Cipriano's just arrived in the custody centre at Guildford Police Station.'

'You want me to come?'

She nodded from across the room.

'You want me to interview him?'

Despite the distance that separated them, Jake was certain he saw a smile flicker on the side of Pemberton's mouth.

'You can watch for the first bit. Then we might decide to bring you in.' It was Bridger who spoke, startling Jake – he hadn't noticed it, but the DS had run away and wandered past them to the canteen to Jake's left. In his hand he held a cup of coffee. 'Come on, mate.'

Jake hesitated a moment. He stared into Bridger's eyes for longer than necessary, contemplating, deep in reflective thought. His gaze moved towards Pemberton at the centre of the room and then to Danika to his left. They glanced at one another quickly.

'I'll leave it, thanks,' Jake said. 'I think Danika should go. The guy just saved my life – I'm not sure how I feel about interrogating him right now.'

'You sure?' Bridger asked.

'Jake—' Danika began, but Jake cut her off. He knew what she was going to say. That she was going to protest against it. But it was done. His mind was made up.

'I want you to go.'

Bridger moved his arm and handed the cup of coffee to Danika.

'Come on then. Seems like you're with us.'

Danika took the mug from Bridger, and as they walked away, she mouthed the words *thank you* to Jake. Jake bowed his head as he watched them leave.

As he waited for Danika to return, Jake found himself a seat at his desk and rested, sighed and collected his thoughts. It had been a long day. And the next few days processing all of the information and details for the Crown Prosecution Service was going to take even longer. But before he allowed himself to think about that, there was something else concerning him. Danny. Freddy. Candice. What the current leader had mentioned to him about Candice mistaking him for someone else. Who? Jake recalled the conversation in his head. It had struck him as odd when she'd started talking about his watch, but then he'd thought nothing further of it. Until… Could that have been it? Had she thought he was someone else because he was wearing the same watch as the person she thought he was supposed to be? Did she think that he was the bent cop who was going to help get Freddy and the rest of them out of the country? But why him? And then Jake remembered. Bridger was wearing the same watch as him. He had only glimpsed it quickly, but he was certain it was the same make and model as his.

No. Surely not. Bridger wouldn't… He couldn't. But then, the more he thought about it, the more it began to make sense.

There was just one final piece of evidence he needed in order to confirm his suspicion.

An hour later, Danika returned, looking happy with herself. Jake thought it was the happiest he'd seen her in a while. It was what she needed right now – a welcome distraction, something to take her mind off everything that was going on in her personal life.

'How was it?' he asked, swinging round to face her.

'Insightful,' Danika replied as she pulled her chair out from beneath her desk. 'Really insightful. He confessed to everything.'

'Nice one. Well done,' Jake said, trying to hide the slight bitterness in his voice. 'Who was leading it?'

'DS Bridger and DI Murphy. I watched for a bit and then they brought me in.'

'Right… Dan, can I ask you something?'

'Yeah, sure.'

'There's something that's been playing on my mind for a

while now. Did you… did you ever hear anything about the traffic accident on the M25 earlier? Was anyone hurt?'

'What traffic accident?'

'Involving a lorry and a bus load of kids?'

Danika shook her head. 'Nope. There've been no reports of that. Why?'

Jake turned his attention back to his desk. 'No reason. Nothing to worry about. I just wanted to make sure everyone involved was OK.'

CHAPTER 63

CONVINCE ME

It was Jake's day off. He had been allowed some respite by Pemberton but had still elected to focus on work in a roundabout way. He had a promise to fulfil.

Jake pulled up to a desolate car park on the outskirts of Elena Miller's estate in Newcastle. Freddy's old partner lived in block ten, floor five, flat twenty-two. Jake removed his warrant card from his glove compartment, exited the car and wandered to the building. On the other side of the car park a group of kids played on their bikes, swerving around the broken bottles strewn across the concrete. One of them carried a basketball in his hand, and the sound of the ball bouncing up and down sporadically on the ground echoed around the grey concrete walls of the estate.

Jake stopped at a flight of steps, checked the small panel on the side of the wall that told him where each flat was, made sure he was in the right place and started up. The stairs stank of alcohol and sweat and decaying cigarettes. Puddles of liquid drenched the steps, and Jake struggled to avoid them.

His legs began to ache as he climbed to the fifth floor. He made a left turn and walked along the outside of the building. To his right, on the other side of the waist-high brick wall, Jake kept tabs on the children playing and, more importantly, his car. He came to a stop outside number twenty-two. The sound of a television played in the background. Jake lifted his hand and rapped his knuckles against the wooden door.

A few seconds later, it opened, and before him was a skinny brunette with thick black bags under her eyes. She wore a thin grey hoodie with disproportionate drawstrings dangling by her collar bones, and a pair of jeans ripped at the knee. In her hand she held a light blue plate carrying a sandwich. Her expression was blank, clearly unimpressed to see the stranger. Jake tried not to take it personally; he suspected she would have been unimpressed to see anyone.

'Can I help you?'

Jake kept his ID in his pocket. 'Elena?'

'Why?'

'It's about Freddy.'

'Don't want to hear it.' She threw the door shut but Jake caught it with his fingers before it closed completely, then pushed with all his might, forcing it open a little. He planted his foot between the door and the door frame.

'Please. I'm a friend of his.' The words felt strange to say.

'The last thing that man has is friends. Who are you?' She hid behind the small sliver in the door.

'My name's Jake Tanner. Would I be able to come in please?'

'No,' she said, scowling at him.

Behind her, from within the house, a call came. 'Who is it, Mummy?'

'Oh, it's – it's no one, Sammy. Just a man who wants to have a chat about adult stuff. Go back to the television.' Elena remained still. She continued to glare through the gap, and he could feel her eyes assessing him, judging him. Eventually, she sighed, stepped aside and allowed him to enter. 'You've got five minutes.'

Jake crossed the threshold and waited in the hallway. Elena closed the front door behind him and pointed to the kitchen.

'In here. I don't want you near my son.'

Jake held his hands in the air. 'It's your house.'

The kitchen was cramped. There was a small table laden with notebooks and textbooks in the far right, barely large enough for two people. Beside it, a fridge that came to the same height as the table. Next to that, an oven, washing machine and a sink. Elena stopped by an overhead cupboard and pulled out a glass.

'What do you do?' Jake asked, leafing through another textbook that was on the surface beside him.

Switching the kettle on, she said, 'I'm studying nursing.'

'That's wonderful,' Jake said.

'But it's a bit difficult with him lying around the house.' Elena nodded towards her son playing in the other room.

'I commend you for it. I have a lot of respect for people in that role…'

'You have kids?' Elena asked, leaning against the kitchen

360

countertop with her arms folded. He sensed she was beginning to warm to him, becoming less hostile to his presence.

'Just the one for now. We had a little scare the other day, but she's fine. My wife was being paranoid, but I think we might try for another one soon. Let's say I won't be disappointed if we get pregnant again. We were told we couldn't have one in the first place.'

'There's a reason they call it the miracle of birth.'

Jake looked to the ground, bit his lip and decided to move the conversation along. He was conscious of the time. 'He wants to see you… and his son, Elena.'

'You can call me Ellie.'

'Right,' Jake said.

'What do you mean, he wants to see us?' she asked, shifting her weight onto the other foot.

'Freddy. He wants to see you. He wants to see his son.'

'Is that what this is about? He sent one of his mates to come and do his dirty work for him? I've been receiving his letters, and they've been going straight in the bin. That man stopped being a father to Sammy the day I found out what he was.' Elena stepped away from Jake, ignoring the kettle that had just finished its boil.

'It's not like that,' Jake said, trying to placate the tension between them. 'It's not like that at all. I promised him I would come here. I also promised him that you would bring Sammy to see him.'

'Who are you?' she asked.

Jake slowly reached into his front pocket and removed his ID.

'Why's he getting a copper to do his grovelling for him?

He paying you? You bent? Wouldn't be the first time I've seen one of them round here.'

Jake pocketed the ID and held his hands back in the air so Elena could see them. 'It's not like that. At all. It's a long story, but—'

'You've got a few minutes left to explain yourself.'

Jake swallowed before telling her everything. He was honest with her. Told her he'd made Freddy a promise. That Freddy had helped him solve the case. That Freddy had proven to Jake he was sorry and beginning to change. That Freddy had lost all of his 'brothers'.

'You can't call them brothers,' Elena said. 'He was the outcast.'

'He was like a father to them. They never had their father growing up, so he stepped into the role.'

'And look how they turned out,' she snapped.

'I didn't have a dad growing up either. He died when we were young, which was worse because we knew him and then he was taken from us. I was the middle child, but I was forced into adopting that role. I looked after my younger brother and I cared for my older sister, who didn't even need me there. But I was, because I loved them. I'm telling you, I didn't know what I was doing. I made mistakes. We all did. I still do. And I can tell you now, we would have been raised so much better if we'd had our dad in our lives. He would have kept us on the right path, told us when to turn left and to turn right. Not that my mum didn't do a great job – she did.' Jake paused to gauge Elena's reaction; she was attentive, her eyes focused. 'Freddy's not asking for much. He just wants to see him. Maybe even speak with him for a bit. You don't have to tell Sammy that Freddy's his father.

Freddy doesn't mind that – he realises he gave up that privilege a long time ago, like you said. Just so long as he's in his life, so long as Sammy knows Freddy exists. I mean, have you prepared for when Sammy begins to get curious? When he wants to find out who his dad is?'

Elena remained silent.

Jake continued without giving her time to answer or think. 'Wouldn't you want to know? I mean, if I could do anything to get my dad back, I would. One hundred per cent.' Jake reached for his wallet, removed a business card that had his work mobile and email address on it, and placed it on the surface. He grabbed a pen from the spine of the textbook beside him and, on the reverse of the card, wrote down the visiting days and hours at HMP Winchester.

'I know it's a long way,' Jake said, 'but if you need me to, I'll be happy to front some of the expense. I can't force you to go, but I hope you'll do what's right for Sammy, because, after all, he's the one that matters in all of this. I'll show myself out. Thank you for your time.'

Jake slid the card closer to Elena, adjusted his wallet in his jeans, then wandered out of the kitchen and out of the flat, closing the door behind him.

CHAPTER 64

WHEN PROMISES COME TRUE

The buzzer sounded overhead and the door clicked open. The prison officer beside him escorted Freddy through the frame and onto his seat. He hadn't been expecting visitors. In fact, he hadn't even known about the visitor – whoever it was – until ten minutes ago. It was out of usual visiting hours and the prison staff had made an exception for him. His assumption was that it would be Jake again, coming back to get help with something. In the years that he'd been locked inside he had only ever seen a handful of visitors. Mostly solicitors coming to bring him bad news, or the sporadic visit from a deranged member of the family who'd found out he was incarcerated and wanted to put it on their blog or their social media channels. Every time, though, whether they were there to exploit him or depress him, he agreed to see them. Prison was a lonely place, and what sort of psychopath would he be to turn down external company?

The visiting room was empty, save for the guards standing to attention in the four corners. Freddy sat there, tapping his knee on the bottom of the table, drumming his fingers on the top. His gaze darted to the clock that hung on the wall to his right. It was nearly lunchtime, and he was beginning to get hungry.

A few minutes passed.

'Is this a joke or something?' Freddy asked, facing one of his favourite guards. 'Because I know how you like to think you're funny, Gabe. But—'

Freddy was interrupted by the door in front of him opening. Two people entered. At first he didn't recognise who they were. And then, as the light reflected off their faces, his heart stopped. Elena and Sammy were right in front of him, strolling towards him. Freddy's eyes were glued to his son. He hadn't seen the toddler in years. Sammy was growing up to be tall and strong. His hair was well kept, and he looked healthy. Elena had been doing a good job, as he knew she would.

Freddy felt a sense of raw elation and euphoria crash over him. A lump swelled in his throat and his eyes began to water.

Elena and Sammy pulled the chairs from beneath the table and sat opposite them.

'You all right, Fred?'

CHAPTER 65

THE CABAL

Bridger slumped into the front seat of his car and slammed the door shut. He exhaled deeply and ran his hands over the steering wheel, bringing himself to make the call. It had been put off for too long now, and the longer he left it, the worse it was going to get.

The ringer sounded in his ear, sending bolts of panic through his brain and into the rest of his body with every tone.

He clapped his knees together as he waited impatiently.

The call was answered but he was greeted by silence.

'Hello?' he said, licking his lips. 'It's me.'

There was a pause.

'You've got some explaining to do,' the voice on the other line said. Bridger didn't know his name. He'd never been given one. He didn't even know what he looked like. All he knew was that the nickname the man had given himself was The Cabal. And in the line of work that he was involved with, it seemed apt to Bridger.

'Do I still get my cut?' Bridger lowered himself in the leather seat.

'Depends whether you can convince me you've earned it.'

'Listen,' Bridger began, suppressing the fear in his voice. 'It's not my fault.'

'You were supposed to get them out of the country. That was your one job. They're either dead or in a cell. That's your problem. Your fault. Not mine. No one else's.'

'There were issues. Delays,' Bridger said. 'This new bloke. Tanner. He got in the way every time.'

'He a threat?'

'Nah.' Bridger shook his head and stared out of the window. He glanced up at the police station just as Jake and Danika exited the building. They were going home for the evening. Together they waved goodbye to one another and headed towards their respective cars. 'Trust me, he won't be an issue.'

'I'll still put him on my radar.'

'He's on mine too.' Bridger breathed in through his nose and out through his mouth. Slowly. Carefully. As if doing it drastically would piss off The Cabal somehow. 'So, do I get my cut?'

'You've still not convinced me.'

'What do you—' Bridger started, preparing himself to release a torrent of anger and frustration, but then thought better of it. This man was the source of most of his income – triple his basic salary from this one job – and he wasn't about to burn his bridges over it. If he played his cards right, there would be more.

'I tried to delay Pemberton for as long as I could, but Tanner was all over me,' Bridger continued. 'The keys. The golf course. He was even wearing the same fucking watch as me. Candice mistook him for me – she thought he was the one who was supposed to be getting them out. And he even had a little friend to help him as well. Danika. Danika Oblak. She was feeding him information on the phone.'

'I've heard her name before. It's cropped up in a few human resources meetings.' There was a pause. 'What about Mark?'

'He tried to get her onside but couldn't get anywhere with it. He's invited Danika out for a drink to see if he can do it that way.'

'She on the turn?'

'Doubt it. Maybe. Have to see what sort of magic Mark can pull out of the bag.'

'And what about this other one? Tanner. Same story for him? Can he be swayed?'

Bridger hesitated before answering. In the distance, to his left, a green Austin Mini Cooper pulled out of its parking space, turned right, drove along the road, past Bridger and headed towards the car park's exit. As the car passed, Bridger and Tanner locked eyes. They waved at one another and Bridger watched the vehicle disappear out of sight.

'Tanner's different,' he began, returning his attention to the call. 'He's too keen. Too eager to do his job. But he's a good detective. Thinks of things in different ways. And he's not afraid to voice them either. He'd make a very good asset, but you either want to cut him loose straight away or win him over. There's no middle ground.'

'I do like a work-in-progress.'

'That one will be one of the hardest grafts of your life.'

'Good. But don't think it's over for you. You're still not done.'

Bridger's brow furrowed and the muscles in his face tightened. 'What?'

'You're not finished. Not yet. The brothers are about to do time. A lot of it. It was your job to get them out of the country. You've made a mess of it. Now it's your job to get them out of jail.

Bridger sighed and shook his head.

'And then I'm done with this job?'

'And then you'll get your cut.'

'And what about Mark? Do the same rules apply?'

'Leave Mark to me. His involvement in this case raises more suspicion than anything else. There are things that he's probably not telling you. You need to keep an eye on who he's getting close with.'

'But I—'

'By the same token, I think it's in your best interests to find yourself some new talent within the team. Get them to help. You might need it because it's going to get dirty. Oh, and don't get caught. Someone a lot worse than Jake Tanner might make life a misery for you.'

EPILOGUE

Following their arrest, Michael and Danny Cipriano were charged with three counts of murder, aggravated assault, armed robbery, possession of a firearms and conspiracy to pervert the court of justice. They are currently being held in remand in HMP Belmarsh where they are awaiting trial. DS Bridger is in charge of the investigation.

Danika Oblak left her husband and two children and now lives in Guildford as a full-time member of Surrey Police. She's started drinking again.

DCI Nicki Pemberton was rewarded with a bravery award for her tactical and strategic decision-making during Operation Corkscrew. She continues to live with her husband and children in their home in Liphook.

* * *

DI Mark Murphy was lauded for his precise and accurate help throughout Operation Corkscrew. He has since dropped DCI Pemberton and made DC Oblak his next "conquest".

Jake Tanner raised his concerns regarding DS Bridger's conduct throughout Operation Corkscrew. DCI Pemberton was in charge of the complaint. No further investigation was made and DS Bridger's record remains untarnished.

Meanwhile, DS Elliot Bridger continues to work for The Cabal in secret.

***

Jake — and some old enemies — return in *The Community*. Coming soon.

Enjoy *The Conspiracy*? You can make a big difference.

Reviews are the most powerful tools in my arsenal when it comes to getting attention for my books. They act as the tipping point on the scales of indecision for future readers crossing my books.

So, if you enjoyed this book, and are interested in being one of my committed and loyal readers, then I would really grateful if you could leave a review. Why not spread the word, share the love? Even if you leave an honest review, it would still mean a lot. They take as long to write as it did to read this book!

Thank you.

Your Friendly Author,
Jack Probyn

ABOUT JACK PROBYN

Jack Probyn hasn't experienced the world. He's never even owned a pet. But he'd like to; there's still time. His twenty-two years on the planet have been spent in the United Kingdom, with a few excursions overseas — a particular favourite of his was Amsterdam. Or Norway. Both of which were lovely.

But what Jack lacks in life-experience, he more than makes up for in creative ingenuity. His Jake Tanner series is the birth child of a sinister and twisted mind, and a propensity to assume the worst will happen in even the most mediocre situation.

Finding himself pigeon-holed as a millennial, Jack decided to stick with the stereotype and do things his own way. After all, he felt entitled and he wanted to destroy industries.

Enter: writing.

The love of writing was rekindled in Jack's life when he (briefly) entered the corporate world, and the passion snowballed from there. No more will the millennial writer find himself working 9-5, indulging in the complexities of business life, or wearing a M&S suit.

He will take the world by storm with his pen (keyboard) and his ability to entertain and enthral readers.

* * *

Why not join him (and his future dog)?

Keep up to date with Jack at the following:
- Website: https://www.jackprobynbooks.com
- Facebook: https://www.facebook.co.uk/jackprobynbooks
- Twitter: https://twitter.com/jackprobynbooks
- Instagram: https://www.instagram.com/jackprobynauthor

Printed in Great Britain
by Amazon